# ONE MONTH'S NOTICE

## KATIE LOU

*Tulip
Rose
Publishing*

For anyone who ever felt they weren't good enough.

You are.

"It's fine. Take as long as you need." Simon smiled at her. "It will be nice for Lucy to have some adult company during the day. I love Louis, but it must be hard work being around a 9-month-old all day long."

"That's definitely a huge bonus of our arrangement—getting to spend lots of time with my gorgeous nephew."

"I know Lucy feels the same about you coming. She never seemed to click with anyone from the baby groups." Simon hesitated for a moment. "The thing is, I'm trying to persuade her she doesn't need to go back to work at the end of her maternity leave. Maybe you could help me talk her out of it?"

"Hmm, I'm the last person you want getting involved in your relationship. I don't exactly have an exemplary track record."

"But it's so ridiculous. She can stay at home. I bring in enough money for the family." Simon drummed his fingers on the steering wheel. "We don't want to pack him off to a nursery every day where he can pick up bugs and diseases. It just doesn't make sense."

"Maybe she *wants* to go back? It doesn't matter whether she needs to. Have you thought about that?" Her brother's old-fashioned attitudes were infuriating, and Nat found it difficult to bite her tongue. But the last thing she needed was a full-blown argument before they even got to his house.

Simon scowled and neither said any more for a few moments until Nat couldn't bear the silence any longer.

"Has Mum said anything to you?" She studied Simon's face for a reaction, but he gave nothing away, focusing on the road ahead.

"She's been asking questions, but I told her she needs to talk to you. You should let her know what's going on."

"I know. It's just she's always so disappointed with me." Nat sighed and picked at her fingernails. "And now, not only do I have another failed relationship to add to the long list, I can't even afford my rent."

"Maybe it's time you started looking for other types of work?"

"And now you sound exactly like her." Nat rolled her eyes.

"Well, maybe she's right." Simon flicked the indicator on the car a little more firmly than it needed. "You've spent your whole life living in this fantasy land of interior design and you can't even support yourself."

"If you're going to be like that, you can drop me off here." Nat folded her arms and bit her lip hard, wishing for a moment she had accepted Lexi's offer instead. But, even though the company of her best friend was preferable to her brother's disapproval, she couldn't turn down the promise of a comfortable bed in a beautiful house over the lumpy couch in a cramped flat.

"And where would you go?" Simon glared at her, but his expression softened as he noticed tears welling up in her eyes. "OK, I'm sorry. No more lectures. I'll leave that to Mum. She's the world champion, after all!" He presented her a smile as a peace offering.

With a heavy sigh, Nat sank back into her seat, the reality of Simon's words weighing her down.

"I know you're only looking out for me, Si. But design is my passion. I can't give up on it yet." She turned in her seat to look at him. "Just give me a bit of time to get back on my feet and I'm sure it will all work out OK. If I haven't got it sorted within the next few weeks, I'll look for one of those 'proper' jobs you keep telling me about."

"Deal," Simon conceded with a nod. "And in the meantime, Lucy and I get some free babysitting."

"That's the least I can do!" Nat squeezed Simon's arm, relieved they had settled on a compromise.

Twenty minutes later, Simon and Nat parked in the driveway of a semi-detached Victorian house in Hampstead, London. Nat felt her stomach drop a little as she looked up at the enormous windows and polished stone steps leading up to the front door. The red-brick exterior, embroidered with white trimmings, was partially obscured by long stretches of ivy that snaked up towards the peaked roof. Whenever she came here, Nat was unable to contain a tiny unwelcome pang of jealousy, despite knowing how hard her brother worked.

Simon had aspired to be a lawyer for as long as Nat could remember, and he put the relentless hard work in to making that a reality. Nat, on the other hand, had always been clueless about what she wanted to do. She just knew it had to be creative.

It didn't seem to matter how hard she tried, she could never get good grades. Where her mum and dad came away from parents' evening singing their praises about Simon and how well he was doing, there was always an air of disappointment after they had seen Nat's teachers. If they had taken the time to see her art teacher, it may have been a different story. But her mum didn't value the creative subjects, and her dad just tagged along, going where he was told. They never really knew how talented she was as an artist. With the struggles she was having getting her interior design business off the ground, maybe they were right all along?

Lucy opened the front door with Louis balanced on one hip and pulled Nat in for a hug. Louis grabbed a fistful of Nat's hair and began chewing it. The dark curls on his head bounced as he fidgeted in his mum's grip, his big brown eyes looking up at Nat with a hint of mischief.

"Hey little man!" Nat carefully extracted her hair from Louis. She kissed him on his head, inhaling the calming scent of baby shampoo. "It's so good to see you. Thanks so much for letting me come and stay." Nat took Lucy's hand and squeezed it gently.

"It's no problem at all. We're really happy to help." She leaned in closer to Nat. "Happier than you will ever know." A look of understanding passed between them. A shared acknowledgement of the challenges of living with Simon and his very particular ways. "Why don't you take Louis into the kitchen? I've set his highchair up ready with his dinner."

Nat lifted her giggling nephew from Lucy's hip and tickled his ribs. He squealed with laughter and slapped a soggy hand on Nat's cheek.

"Lovely!" Nat grimaced and wiped the saliva with her sleeve. Lucy picked up Nat's rucksack and made her way towards the house.

"We'll take your things up to your room and then we can then sit down and eat together. We could maybe have a glass of wine to celebrate the arrival of our new housemate."

"Becoming homeless is hardly something to celebrate, is it?" Simon said. Lucy and Nat turned and stared at him, their mouths wide open. "Oh, sorry. That came out wrong," he muttered, trying to rectify the situation with an apologetic smile.

"For someone so bright, you really can be quite dumb at times." Lucy glared at him. "As punishment, you can open one of the expensive champagnes."

"Now that sounds like my kind of welcoming party!" Nat's eyes lit up as she followed Lucy into the house. Simon reluctantly conceded defeat and carried in the suitcase, trailing behind the two women as they chattered.

Later that evening, with her head somewhat hazy from the wine, Nat stood in the en-suite bathroom and wiped a damp cloth across her face to remove the dirt from the day. She leaned into the mirror, pressing at the puffy skin underneath her eyes, and studied the green of her irises. With the sun catching them at the right angle, they were usually a vibrant jade with flecks of gold. Today they reminded Nat of pond water. Her hair, a rich brown emphasised by natural chestnut highlights when styled, hung limply around her face like dark curtains ready to shut out the world.

Nat finally climbed into bed, utterly exhausted and mentally drained from the day. She propped herself up onto the pillows, struggling to get comfortable and knowing that sleep would not come easily to her. Even the faint aroma of lavender from her pillow spray did little to settle her. Although she had slept in this room many times before, the circumstances of her being there created a sensation of uncomfortable unfamiliarity.

The only light in the darkness came from her phone as she scrolled through photographs, torturing herself with memories of happier times. On holiday in Rome, noses almost touching as they attacked an enormous gelato. Out for dinner on Valentine's Day, hands held together in a heart shape next to the soft glow of candlelight. Dressed up for a Halloween party, matching vampire costumes with fake blood dripping from cheesy grins.

She tapped into her messages and read the last one he sent her a few weeks ago.

> I'm really sorry. I didn't mean to hurt you. I wish things hadn't ended like this
> xx

Nat had tried to respond at the time, but never found the right words. Her clumsy fingers always tripped themselves up as she typed, hitting delete every time until there was just a blank space. What do you say to the person who broke your heart and walked away with barely a backward glance?

It wasn't that their relationship had ended in a big argument. Maybe that would have been better. For Joe, their time together had run its course and whatever Nat offered, it just wasn't enough for him. She wasn't enough. He faded into the distance, shrugging off his feelings for her like a tatty coat that didn't fit any more.

She began to type.

I miss you…

Delete. Delete. Delete.

# Chapter Two

**Tuesday 5ᵗʰ April**

"One, two, three, go!"

Nat and Lexi flipped their heads back and downed shots of tequila, slamming the empty glasses onto the bar. They both shuddered as the amber liquid burned their throats and warmed their insides. The cocktail bar, tucked away in a corner of Croydon, was a hidden gem and one of Lexi's favourites.

Shelves full of bottles shimmered behind the bar, where a hipster bartender meticulously lined up polished cocktail glasses.

"That's my girl!" Lexi pulled Nat in for a drunken hug. "See, I told you everything would feel a lot better after a few drinks."

"They won't feel so great in the morning with a massive hangover." Nat groaned as she steadied herself against the bar. "And I promised Lucy I would have Louis tomorrow so she could go shopping."

"You deserve to blow off a bit of steam, even on a school night." Lexi signalled to the bartender. "You've been through a rough time."

"I don't think Simon would agree." Nat sighed and rolled her eyes. "He keeps emailing me boring jobs I could apply for, even though I said I wanted to keep going with my interior design business for a bit longer. I just wish I had more experience so I could get the contracts that paid more money."

"Well, that sums up Simon perfectly. Boring with a capital B. Captain of the boring brigade. King Boring."

"Don't be mean!" Nat jumped to his defence, even though, deep down, she agreed with Lexi. "He's my big brother and he's looking out for me. Although, I was hoping he would give me a bit of breathing space before he started with the nagging. I've barely been there a week." She slumped down into her seat.

"Maybe your mum put him up to it?" Lexi suggested, turning to order two more shots of tequila.

Nat thought for a moment. It wouldn't be the first time her mum had gone behind her back. She could just imagine her talking with Simon, dissecting each disaster. If only she knew how much her interfering made everything worse. Nat already felt like a failure, and her need to get involved all the time just proved her mum thought the same.

"It wouldn't surprise me." As Nat rested her chin on her hands, she noticed a faint glow from inside her handbag and reached in for her phone. The shot of tequila immediately churned in her stomach as she saw the name on the screen indicating a new text message. A shiver went down her spine—it was like she knew they were talking about her.

> Hello darling. How is the job hunting? I hope you can come to Sunday lunch with Simon, Lucy, and Louis. I don't want you sat moping around on your own. Love Mum x

Nat fought the urge to slam the phone down on the bar. Even when her mum was trying to be nice, she still said the exact thing that would get under her skin. Lexi leaned in to read over her shoulder. Nat turned and raised an eyebrow at her intrusion.

"What?" Lexi threw her hands in the air. "I'm just checking it's not that dickhead messing your head up again."

Nat laughed. Lexi had always been so protective of her. They had been close friends since they met at university almost ten years ago. After bonding over a shared love of contemporary art and jazz music, they had become inseparable.

Lexi was the more daring one when it came to adventures. She loved pushing Nat out of her comfort zone and seemed to enjoy it all the more when Nat came kicking and screaming. Sweat-drenched music festivals in the middle of nowhere, where days passed in a dreamy haze of loud music, glittered faces and overflowing beer cans. A spontaneous coach trip to Amsterdam with the cheapest of last-minute tickets. After Nat's objection of "but I've got an assignment to finish", Lexi had simply laughed at her, packed a small suitcase, and showed up at her door, regardless. Everything was so much easier back then.

"Why is everything falling apart? What is wrong with me?" Nat blinked hard, fighting against the tears. "My business has failed before it even got off the ground. I can't afford my rent, so I've had to move in with my brother and my cheating boyfriend dumped me. I am not winning at life right now."

"Well, bad things happen in threes. So, look on the bright side." Lexi flashed an encouraging grin. "You've probably had your fill of terrible luck and things can only get better now!"

Nat frowned. "Are you *trying* to tempt fate on my behalf?!"

"OK, I can't look at that sad face any more." Lexi pushed herself away from the bar. "I'm going to the toilet, and when I get back, we are downing these shots and finding some gorgeous men to spend the rest of the night flirting with." Lexi put her hands on her hips and wiggled them from side to side, showing off her beautiful curves in fitted leather trousers. Her body moved effortlessly in time with the music. She had a natural rhythm that came from deep within and always drew attention from across whichever room she was in. Nat admired her confidence, wishing she could borrow just a little.

"Someone, or something, will put a smile on your face tonight if it kills me." She winked at Nat and strutted away, deliberately crossing her feet like a catwalk model as her almost jet-black hair, with perfect mermaid waves, swished against her back. Nat laughed at her best friend, desperately trying to grasp onto the fleeting sensation of light relief that always came with her company after a what had been a miserable week.

As the night wore on, Nat's troubled thoughts began to fade. She laughed and chatted with whichever group of people Lexi had decided would be most interesting before she moved them along to the next group. The taste of tequila lingered on her tongue as she allowed herself to be cocooned by the background music and gentle flow of conversation.

After a while, Nat slipped through the crowded bodies and stepped into the bathroom, eyes squinting as the harsh lights bounced off the tiles. A thin line creased her forehead as she studied herself in the mirror. Her cheeks were pale, a stark contrast against her dark hair that seemed even darker under the unforgiving lighting. Shadows hovered under her eyes, the effect worsened by smudged traces of mascara.

She rummaged through her handbag and pulled out a clear lip gloss, swiping it across her lips and pressing them together. Her throat was dry from hours of conversation and too much alcohol. She needed water. As she zipped up her bag, the bathroom door swung open and a group stumbled in, their laughter echoing against the hard surfaces. Nat smiled at the girls, a fraction jealous at how carefree they seemed, before making her way back towards the bar.

With an unexpected jolt, Nat collided with someone, causing her to stumble. She steadied herself on a nearby pillar and looked up, meeting the gaze of the person responsible. Time froze as recognition flickered across her face.

"Er... hi." The awkward smile on Joe's face settled into an unattractive grimace.

"Hi." Nat's chest tightened under the weight of the unspoken words she carried within her. They stood looking at each other for a moment. The woman beside Joe fidgeted from one foot to the other, her eyes dropping to the floor. Nat's eyes shifted to trace the lines of a stranger who had unknowingly caused nights filled with tears and anger.

She was a few years younger than Nat and wearing a casual outfit that, on anyone else, would have looked out of place in a cocktail bar. But she had matched it with just enough jewellery and make-up to elevate the effect. Even the way she had styled her blonde highlighted hair into a messy bun gave it an effortless look.

Nat looked down at her own outfit. Fitted jeans that had been worn too many times and were losing their shape. A plain jumper that, when new, was luxuriously soft and the deepest midnight black. But now, was losing the richness of colour and had developed a fine layer of bobbles, signifying it was heading rapidly towards the end of its life. And let's not even go there with the make-up.

She looked back at Joe, noticing he was holding onto the woman's hand—a reminder that his life had moved forward, even if hers had yet to start up again. Nat's heart drummed in her chest, the intensity of the moment threatening to overwhelm her. She was torn between wanting to turn and flee and a strange desire to confront what had been left unresolved.

"How have you been?" Joe's voice broke the tension, though his attempt at casualness only seemed to heighten the strain.

"Yeah, really good, thanks." Nat managed a tight smile, glancing again at the woman.

"Oh, this is Emily." Joe nodded towards his new girlfriend.

"Nice to meet you," Emily said, a touch of uncertainty in her tone.

Nat's lips unwillingly curved into a polite smile. "I'm Nat, Joe's recently ex-girlfriend. It's nice to meet you too."

"Oh, I see." Emily looked at Joe with a look of surprise across her face, telling Nat all she needed to know.

Joe's eyes darted nervously between the two women. Nat weighed up her options. She could linger in the uncomfortable silence, unleash a barrage of accusations on him, or walk away with some dignity intact. She chose the latter.

"Well, it was... nice to run into you. Take care." Without giving either of them a chance to respond, Nat walked away.

She had been fighting so hard against the feeling that everyone thought she was a disappointment, incapable of looking after herself. How many times would she have to be rescued by someone else? Her heart pounded in her chest while her mind raced until she made a resolution—a vow that she wasn't going to allow bad things to just keep happening to her. As her steps grew more confident with each beat of the music, she left Joe and Emily behind and made her way back to the bar.

"Are you OK?" Lexi's voice broke through Nat's trance.

Nat blinked, her gaze shifting from where she had watched Joe and Emily disappear out of sight. She turned to Lexi, offering an uncertain smile.

"Yes, I... I just didn't expect to see Joe here tonight." Although it felt like the universe was conspiring against her, Nat knew this was just pure bad luck and coincidence. Lexi had introduced Nat and Joe to this bar a few months ago, well before the break-up. It was just typical of Joe to forget the reason he knew the place even existed. If he had remembered, Nat would like to think he would have kept away out of respect for her. Especially when it came to parading around his new girlfriend.

"Eurgh, what's that idiot doing here?" She glared towards where Nat had been looking. "I know it's been tough." Lexi's tone softened. "But remember, you're stronger than you think. And tonight, we're here to relax and have fun."

Nat swallowed, her eyes searching Lexi's for a moment. Their student days seemed like a distant memory, back when they were eager to make their mark on the world. Nat had left home with a newfound sense of independence and resilience, determined not to need anyone's help or approval to succeed. How had that slipped away from her so quickly?

She had lost her way, swept up by the daily trappings of adult life. The late-night talks with Joe seeking reassurance about her designs, the need for approval from her mother that never came. Her constant desire for acceptance and validation had turned into an unhealthy crutch that was hurting more than helping. It was time to stop relying on others and start depending on herself.

"You're right." She flashed a small but genuine smile. "I *am* here to have fun."

They lifted freshly filled shot glasses and clinked them together. Lexi's unwavering support was just enough to boost Nat's new determination, shifting it to less shaky ground. She downed her shot. It was time to take back control. Life was going to be on her terms from now on.

# CHAPTER THREE

**Tuesday 12ᵗʰ April**

"So, Natalie. Tell us about your most recent design experience." Harriet, the interviewer from Summit Financials, looked up from a notepad and peered over the top of her glasses. Nat almost shivered from the coolness of her stare. Harriet was wearing a well-tailored dark suit that complemented the air of superiority she carried with her. The soft hum of the air conditioning filled the room as Nat twisted a silver ring on her little finger to steady her nerves—a thoughtful gift from Lexi to wish her luck and give her something to focus on if she needed it. And she definitely needed it today. Since the incident with Joe last week, she had focused all her attention on getting her life back on track. The interview offer had come quickly following the application she sent only a few days ago, so she took that as an encouraging sign.

"Erm. So, I finished university seven years ago and since then I have been building my interior design business. I have been working with a range of small companies with a focus on creating a fresh, welcoming look for their clients and staff."

Nat pulled out a large black folder from her bag. She had spent countless hours perfecting her portfolio, selecting the projects that showcased her skills in the best light. Several pieces of paper and fabric scattered across the floor as she opened the cover.

"Oh gosh, sorry." Nat stood up, rushing to gather the escaped contents. Her face flushed as she sat back down, noticing a smirk on the face of the other interviewer, Josh. He was younger than Harriet, and emanated a confidence that Nat wished she had right now.

"Here are some photographs from a client I worked with earlier this year to restyle their bakery." Nat passed a handful of photographs across the table. Harriet and Josh glanced at them, remaining deliberately silent and keeping their expressions neutral.

"And here are the designs for a new Turkish restaurant that launched last month." Nat opened out a large piece of paper and laid some fabric on top. "I imported these fabrics directly from the hometown of the owners of the restaurant, as they

were keen to have an authentic experience for their diners."
Her words flowed with passion as she detailed the challenge she
had undertaken. Nat watched Harriet as she scanned over the
designs, wrinkling her nose before making some brief notes on
her pad.

"These are very, er, pleasant. I can see you have had plenty
of experience dabbling in design and playing with shops." She
tapped her pen on the edge of the table. "But do you have
anything a bit more corporate? Something that might be more
suited to an accountancy firm?"

Nat began flicking through her folder, her heart racing as she
rushed to find a particular project that might impress.

"I think I have just the thing." She turned a double spread
out towards them, letting out a quick sigh of relief. "Here we
go. This is an estate agency I did a re-branding for last year.
The son had recently taken over the company, and he wanted
to update the imagery and interior so that it had a modern,
professional feel." Her eyes shifted between Harriet and Josh,
trying to establish a connection beyond the professional façade.
The pair took a little longer to look over the images than Nat's
other work, so she talked them through the stages of the project
with a little boost of confidence.

"I used my knowledge of psychology to build a sense of trust
and reliability for my client's brand. I developed a colour palate
using blues, focusing on the lighter end of the palate to create
space and openness. There's a lot more to interior design than
most people think!" A genuine laugh escaped Nat's lips as she
attempted to inject a touch of warmth into the atmosphere.
However, their response was more stoic than she had antici-

pated and the chill remained. She hoped her enthusiasm might elicit a shared chuckle, but their expressions remained serious.

"What would your initial thoughts be on designs for this company, Natalie?" Josh's voice cut through the air as he folded his arms. She met his gaze squarely, her eyes conveying determination.

"The first stage of any design process is to get to know the client before making recommendations. From the brief you provided, I can see you want a professional feel for your staff and customers. I would like to spend some time in your offices getting an understanding of what it's like to work here and what the current experience is for your customers. Then I can make some suggestions for how we can create memorable designs that will make a lasting impression."

Natalie paused, relieved that she had delivered the introduction to her pitch without stammering. She waited for further questions. They never came.

"Well, thank you for sharing your work with us." Harriet stood up, signalling the interview had concluded.

"I appreciate you giving me the opportunity to be interviewed." Nat reached out and shook their hands in turn. She maintained a firm grip to show her professionalism, even as a flicker of vulnerability danced across her face.

"We have a few more people to see, so we will let you know our decision as soon as we can."

Harriet ushered Nat towards the door and out into the foyer before she could ask any further questions. As she was left alone, the vast office space loomed around her and the weight of the moment began to sink in. A mixture of hope, uncertainty, and a dash of pride swirled within Nat as she made her way outside. Spotting a nearby cafe, its inviting aroma beckoning to her, she couldn't resist the pull.

The warm hum of conversation and the gentle hiss of the espresso machine filled the air as she approached the counter. After ordering her cappuccino, she leaned against the counter, grateful for a moment of respite after the tension of the interview. With a deep breath, she found Lexi's name in her phone and pressed the call button. It rang twice before Lexi's voice chirped through the line.

"Hey! How'd it go?"

Nat chuckled softly. Lexi's voice always lifted her spirits. "I think I did alright. I mean, I had their attention, and they seemed interested in the project I presented." Her fingers toyed with a sugar sachet. "But there's this professional poker face thing they've got going on. It's hard to gauge their real thoughts."

"Oh, come on. You know those corporate types." Lexi's laughter bubbled through the phone. "They're all about being stoney-faced and mysterious. But seriously, I'm sure you aced it."

A grateful warmth filled Nat's chest at Lexi's infinite confidence in her.

"Thanks. I talked them through the re-branding project for the estate agency, how I used psychology in the design process, and how I plan to tailor the designs to their needs."

"You've got this. Seriously. Remember, you've got the charisma of an authentic artist. They probably left that room with hearts in their eyes."

Nat smiled to herself. Lexi always knew the right thing to say. Her gaze wandered out the cafe window, contemplating what the immediate future might hold.

"They mentioned they had a few more companies to see, so they'll get back to me as soon as they can. I guess now I'm in that nerve-wracking waiting game."

"Well, until then, let's just celebrate the fact that you nailed that interview, OK?" Lexi's words were filled with genuine excitement. "Although I am concerned if you get this job, you won't have time for my little project. I'm due to get the keys next week!"

"Don't you worry, you're my number one priority. I will make sure there's plenty of time to get that place looking absolutely perfect for you."

"You are a beautiful person, Natalie Jane Cavendish. Make sure you let me know what happens."

"I'll let you know as soon as I hear from them."

"Awesome. Now go enjoy your victory coffee and bask in the glow of a job well done. Talk to you later!"

Lexi's words left Nat with a sense of renewed energy and a profound gratitude for the friend who always knew how to build her confidence.

# Chapter Four

**Friday 15th April, daytime**

Nat pushed open the heavy door of 'Le Jardin d'Hiver' in central London and a gust of fresh spring air swirled in behind her. The restaurant was the epitome of elegance, with its high ceilings adorned with intricate mouldings, white linen-draped tables, and walls lined with tall arched windows that bathed the room in soft natural light. The gentle hum of conversation blended with the clinking of fine china and the subtle notes of a live piano being played in the background.

She spotted her parents at a table near the grand fireplace, its marble mantle boasting a display of fresh flowers that perfumed the air. Her mother, Anita, looked up from the menu, eyes sharpening as Nat approached. Geoff, her dad, offered a warm, reassuring smile that eased some of the tightness in Nat's chest.

"Nat, darling, you look thin. Are you eating enough?" Anita's voice carried a tone of concern wrapped in critique as she stood to embrace her daughter.

"Hi, Mum," Nat replied, offering a small smile while shrugging off the comment. She turned to her dad for a more genuine hug, feeling the familiar comfort in his steady presence.

"Looking good, love." Geoff squeezed her shoulder gently before they all sat down.

Anita wasted no time diving into Nat's personal life. "So, tell me about Joe. I heard things ended badly. What happened?"

Nat tensed, her hands fidgeting with the silverware. "Mum, it's not really—"

"Anita, leave the girl be," Geoff interrupted with a soft but firm tone, giving his wife a look that bordered on admonishment. "Can't we just enjoy our lunch without turning it into an interrogation?" He turned to Nat. "I hope you don't mind love, but we ordered for you. Your mum was worried we might be late for the theatre."

Anita pursed her lips but relented, shooting Nat a pointed look that suggested this conversation wasn't over, merely postponed. Nat exhaled quietly, grateful for her father's intervention. She didn't need another reminder of her perceived failures, least of all when it came to her romantic life—or lack of.

The waiter arrived at their table, balancing a tray overflowing with artfully arranged dishes. As he placed the plates of gourmet food, Nat couldn't help but admire the vibrant colours and intricate presentation that made everything almost too pretty to eat. The restaurant's lavishness was evident through the whole dining experience—from each perfect morsel to the plush seats, gleaming cutlery, and the low buzz of quiet chatter mixed with gentle laughter.

"Simon mentioned you went for an interview. Something about interior design for an accountancy firm?" Anita's question sliced through the ambiance.

Nat felt her irritation bubble at the mention of her brother. Trust Simon to spill details she wasn't ready to share. Still, she knew better than to let her annoyance show. "Yes, it was an opportunity I wanted to explore," she said, keeping her tone neutral as she nudged a seared scallop around her plate.

"Tell us a bit about it," Geoff encouraged, attempting to navigate the conversation into safer waters.

"It was... interesting." Nat paused, gauging how much to reveal without inviting more scrutiny from her mother. "I think it went well, but you never can tell with these things." She offered them a small smile, hoping to convey both optimism and reality without showing too much of her self-doubt.

They settled into silence as each of them took polite bites of their food, nodding appreciatively as they savoured the intense flavours. Nat's phone vibrated sharply against the tablecloth, interrupting the peace. Anita tutted loudly. A quick glance at the screen showed a familiar number. She excused herself, pushing back her chair and stepping outside.

"Hello?" Her voice was steady despite the flutter of anticipation in her chest.

"Ms Cavendish?" The voice on the other end of the line was brisk, similar to the tone Nat had been met with during her interview. "This is Harriet from Summit Financials."

"Hi, Harriet," Nat said, her heart rate picking up as she braced herself. She shifted her weight from one foot to another, waiting for the response that could potentially shape her future.

"I'll cut straight to it." Harriet's words were clipped and efficient against the low rumbling of the traffic as it hummed in the background. "Your portfolio is creative, certainly, but it lacks the commercial insight we need for our industry. Frankly, your experience doesn't quite match our expectations either."

Nat's grip on her phone tightened, the sting of criticism sharper than the chill in the air.

"I'm sorry to say," Harriet added, almost as an afterthought, "we've decided to go with a much stronger candidate."

"Right, I see," Nat managed, her throat tight. "Thank you for letting me know."

"Best of luck with your future endeavours." Harriet ended the call before Nat had a chance to respond.

Steeling herself, she returned to the restaurant, the sound of clinking cutlery and background chatter suddenly overwhelming. Her parents looked up expectantly as she approached the table. The hopeful gleam in her mother's eyes made what she had to say next even harder.

"They gave the job to someone else." Nat forced the words out like bitter pills. "They thought my work wasn't commercially viable enough."

Anita's brows knitted together in a frown that wrestled between concern and disapproval. "Natalie, really, I think this just shows you should focus on finding a proper job. Something stable, not these... artistic whims."

A hollow laugh threatened to bubble up in Nat's throat, but she suppressed it. 'Proper job'—the phrase was an all too familiar one, a pointed reminder of how far her dreams strayed from her mother's definition of success.

From across the table, Geoff caught Nat's eye. She was comforted by the softness in his expression. He opened his mouth as if to intervene, perhaps to offer consolation, or maybe challenge Anita's harsh critique. Instead, he simply offered Nat a sympathetic smile, a silent acknowledgement that some battles weren't worth fighting—at least not here, not now.

"Maybe you're right," Nat conceded with a shrug, tucking away the hurt for later reflection. She wouldn't let her mother see the depth of her disappointment. Not when there was still a glimmer of hope that one day, her aspirations would become reality.

Nat pushed her food around on the plate, no longer interested in its colourful presentation. What appeared appetising just moments ago now looked like a messy art project from school, trying its best to impress but lacking any real substance. Her appetite had vanished, leaving behind only the sour taste of rejection.

"Nat, aren't you hungry?" Anita glanced at her daughter's barely touched meal, her voice laced with impatience rather than concern.

"Lost my appetite, I guess." Nat forced a small piece of food past lips that struggled to accept it.

"Geoff, we really should be going." Anita checked her watch. "Can you get the bill?" She stood up with a sense of urgency, excusing herself to visit the ladies.

As her mother's clicking heels faded into the distance, Nat felt the tension in her shoulders ease slightly. The absence of her mother's scrutinising gaze brought a brief respite. It was just her and her dad now, sitting in the aftermath of yet another clash of dreams and expectations.

"Nat," Geoff began softly, reaching across the table to cover her hand with his—a gesture so gentle it felt like a whisper, calming the chaos of her thoughts. "Are you going to be OK? I can stick around this afternoon if you'd like some company."

She looked up, meeting her father's kind eyes. There was a depth of understanding there that she rarely found in her mother's pragmatic stare. Nat managed a half-smile, appreciating the offer more than words could convey.

"No, Dad, it's fine. Really," she reassured him, although part of her yearned to take him up on his offer. "Mum would never let you hear the end of it if you missed the show."

"Alright, but if you change your mind…" he trailed off, giving her hand a comforting squeeze before letting go.

"Thanks," Nat whispered.

At that moment, the waiter arrived with the bill. Geoff pulled his wallet from his jacket pocket and handed over a credit card without a glance at the total. The noisy clatter of Anita's heels announced her return. She swung her coat over her shoulders, buttoning it up as if sealing herself away from the afternoon's disappointments.

"Come on then," she said sharply, her eyes darting to the ornate clock that hung above the bar. "We can't dawdle, or we'll be late."

Nat and Geoff exchanged a glance—his apologetic, hers resigned—as they rose from their seats. The overstuffed velvet chairs released them reluctantly, as if they too sensed Nat's need for comfort. Geoff rounded the table, reaching for his own coat and offering a supportive arm to guide Nat towards the exit.

"Thank you for lunch," Nat managed to say, her voice steadier than she felt.

"Of course, darling," Anita replied, her attention already focused on the door and getting out onto the bustling London street.

"Take care, sweetheart." Geoff's eyes were warm with unspoken empathy.

"Chin up, Natalie. This is just a small bump in the road." With a final adjustment to her scarf, Anita shepherded Geoff down the pavement, an urgency to her stride.

"Call us later," Geoff called over his shoulder, his figure receding as he was propelled by his wife's single-minded determination towards their important prior engagement.

Nat stood still, watching as they disappeared into the sea of people in the city. She felt a pang in her chest where her mother's support should have been. But amidst all the bustle and cool bite of the breeze, she couldn't help but feel grateful for the quiet ally she had in her father. His kindness a warm light that helped her through the darker moments of the afternoon.

# Friday 15<sup>th</sup> April, evening

"I'll be serving dinner in five minutes," Lucy called out from the kitchen. "Would you mind letting Simon know? He's in the study, no doubt with his head buried in paperwork."

Nat folded the lid of her laptop shut and picked up Louis as he writhed around in his ball pool.

"Come on, little man, let's go find Daddy." Louis was clinging onto a plastic ball, which he happily banged against Nat's head.

"Ow!" Nat cried out and pretended to be upset. Louis' eyes opened wide, and he dropped the ball to the floor, his bottom lip trembling. "I'm only teasing!" Nat covered his face in kisses and his frown transformed immediately into a wide smile. She knocked on the door of the study before opening it.

"Dinner is being served." She sighed as she watched her brother, hunched over a pile of paperwork and rapidly flipping through pages. He took life so seriously and worked such long hours, Nat wondered how different he might be if he took time to unwind.

It had been the same even when they were children. While Nat came home from school and wanted to relax and play with her toys, Simon wouldn't even think about joining her until he had done all his homework. But when he had finally finished, they would spend their summer evenings in the back fields playing with a ball or finding insects. In winter, they would play card games and eat hot buttered toast by the fire. Although he was almost four years older, he still made time for her, even when it wasn't cool to play with your little sister.

Things changed when he left for university. He entered a new world of adulthood that was a distant future for Nat. When he returned home for the holidays, he aligned himself more to their parents with his newfound maturity and grown-up conversations. As the only teenager in the house, Nat had been left behind, and they never properly reconnected after that.

"Huh?" Simon looked up, his forehead creased with a deep frown.

"Food." Nat rolled her eyes. "You know—that stuff you put in your mouth, and you do this..." She faked chewing a large mouthful of food. Louis giggled and squeezed the side of Nat's face.

"Oh, OK." He scribbled something in his notebook. "Sorry, we've got a big case on at work, and I just needed to get this briefing ready for a meeting tomorrow."

"Don't be long."

Nat took Louis into the kitchen to get him sat up at the table. She sang nursery rhymes as she cut slices of toast into triangles and placed a little bowl of golden scrambled egg onto the plate.

"Oh, I forgot to mention earlier. I saw a couple of interior design positions you might be interested in." Lucy placed two plates of food on the table. "I'll fire them over on email."

"That sounds fantastic!" Nat's eyes lit up with excitement. "Thanks so much."

Simon, who had finally emerged from the study and taken his seat at the table, joined in with a condescending tone. "Interior design? Are you still going for those jobs? I would have thought that last interview put you off for good."

The reminder of the brutal feedback she received from the accountancy firm made her wince. She was still feeling bruised over their harsh words that afternoon and her confidence was nowhere near returning any time soon. Nat hadn't had time to speak to Lexi and knew she needed her reassuring words before she would feel better.

"You're smart," Simon continued. "Surely you could do something more practical, like finance or project management? Something that might give you a bit more of a steady income?"

Nat felt her earlier enthusiasm wane as her brother's disapproval weighed on her. She glanced at Lucy for support, who immediately placed a comforting hand on Nat's and countered Simon's argument.

"People should follow their passions and pursue what makes them happy. Nat's talent for interior design shouldn't be underestimated. Besides, she's still in the early days of her career journey, and who knows where it might lead her?"

Nat gave Lucy a grateful smile and decided it was time to change the subject, knowing that her sister-in-law was thinking about her own job and her own dreams.

"I've been meaning to ask, when does your maternity leave finish? Have you thought about when you might be going back to work?"

The atmosphere at the table became tense as Simon put down his fork, clearly displeased with the change in topic.

"I've told her she doesn't need to go back to work," he cut in, his voice somewhat controlling. "We're financially stable, and we can manage just fine without the extra income."

"Oh sorry, I didn't realise we were living in the 1950s." Nat glared at her brother.

"It's not just about the money," Lucy said, her gaze steady and unwavering. "I love being a nurse, and it's fulfilling in ways that go beyond the financial aspect. It's important to me to help people and feel like I'm making a difference in the world."

"But you are making a difference." Simon's voice softened a fraction. "You're making a difference to our family."

"I know that." Lucy placed her hand on Simon's shoulder. "But this is important to me."

"This is the 21$^{st}$ century," Nat added. "Plenty of women find a balance between career and family. If Lucy is passionate about her job, it will make her a happier and more fulfilled person. That must be better than staying at home and picking up your dirty socks all day long."

Simon grumbled in response but said nothing more, returning to his meal with a slightly discontented expression.

The rest of their dinner passed in strained but polite conversation, away from any topic that might be controversial. Nat knew her brother was still stewing over her 1950s comment. She cleared the plates from the table, noticing Louis was covered in sauce. She held him at a slight distance as she lifted him up out of his highchair.

"Time to get you clean." She wrinkled her nose as he swiped his grubby hands towards her.

"I'll do that." Simon offered his arms out to take Louis from Nat. "Why don't you get the laptop set up at the kitchen table and get your CV ready? As soon as I have put him to bed, I'll be back down. Maybe I can help you send some job applications off?" He put his arm around Lucy's waist and kissed her on the cheek. "Maybe we could have a look at yours as well so you can think about that promotion you've talked about before?" He threw them both an apologetic smile.

Nat was surprised at Simon's realisation that his words might have hurt both of them. Emotional intelligence had never been high on the list of his abilities.

"Thanks." She gave him a nod of forgiveness, then began loading the dishwasher.

# CHAPTER FIVE

**Monday 18<sup>th</sup> April**

"The interview is in a coffee shop?!" Lexi's voice echoed from Nat's phone speaker.

"Yes," Nat said, with a sigh. "And I have absolutely no idea what to wear." She flicked through the sad selection of clothes that hung in her wardrobe.

"Remind me which one this is again."

"It's the PA job for the CEO of a small tech company." Nat couldn't hide the disappointment in her tone. "They run a social media platform aimed at people with an interest in health and fitness." She pulled out a flowery dress, held it up to herself and looked in the mirror. She decided it was too short and changed it for a navy shift dress.

"Oh. I can see why you're not jumping up and down with enthusiasm. That doesn't sound like your cup of tea at all. And it is pretty unusual having an interview in a coffee shop."

"I know, but I've had five interviews for different jobs now, and no luck so far." Nat pulled the dress over her head and smoothed it flat across her stomach. She noticed something in the reflection and looked down. There was an obvious stain right in the middle. She sighed and lifted it up again before tossing it into the corner of her room and the growing pile of cast-offs. "And that's not even counting the number of jobs I've applied for that I haven't even got to the interview stage." She slumped down onto the bed. "I don't think I'm in a position to be choosy. Anyway, at least this pays good money."

"Well, whatever you do, don't order a cappuccino." Lexi burst into laughter, snorting loudly. "You always get foam on your face, and you'll never get the job if you sit there with a milky moustache!"

"Thanks for the advice." Nat took in a long breath, then exhaled. "I'd better finish getting ready. I'll call you later."

"Good luck!"

Nat ended the call and threw her phone on the bed.

"How are you getting on?" Lucy popped her head around the door.

"I've got nothing to wear."

"Give me one minute..." Lucy returned a few moments later and handed Nat a black pencil skirt and cream silk blouse. "These should fit you."

She buttoned the blouse up and tucked it into the skirt. They fitted perfectly, although they didn't feel as comfortable as her usual relaxed choice of clothing. She took comfort in knowing it was only for the next couple of hours.

"I don't suppose you—" Before Nat could finish her sentence, Lucy held out a pair of black high heels.

"You are a lifesaver. Thank you!" Nat beamed and gave her a big hug.

"Shhh, I've not long put Louis down for his nap!"

"Oh, sorry!" Nat whispered, taking the shoes and creeping downstairs. She took a last look in the hallway mirror at her hair and make-up and left the house.

The bustling coffee shop was in the heart of Shoreditch and Nat felt out of place as soon as she stepped through the door. The air was thick with the rich aroma of freshly brewed coffee and warming pastries, further unsettling her queasy stomach. She scanned the trendy décor. Artsy black and white photographs punctuated exposed brick, dotted with plants that made an extravagant show of their foliage cascading down the walls. She wondered who they had hired to do their design work. It was very... fashionable. Perfect for the Instagram crowd.

People engrossed in their laptops occupied sleek wooden tables. They chatted occasionally with their companions, creating a soothing melodic hum. The place exuded effortless cool—a stark contrast to how Nat felt at that exact moment. She looked at the chalkboard menu suspended from the ceiling. As suspected, this haven for hipsters offered an almost endless choice of drinks, and endless variations on those choices. There were cold brews, matcha lattes, avocado espressos, beetroot cappuccinos—Nat had never heard of most of them and hoped they would offer just a simple coffee.

As she stood near the entrance fidgeting with the strap of her bag, she couldn't help but notice a man in the corner deep in conversation on his phone. He was wearing a dark grey jacket with slim black jeans. The top buttons of his crisp white shirt were undone, revealing a silver chain that rested on smooth tanned skin. The man ended his call and looked up, catching Nat's eye. She quickly turned to walk to the counter, realising she had been watching him for so long it almost bordered on inappropriate.

As she approached the barista to order her drink, the man appeared by her side and touched her arm.

"Natalie?" His voice was rich and deep.

Nat jumped and swung round. Her eyes widened as the man she had been staring at moments ago now stood next to her with an expectant look on his face. She cleared her throat to compose herself.

"Yes, hi. You must be Michael. Please call me Nat." She thrust her hand out to shake his, grabbing it clumsily. "I was just about to get a drink. What would you like?"

"Let me get these." He turned to the barista. "I'll have my usual please, Jack, and...?"

"Oh. An Americano, please." Despite desperately wanting a cappuccino to calm her nerves, Nat remembered Lexi's advice.

"Great." The barista flicked a cloth over his shoulder and smiled. "Take your seats and I'll bring them over to you."

Nat followed Michael to the table in the corner and took the seat opposite him. With his defined features and composed demeanour, Michael radiated an air of authority that only intensified her unease. His piercing blue eyes studied her every move, causing her hands to tremble slightly underneath the table. She steadied them by straightening out her skirt, hoping it would have the same effect on her nerves. She was so out of her depth.

"So, Natalie," Michael began, his voice smooth and confident, but with a hint of impatience. "Why don't you tell me a little bit about yourself."

Nat swallowed hard, trying to remember back to the interview practice Simon had drilled into her the night before.

"Well, my main experience is as an interior designer. I have been running my own design business since I left university a few years ago." She paused as the barista arrived at the table with their drinks. "But I'm a quick learner and I'm eager to take on new challenges."

"I can see that." A flicker of amusement danced in his eyes as he leaned back in his chair. "You certainly took a leap by applying for this position."

Her cheeks flushed. She refused to let her lack of experience define her. This opportunity would not be taken away from her like everything else in her life at the moment.

"Yes, it might seem unconventional, but I believe the skills in organisation, attention to detail and creative problem-solving I have developed in running my own company would be valuable assets in this role." She nodded her head as if agreeing with herself, hoping Michael found the conviction in her voice persuasive enough to believe her.

He took a steady sip of his coffee, studying Nat's face while he drank. Her heart skipped a beat, unsure of what he might be thinking. Had she completely blown the interview with the truth that she had no experience of being a PA and didn't have the first clue about what it might entail? Simon might have helped prepare her with the words, but they felt hollow and lacking conviction as she said them out loud.

After what felt like an eternity, he placed down his cup.

"Do you know what, Natalie? I appreciate your honesty. It's refreshing."

A tiny flush of confidence caused Nat to sit up a little straighter, and the tension seemed to ease. They continued to discuss her experience and skills, and the challenges of the role. The weight of the interview began to lift, replaced by a spark of hope. Nat's focus was on Michael and the opportunity to prove herself.

The sound of a bell momentarily distracted her as the cafe door swung open. Her gaze locked onto Joe's figure as he entered the coffee shop. A wave of shock washed over her and her heart began to race. She immediately felt sick, her stomach twisting and turning as he took off his jacket, revealing an all too familiar red jumper—the one she used to tease him about for looking like Father Christmas. His messy blonde hair and the way he always seemed to carry a permanent smirk on his face—she found those endearing at the start of their relationship. Now she found them irritating. Everything about him filled her with old emotions. Ones that she had been fighting to keep at bay.

This was the last thing she needed at that exact moment. In a city the size of London, bumping into him twice in one week seemed like terrible luck. Either that, or she had left her location tracking on her phone and Joe was going deliberately out of his way to wind her up. Despite how their relationship ended, she didn't believe he would be that cruel. She really did just have terrible luck.

Nat watched as he settled at a table, his new girlfriend beside him. The affection in their gestures was crystal clear, even from a distance. As much as she was doing her best to move on, seeing Joe with someone else was a stark reminder that her heart still carried the scars of their recent history. The interview, her newfound confidence—it all felt insignificant in the face of this unexpected encounter.

She looked back at Michael, struggling to regain her composure. His voice seemed distant as he continued to talk, but Nat's mind was consumed by memories and the feelings she was struggling to suppress.

"Is everything OK?" Michael said. It was difficult not to notice the uncomfortable look on Nat's face.

"Oh, it's nothing." Nat waved her hand to brush away his question.

Michael frowned, but then continued to talk Nat through the key responsibilities of the job and what he expected of the successful candidate.

"So, how do you feel about that?"

Silence.

"Natalie, how do you feel about that?" he said again, more impatiently.

"Oh, I'm sorry." Nat's face fell. "I was totally distracted."

"What's going on?" Frustration flashed across Michael's face. "You're supposed to be here for a job interview. And perhaps I should remind you, it's a job you don't even have any experience in so the odds aren't stacked in your favour."

Nat winced as the words, delivered with an acid tone, cut her deeply.

"I'm really sorry. My ex-boyfriend just walked in with his new girlfriend."

Michael raised an eyebrow and Nat realised she would have to explain further if she was going to salvage the situation.

"We only broke up a few weeks ago. And he's with the girl I'm pretty sure he started seeing before we actually split up." Nat sunk down into her seat, trying to make herself invisible and forgetting for a moment who she was with and why she was there. "This just gives him even more reason to think I'm a loser. My business has failed, I'm living with my brother, and I'm sitting in a coffee shop being interviewed for a job I don't even want."

Nat instantly regretted the words that had just tumbled out of her mouth, especially as Joe had just noticed her and lifted his arm to give an awkward wave. Michael looked over at Joe and frowned. Then his face softened and he moved closer to Nat, taking her by surprise.

"Well, why don't we give him something else to think about you instead?" He waited until he was sure Joe was looking, then reached over and took her hand in his. He pulled it up to his mouth and planted a gentle kiss on her knuckles.

There was a long silence as Nat held her breath. Eventually, Michael let go of her hand, but she could still feel the warmth of his touch on her skin.

"Can I get you another drink?" Michael stood up as if everything was completely normal.

Nat stared up at him, trying to process what had just happened. If it was any other man in any other place, the moment would have seemed entirely inappropriate. But something about the exchange felt natural, like it was meant to happen.

"Natalie?"

She nodded slowly. She couldn't face the thought of another black coffee. Screw it.

"I'll have a cappuccino, please." There was no way she was going to get this job anyway, so what did a bit of milk froth on her lip matter?

She watched him as he walked up to the counter with a determined stride, his broad shoulders carrying an unmistakable confidence. Nat felt a wave of warmth wash over her. Michael's gesture in front of Joe had taken her by surprise, and although it meant nothing to him, it meant everything to her.

"Er, can I ask why you did that?" Nat said when Michael sat back down. She needed to understand why this man with his cool, almost stand-offish exterior had done something so unexpected. Michael was silent while he stirred his drink before looking at her and staring, his gaze intense.

"I can't stand infidelity and it's clearly had a nasty effect on you. To me, it looks like he's the loser if he thinks it's OK to do something like that to someone like you." He stopped speaking and looked down into his cup.

Michael's words echoed in Nat's mind. What did he mean, *someone like you*?

"Plus, we're in the middle of an interview and I don't have all the time in the world." Michael looked down at his watch. "I was hoping we might be able to get to the end of it before this place closes. As you know, I don't currently have a PA and the thought of having to reschedule my diary myself terrifies me."

They continued the interview, and, to Nat's relief, she made it to the end with no further interruptions or disasters. She tipped her head back and finished the last dregs of her cappuccino.

"Well, thank you for taking the time to interview me," Nat said, reaching for her bag. "It's been really nice to meet you."

"Do you mind?" Michael held up a tissue and Nat's face clouded with confusion. He reached forward and gently wiped something off the tip of her nose. The look of concentration on his face and his close proximity caused Nat's heart to beat so fast and loud, she was sure he could hear it. He held up the tissue to show Nat a smudge of cappuccino foam with chocolate dusting. Her cheeks flushed as she brought her hand up to her nose. The scent of his warm, spicy aftershave had lingered on the hand he had kissed and sent a shiver up her spine.

"It's OK, I got it all." Michael smirked. Nat couldn't decide whether to laugh or cry. But before she did either, they were interrupted by a message pinging on Michael's phone. He read it, then grabbed his jacket from the back of the chair.

"I need to get back to the office." Michael glanced over his shoulder to where Joe was sitting. "Why don't you walk out with me so we can keep the pretence up a bit longer? We can remind him what he's missing out on." He stood up, tilting his head to one side with a broad smile, and held out his hand.

Nat's stomach flipped as she was momentarily stunned by both his gesture and how his face had been transformed by a simple smile. There had been no doubt he was handsome—the serious expression he held for most of the interview gave off dark and brooding vibes. But the shift in his features to something even more good-looking took Nat by surprise. This was a man that could be relaxed and carefree, but only on his terms.

She timidly accepted his outstretched hand. Her hand tingled where it met his warm grip as they walked out of the coffee shop together, before going their separate ways as if nothing had happened.

# Chapter Six

**Tuesday 19<sup>th</sup> April**

Nat pushed hard against the wooden door with her shoulder, being careful not to spill the contents of the two steaming cups she was holding in each hand. As she took a step into the shop, the door swung back towards her more quickly than she was expecting.

"Oh shit!" Nat twisted awkwardly to stop the large folder tucked under her arm from slipping to the floor.

Lexi was sitting at a rickety table in the centre of the shop, concentrating on her laptop screen. She turned towards the sound and her face lit up.

"You made it! And you brought coffee! You're my saviour."

Lexi rushed over, grabbed a cup from Nat and took a big swig.

"Slow down!" Nat laughed. "You'll scald yourself. I could do without a hospital trip, thank you!"

"Alright, Mum! Come on, let me show you around."

Lexi talked non-stop as she walked Nat around the shop. The estate agency had only given her the keys that morning, and she was eager to get started. Nat tried to block out the chattering as she took in every little detail, imagining the possibilities for how the space could be transformed into something beautiful.

Lexi had dreamed of owning a music shop or a cafe since she was a little girl. The space she had rented would allow her to do both, with enough space for the shop and the facilities to run a cafe alongside. It was no surprise that Lexi would want Nat to do the interior design of the shop, but she still felt honoured to play a part in fulfilling Lexi's dreams.

"So, what do you think?" Lexi's eyes were wide with expectation.

Nat took her time to look around the shop, giving nothing away.

"It's like walking into a song that's just waiting to be sung." She grinned as Lexi jumped up and down, clapping her hands together.

"I knew you'd love it!" Lexi twirled around in a full circle. "I can't wait to see you work your magic on it." She pulled another chair over to the table and they both sat down.

Nat opened the black folder, revealing a collage of images, fabric samples, and magazine clippings. Lexi leaned in, eyes brimming with delight as they skimmed over visions of what the future might look like for her business. Nat took a fresh sheet of paper and began sketching. Before long, drawings filled every corner of the page, showing the different parts of the shop and how they could be designed to be both stylish and practical.

"Imagine this," Nat said, pointing at a sketch of a counter near the entrance. "We could set up a counter here for the cafe side."

"I see." Lexi nodded as she scanned over the drawings. "Yes, that's perfect!"

"And over there, by the window, we could create a special nook with soft armchairs and bookshelves filled with sheet music."

"Maybe we could find an old record player and keep records there, too?"

"That's a fantastic idea!" Nat loved Lexi's enthusiasm. "Then, I was thinking we could hang instruments on the walls, like art pieces. Guitars, violins—"

"—pianos!" Lexi finished, her voice bursting with excitement.

Nat raised an eyebrow. "Somehow, I don't think these walls were designed to take the weight of a piano!"

Lexi ginned sheepishly.

"Anyway, here is the really special bit." Nat turned the page and nodded towards the other side of the shop. "That's where we are going to build a retractable stage."

"How's that going to work?"

"You leave the mechanics of it to me." Nat winked. "You just need to apply for a licence so you can stay open later in the evenings. And with the push of a button, you will have a stage for live performers."

Lexi's jaw dropped. "Oh, it's going to be even better than I could have imagined! I'm so excited for the launch party—it's booked for the 27th May so we have just under six weeks."

Nat couldn't stop laughing as Lexi pulled her in for a hug and planted kisses all over her face.

"OK, enough!" Nat pushed her off. "Hold on, I can hear buzzing. Is that me or you?"

The women patted their pockets, checking to see whose phone was the source of the noise.

"Oh, shit!" Nat pulled her phone out of her bag. "It was mine, but I missed it." Her face fell as she unlocked the screen.

"Who was it?"

"It's the man from the job interview I had yesterday."

"Oh, of course!" Lexi's hand flew up to her mouth. "I'm so sorry. I was so wrapped up in my shop and I completely forgot to ask you how it went."

"You know the feeling in a dream where you are in front of a crowd of people, and you realise you are totally naked? Well, it was like that, but a million times worse."

"It couldn't have been that bad?" Lexi frowned. "Could it?"

"It was great, apart from the stumbling over my words, feeling completely out of place and being not at all suited for the role. Oh, and the cappuccino foam on the nose."

"What did I tell you?" Lexi fired her a scolding look before relaxing her expression. "I'm sure you did fine. That sounds like any job interview and you have got so many transferrable skills. You're just putting yourself down, as usual."

"I haven't finished. Guess who walked into the coffee shop?"

Lexi shrugged her shoulders.

"Joe."

"Oh, what happened?"

"It wasn't just Joe. It was Joe and his new girlfriend. After I saw them, I was totally distracted and couldn't concentrate."

"Of all the people to walk in." Lexi rubbed Nat's arm. "It might still be OK though?"

"I doubt it. Michael did the strangest thing, though. Which, now I think about it, must have been because he knew he wasn't going to give me the job and felt even more sorry for me. This is going to sound unusual—" Nat paused, taking a slow breath "—but he waited until he knew Joe was looking over, then he took my hand and kissed it."

"I'm sorry, what?" Lexi's jaw dropped.

"I know, right? It sounds a bit creepy now I've said it out loud. Although, it didn't feel like that at the time." Nat thought back to the coffee shop and his soft lips as they traced her hand. The memory of the intimate gesture sent a tingling sensation down her spine. She remembered the smell as she lifted her hand to brush her hair off her face. She almost hadn't washed her hands as she didn't want to remove the traces he had left behind—the warm, spicy scent that made a statement without being overpowering. A scent she could definitely get used to and nothing like the cheap fake stuff Joe used to buy off the internet.

"He's good-looking, isn't he?" Lexi narrowed her eyes at Nat.

"I suppose some people might think that." Nat's cheeks flushed.

"Bloody hell." Lexi sat back in her chair. "That's definitely not your average job interview."

Nat's phone buzzed in her hand. There was a new voicemail, so she dialled the number and put it on loudspeaker.

"Hi, Natalie. It's Michael. Thanks for coming to the interview yesterday. Could you give me a call back when you have a few minutes? Thanks."

"Oh, sexy voice!" Lexi purred like a cat.

"I suppose that'll take the edge off when he tells me I haven't got the job."

Despite Nat's usual sunny disposition, the recent spate of rejections had really knocked her confidence. She was finding it difficult to summon any kind of positivity. "Well, here goes nothing." Nat lifted the phone to her ear and waited for Michael to answer.

"Hello?"

"Hi Michael, it's Nat."

The momentary pause caused Nat's stomach to lurch. He couldn't have forgotten who she was already?

"Oh Natalie, thanks for calling back. I wanted to have a quick chat with you about the interview."

Nat drew in a long breath to brace herself for the bad news.

"So, obviously, you don't really have any direct experience in being a PA..."

Nat nodded along as she listened to Michael speak, willing him to get to the end so she could hang up and move on. It was clear she hadn't impressed him, so she didn't want her humiliation to drag on any longer.

"...but compared to the other candidates, and the poor decisions the HR team has made recently on who they have appointed for this role, I thought I would give you a chance." Michael coughed. "You do seem to have good transferrable skills and hopefully you will be a quick learner."

The phone went silent. Nat was too stunned to speak.

"Are you still there?"

"Oh yes, sorry." Nat's voice wavered. "I don't know what to say."

"Well, the most common response when someone is offered a job is 'yes'. Even for someone who says they don't actually want the job during the interview."

Nat cringed at the reminder. "I just wasn't expecting this. I didn't really think I would get the job after what happened. Are you sure?"

"Are you questioning me about whether I want to offer you the job?"

Out of the corner of her eye, Nat spotted Lexi wriggling around on her seat and waving her hands around.

"TAKE THE JOB!" she mouthed. "YOU CAN DO IT!"

"OK, if you're happy to give me a chance." Nat bit down on her lip. "I'd love to accept the offer." She let out a sigh of relief.

"Only if you're sure I'm not putting you out?"

Nat couldn't tell from Michael's tone whether he was being serious or not.

"I'll get the HR team to email you across the contract and we can agree on the start date. The sooner the better for me."

"That sounds great." Nat allowed a smile to form on her face. "I'm looking forward to working with you." She slipped the phone back into her pocket and looked up at Lexi, now unable to stop grinning.

"I can't believe it," Nat squealed. "I've finally got a job!"

"This calls for a celebration tonight!" Lexi leaped out of her chair, pulling Nat out of hers and began dancing her around. "Not only are you going to work magic on my shop and turn it into the most successful music cafe in the world, but you have also got yourself a job—" Lexi paused dramatically, a cheeky grin on her face, "—working for a hot CEO. Things are most definitely looking up for you!"

The initial excitement of the job offer didn't last long as Nat quickly became overwhelmed at the thought of what was ahead. How would she juggle starting a new job and help Lexi get her shop ready in time for the launch party?

"Hey." Lexi punched Nat playfully on the arm. "You don't look so happy for someone that has finally got her brother off her back."

"I'm just worried about how I'm going to manage everything." Nat was terrified she would let her best friend down and didn't know if she could cope with any more failures. "I want your shop to look amazing, and I'm about to start a job I don't have the first clue about doing."

"First of all, the plans you have drawn up for the shop are amazing. You tell me exactly what we need and I will get that sorted so you don't have to worry. We have a month and a half until the launch party, which is plenty of time." Lexi put her arm around Nat's shoulder. "Second of all, you will absolutely smash that job. Michael has given you a chance, and he sounds like the type of person who wouldn't take a risk on someone he wasn't sure about."

"You're right." Nat forced a smile. "I need to think more positively." She turned to give Lexi a hug. "Thanks for your support. Let's get these designs finished and then the first drinks are on me!"

As Nat added notes onto the sketches for Lexi's shop, she finally allowed a fraction of excitement and hope to build inside her.

# CHAPTER SEVEN

## Monday 25<sup>th</sup> April

Nat took a deep breath as she opened up her laptop. She had spent the last week preparing for her first day, reading up on the company's background and its mission statement. She was determined to make a good impression. Just because she didn't see a long-term future there, it didn't mean she wanted to look a complete novice. Michael had founded HealthLink a few years ago and the company had grown quickly, with their user base of people looking to connect and share their health journeys now in the millions. They were known for being a forward thinking company and took a strong stance against exploitative behaviours, both for their employees and customers.

The company was flexible and allowed staff to work from home, so Nat was sitting in the kitchen. The table was sturdy and made of dark wood, with a few scuff marks and stains from years of use. Light streamed in through the windows and illuminated the space, creating a bright and airy feel. A vase of fresh daffodils sat in the centre of the table, adding a splash of colour to the room.

Nat loaded her emails and saw a message from Michael at the top of the list. He had welcomed her to the team and given her a brief overview of what was expected of her that day. She was to familiarise herself with his daily schedule and spend some time learning how to use the company's specialised software.

She looked at the time on the corner of the screen. There was an hour until she was due to have a video call with him to run through the urgent tasks. Nat noticed there were some other emails waiting for her, so she opened each one taking in the minutiae of everything she read and jotting down notes in the new notebook she had treated herself to. It was a deep burgundy colour, with gold embossed flowers on the vegan leather cover. The pages were thick and velvety, lined with perfect black ink and calling out for the owner to fill the blank spaces.

"Morning!" Lucy breezed into the kitchen and flicked the switch on the kettle. "Can I make you a drink? I was going to do a pot of tea."

"That would be lovely, thank you."

"How are you getting on?"

"OK, I think." Nat placed her pen down. "Michael has a very busy diary and there's a lot to get my head around."

"Well, it's only your first day, so it's bound to feel a little overwhelming. I'll stop distracting you." Lucy smiled and disappeared into the utility room with a basket overfilling with dirty laundry. Nat returned to her notepad and emails.

"Oh, shit." It was just after ten a.m. and she had missed the start of her first meeting with Michael. She clicked on the video link and adjusted the headset while she waited for the call to connect.

"So, you finally decided to join me?" Michael was leaning back into a large black office chair with a neutral expression on his face.

"I'm so sorry," Nat spluttered. "I was busy reading emails and didn't notice the time." She couldn't tell whether Michael was angry. He was like a closed book and this frustrated her. Even though they had only met twice, she was normally so good at reading people.

"I'll get one of the tech team to show you how to set notifications up. Then you won't forget again."

Nat squirmed in her seat. This really wasn't a good start.

"OK, let's run through everything." Michael sat forward, bringing his face closer to the camera. "There will be some key meetings over the next few weeks you will need to be at, taking minutes and ensuring we have an accurate record of any decisions."

As he began to talk, Nat was mesmerised by the colour of his eyes. The glow from his laptop screen lit up the deep blue in a way she hadn't noticed under the lights of the coffee shop.

The protection she felt from being behind a computer screen allowed her to study him in detail. His dark hair was styled loosely and a day or two of stubble framed his mouth. The plain white t-shirt hugging his muscular frame contrasted perfectly against his tanned skin.

Michael paused for a moment. "Are you still with me?"

Nat brought her focus back to the words coming out of his mouth and nodded to show she was listening. "OK, that sounds good. Decisions." Nat wrote carefully in her notebook.

Lucy came back into the kitchen and switched on the radio. As loud music echoed around the room, Nat waved her arms to get her attention and show she was on a call, forgetting that Michael could see every move.

"Oh, I'm so sorry!" Lucy mouthed, shutting off the radio.

"I hope those aren't your dance moves?" Michael raised an eyebrow.

"Sorry, carry on." Nat smiled apologetically.

He began talking again, but then paused for a moment as Lucy's arm appeared on camera. The hand placed a cup of tea down on the table and slid it towards Nat. Lucy's face appeared momentarily. She nodded at Michael and then slipped quickly out of view again. Nat put her hand up to her mouth to hide a smile, which disappeared quickly as soon as she heard Michael sigh heavily.

"Sorry, again. As you can see, I'm not used to working from home."

"I'll call you a bit later on." His tone was blunt. "I've got a meeting I need to get to now." The call disconnected before Nat was able to respond.

"I'm so sorry." Lucy's face was etched with guilt.

"Honestly, don't worry about it." She gave Lucy a forgiving smile, but couldn't help feeling a little uneasy at the rocky start to her first day. Was Michael always going to be so serious?

The rest of the morning passed quickly as Nat worked through her growing list of jobs. She kept an eye on Michael's emails to ensure anything urgent that came through was flagged for his attention. The first few pages of her notebook had already started to fill up, the handwriting getting messier with each new task.

"I'm going to make some sandwiches." Lucy placed Louis in his highchair with a beaker of water. "Would you like tuna or cheese?"

"Tuna please." Nat tickled Louis under his armpit and he let out a squeal. "Do you want a hand?"

"Oh no, don't worry. You can entertain the little terror for a while. How's the job going so far?"

"Well, it may not be the most life-changing of jobs, but at least it's busy, so the days aren't going to drag." Nat stuck her tongue out and Louis stuck his out in reply.

"What's your boss like?"

"He's..." Nat paused, trying to think how to describe Michael. "He seems like a reasonable person, but can be a little stern at times. A little difficult to read. I need to give it more time before I give my final verdict."

"Oh, dark and mysterious!" Lucy grinned at Nat. "Well, from the quick peek I got earlier, he's extremely good-looking."

Nat rolled her eyes. She contemplated telling Lucy about the coffee shop kiss, but decided against it. It was only Michael doing her a favour and didn't mean anything. She was sure of it. Louis picked up his beaker and banged it on the table, frustrated at not having Nat's full attention.

"Hey there grumpy!" She placed her hand on his chubby fist to calm him down. "Don't worry, you're the only boy I'm interested in."

Louis grinned, showing off his two new bottom teeth. With a shriek, he launched the beaker across the table. As it landed, the lid came loose, the contents drenching Nat's notebook. She grabbed it before the water could do too much damage, spraying her laptop in the process.

"Oh shit, here!" Lucy threw Nat a tea-towel so she could mop up the mess. "I'm so sorry. I thought the lid was on properly."

"Honestly, you really don't need to apologise. You and Simon are doing me a huge favour letting me stay. It's only a bit of water, no harm done." Nat rubbed Lucy's arm. "Come on, I'll help you finish making lunch. I could do with a break from the screen, anyway."

It was almost three p.m. and Nat was determined to be on time for the next video call with Michael. She checked her hair and applied some tinted lip gloss before starting the call. As she waited for him to join her, she fiddled with her pen and doodled on the corner of a page.

"How are you getting on with everything?" Michael's face appeared and his voice made her jump.

"Oh, hi!" Nat sat up straight. "Good, I think."

"Have you confirmed the arrangements for the investor meeting with Spinigma and restaurant booking next Sunday?"

Nat flicked through her notebook, peeling some of the damp pages apart. Some of the ink had smudged a little so she could only just make out the writing.

"Not yet. The restaurant wasn't answering when I called them, so I will try again later."

"OK." Michael frowned. "That's really important as they are flying in from the States, and we only have a few weeks to agree the details of any potential deal."

"Of course. I'll get straight on it when we've finished this call."

"And the other investor, Ethica. How are you getting on reading their proposal and pulling together a summary?"

"Yes, good. I've nearly finished reading it." Nat was frustrated that he kept asking about the tasks she hadn't completed. Her stomach churned a fraction as she saw the stony expression on Michael's face. "But the report will be done by first thing tomorrow morning."

Just as Michael was about to speak, a deafening scream echoed around the kitchen. Louis' baby monitor was on the sideboard, and he had chosen that exact moment to let the household know he had woken up from his afternoon nap.

"What the hell was that?" Michael screwed up his face.

"Oh sorry, that's my nephew." Nat leapt out of her seat to turn the monitor down. "It's not normally this noisy here."

Michael paused for a moment, before returning to the list of work Nat needed to get done before the end of the day.

"OK, well, I'll leave you to it." Michael spoke quickly, his efficiency leaving no time for small talk or niceties. "We'll have another call tomorrow morning after you've finished the report."

"OK, bye—" But Michael ended the call before she could wish him a nice evening.

Nat slumped in her chair, disappointed that he seemed so unimpressed with everything she was doing. She eventually motivated herself enough to continue reading the proposal, trying to ignore the gnawing sensation of self-doubt that was beginning to work its way through her body.

# CHAPTER EIGHT

**Sunday 1ˢᵗ May**

The gravel crunched under the tyres as the car pulled up onto the driveway of Nat and Simon's parents' home nestled in a small Surrey village. The cottage was a vision of rustic beauty, with walls adorned in wisteria vines, thick with purple pendants on the cusp of blooming. They climbed gracefully towards the thatched roof, giving it a fairy-tale feel. A cobblestone path meandered through a well-tended garden, bursting with colourful flowers. Her father's place of respite when he needed time to himself.

Nat stepped out of the car and stretched, taking in the spring sunshine and fresh air. Although the journey had taken less than an hour, travelling by car always made her sleepy. She walked around to the other side and unclipped Louis from his car seat. He was still fast asleep, so Nat cradled his head into her neck, hoping to keep him that way for as long as possible. She loved the sensation of his gentle, rhythmic breathing and the little puffs of hot air against her skin.

"You grab the wine and pudding," Simon called to Lucy. "I'll bring the changing bag."

"Shh!" Nat glared at Simon. "Louis is fast asleep."

"Oh, sorry," he whispered. "Although he won't be allowed to stay that way as soon as Mum gets hold of him!"

The front door swung open and Anita rushed out, her apron covered in flour and a tea-towel slung over her shoulder. Her cheeks were flushed red, likely from the hours spent preparing lunch by the hot oven.

"My baby is here!" She clapped her hands together and went straight towards Nat, arms outstretched. "Come to Granny."

"And there I was thinking you were pleased to see me." Nat teased, handing over Louis. "Be gentle. He's still fast asleep."

Anita landed several noisy kisses on the top of his head and he screwed his face up in response. His eyes flickered open and his mouth immediately turned downwards.

"Oh no baby boy, don't cry." Anita patted his back and gently bounced him up and down. "There we go, that's better."

Before long, Louis was giggling at the sight of his grandad as he crept up behind Anita, pulling silly faces. He stopped to ruffle Louis' hair before walking over to Nat.

"Hi, love." Geoff pulled his daughter in for a crushing hug. "How are you?"

"I'm good, Dad." Nat kissed him on the cheek, then checked him over. As always, he was wearing smart chinos and a checked shirt with the collar peeking out of a soft woollen jumper. "You're looking really well."

"Your mum has me on a special diet." He patted his stomach. "I'm hoping she will let me off today because lunch is smelling delicious. Lucy! Simon! Come on, let's get you all inside."

Nat's mouth watered as soon as she walked into the hallway. The familiar smell of her mum's famous roast beef drifted out of the kitchen, tantalising the house with its rich and savoury aroma.

"Do you need anything doing, Mum?"

"You could help me with the vegetables. I'll get your father to carve the meat in a little while, then we can serve."

"Of course." Nat followed her mum into the kitchen. She smiled as she was quickly reminded of the comforting routine of Sunday roast dinners. As expected, there was a glass of dry sherry on the side and a play on the radio to keep her mum company while she took her time preparing everything for the feast.

Nat rummaged around in the drawer and eventually pulled out a peeler and a small knife. As she began to scrape the skin from the carrots, she felt a slight pang of nostalgia for when she was younger and still lived at home. When the only stress in her life was passing her art exams and deciding what colour to paint her bedroom.

"Something on your mind?" Her mum's voice cut through her thoughts and the steady rhythm of the peeler.

"I'm fine." Nat dropped another layer of orange into the food waste bin. "It's been lovely getting to spend so much time with Louis."

"It's so good of Simon to let you stay with him." Anita took a large head of broccoli out of the fridge and handed it to Nat. "It's such a shame you couldn't work things out with Joe. He seemed like such a nice boy."

Nat bristled at her mother's words and she placed the broccoli roughly onto the chopping board, scattering tiny green florets across the surface.

"It wasn't that I couldn't work things out with Joe," she said, her tone hardening. "It's that he'd already moved on with somebody else. There was nothing to work out."

"Still, maybe if you'd tried a little harder..." Anita's voice trailed off when she saw the look on Nat's face. "Well, anyway. There's plenty more fish in the sea."

They carried on preparing dinner in silence. The brief nostalgia Nat had felt before rapidly evaporating at the reminder of why she had been so keen to leave home at the first opportunity.

"How's the new job going?" Anita smacked Geoff's hand as he reached over to take another roast potato from the dish.

"It's only been a week, but so far it's OK."

"What's your boss like?"

"Yes, he's fine." Nat glanced over and spotted the silly grin on Lucy's face. She kicked her under the table and looked away to avoid giggling. "He's a little moody at times, and it's not like I really have any other option. Those job offers weren't flying into my lap. Hopefully, I won't have long to wait until a design contract comes through and I can get my business back on track."

Nat glared as Simon let out an involuntary grunt. The way he dismissed her career infuriated her. Just because he was a hot-shot high paid lawyer didn't make him any better than her. Interior design was her passion and what made her happy, even if it didn't always pay the bills. But she bit her tongue. She didn't want to start an argument in front of their parents, and she was grateful for the fact he was letting her live with them.

"Well, it's good you finally have a job." Anita piled some extra vegetables onto Geoff's plate. "And who knows what that might lead to? Working for a tech company sounds exciting!"

"I'm still looking for interior design work." Nat struggled to keep her tone neutral.

"I'm just saying, maybe a change in career wouldn't be such a bad idea?"

"Well, we're behind you, whatever happens, sweetheart." This time Geoff managed to swipe a final potato while Anita was distracted feeding Louis. He winked at Nat, before popping it in his mouth whole, wincing at the nuclear heat that hid within and forcing out quick breaths for the steam to escape. Nat shook her head at him, unable to hide a smile.

Anita took advantage of the lull in conversation, relishing the opportunity to update everyone on the latest village gossip.

Nat nodded along politely, doing her best to keep up with the different names and how they related to each other. The plates emptied one by one as Anita worked her way through the sordid tales from what, to any outsider, appeared to be a picture-perfect slice of sleepy middle-class countryside heaven.

"I'll start clearing the dishes away." Nat stood up, relieved to have avoided any further discussion about her career, or lack of it.

"I'll help you." Lucy reached across to take Simon's plate.

"How very 1950s housewife of us!" Nat winked at Lucy, who curtseyed in response.

"It's OK," Lucy said, interrupting Simon just as he was about to protest. "Simon is a very modern father and was just about to change Louis' nappy, weren't you?!" She rushed out before he could object, and Nat followed her into the kitchen.

As Nat brought through the last of the dishes, her phone buzzed in her back pocket. She pulled it out to unlock the screen and was surprised to see an email from her favourite university tutor from her last year of studying. They had kept in touch since Nat had graduated a few years ago and Sylvie was always keeping an eye out for new opportunities for her.

Subject line: Exciting opportunity

Hi Nat,

I hope you are keeping well? I have just had this come through my network and I think it's right up your street. You only have a month to prepare your portfolio, but I have already put in a good word, and they want to interview you on the 31$^{st}$ May at 10 a.m. I've attached the brief. Give me a call if you want to talk it through.

Good luck!

Sylvie x

Nat clicked on the attachment, her eyes growing wider as she took in the detailed information on the screen.

"Are you OK?" Lucy patted her on the arm to get her attention.

"I don't believe it!" Nat turned her phone towards Lucy. "There's an opportunity to bid for an amazing design contract. It's for the owners of a grand country house in the Cotswolds. They want to turn it into a luxury hotel. If the successful designer does a good job, they could end up being the official partner working on properties they are securing all over the world." Nat couldn't believe the words that were coming out of her mouth. "This is my absolute dream job."

"That sounds fantastic!" Lucy's smile shifted into a frown. "So why don't you look happy about it?"

"I don't know how I'm going to manage it all." Nat scrolled down through the portfolio requirements. "I'm only one week into the new job and I've got to do so much work on Lexi's shop to get that ready for the launch. How on earth am I going to fit in preparing a portfolio good enough to win the contract alongside all of that in a month?"

"You absolutely can, and will, do it." Lucy placed her hands on Nat's shoulders. "Whatever you need, just let me know and I can help. I'm sure Simon will help, too."

"No." Nat shook her head. "Please don't say anything to Simon about this. I couldn't bear the disappointment at another failure of mine."

Lucy sighed. "Look, I know he can come across like that, but he really is very supportive of you. We both are."

"I know. But let's just keep this between us for now. I'll have a think about it."

"OK, but don't let this dream slip through your fingers. You know you'll regret it if you don't try."

As they travelled home later that day, Nat stared out of the window, watching the world pass by in a blur. The sun was setting and pastel hues filled the sky with shades of pink, apricot, and violet. The last few weeks had not been easy, and Nat knew Lucy was right. This was the contract she was waiting for, and she couldn't let this opportunity pass her by.


That evening, Nat lay back in the bathtub, a cloud of lavender-scented bubbles surrounding her as she allowed her body to relax. She closed her eyes and drifted into a daydream, imagining the country house and how she might transform it into something beautiful. There would be plush fabrics covering the walls and elegant chandeliers hanging from the ceilings. Carefully selected pieces of art and furniture would make a statement to those lucky enough to be staying there. She could really make a name for herself with this opportunity.

"Imagine that," she murmured to herself, a smile gracing her lips at the thought of finally achieving her lifelong dream.

Her thoughts shifted to the week that had just gone by—a whirlwind of meetings, paperwork, and endless cups of coffee. Despite her lack of experience, Nat felt a growing sense of accomplishment. She had managed to keep up with the frenetic pace and adapt to the demands of her new job.

As she soaked in the warmth, Nat thought about the new colleagues she had met over the previous week. They had mostly been kind and supportive, offering advice when needed or simply lending a sympathetic ear when she felt overwhelmed.

Her favourite was Jamie, one of the technical team who had been exceptionally welcoming from the start. He was a far cry from the stereotypical geek, with his perfectly trimmed beard, easy smile, and bright green eyes that sparkled with mischief. He had greeted her on the first day she had worked in the office with a steaming cup of caramel coffee and a box of fresh donuts. This small act of kindness had touched Nat, even though he proceeded to work his way through most of the contents of the box before she had even managed to eat one.

Could managing the new job and preparing the portfolio be possible after all? Her fingers traced patterns in the bubbles. The steep learning curve hadn't deterred her spirit. If anything, it had only served to fuel her determination to do well.

Her phone buzzed on the side, interrupting her thoughts. The screen displayed Michael's name, and a knot began to tighten in her stomach. Why would he be calling her this time on a Sunday night?

"Hello?" she said, her voice wavering.

"Natalie." Michael's tone was sharp. "Did you confirm the reservation for us at La Maison tonight?"

"Yes... yes, I did," she stammered, racking her brain to remember the details of the phone call she had made earlier in the week.

"Well, it appears they don't have any record of it. I am standing here with the representatives from Spinigma. What the hell am I supposed to do?" Michael paused for a moment.

"Do you want me to come over there now?" Nat sat bolt upright, sending water cascading down the side of the bath. "I could speak to someone and sort it out."

"Don't bother, by the time you get here I will have found somewhere else. It's a bank holiday tomorrow, so we'll talk about this Tuesday morning. I need you to come to my apartment first thing. I'm waiting for a delivery and can't go out."

"Of course. I'm so sorry. I don't know what happened," she said, her voice thick with regret.

"Just be there by eight a.m. sharp." He hung up before she could respond.

The knot in her stomach twisted tighter as she stared at the screen and panic swirled within her, threatening to overwhelm her. She needed advice, comfort—someone to help her process her thoughts. Her fingers hovered over the screen, scrolling down to Lexi's name, and pressed 'Call'.

"Hey! How's it going?" Lexi chirped as she picked up the call, her bright tone a stark contrast to Michael's irritation.

"I messed up," Nat sighed, feeling tears pricking at the corners of her eyes. "I messed up big time."

"Hey, slow down. What happened?"

"Michael just called me. I was supposed to sort out a reservation for dinner with an important investor. I must have forgotten to book it with everything being so busy at the house with Lucy and Louis, and now he's furious with me," Nat said, her words tumbling out in a rush. "He wants to talk Tuesday morning, and I'm pretty sure he's going to fire me."

"OK, first things first—take a deep breath," Lexi instructed. "It sounds like an honest mistake. Just explain what happened, apologise, and make sure it doesn't happen again. Just be professional—it's your first week and you're still learning."

"You're right." Nat exhaled. The breath she didn't realise she was holding escaped her lips. "It's just so hard when everything is so new, and I feel like I'm constantly trying to prove myself."

"I get it," Lexi reassured her. "But remember, nobody's perfect and everyone makes mistakes. You'll learn from this and become even better at your job."

"Thanks, Lexi. You always know what to say," Nat said, feeling more settled as she wiped away a stray tear.

"Anytime. Just call if you need anything, OK?"

"Will do. Goodnight."

"Goodnight. Chin up."

Nat rested her phone on the edge of the bath, staring at it for a moment before letting out a shaky breath. She closed her eyes and submerged herself under the water, feeling the weightlessness as her long hair floated around her. As she held her breath, she replayed the conversation with Michael in her mind, his frustration clear in every word he had spoken. Would this one mistake be enough for her to lose her job? Simon would be furious with her.

Resurfacing, Nat gasped for air and wiped the water from her face. As she looked around the bathroom, her gaze fell upon the assortment of design magazines that she had sprawled across the floor earlier. They served as a reminder of the future that might be even further out of reach if she was going to be spending her time finding another job.

Taking a deep breath, she resolved to face the upcoming confrontation head-on. Tuesday will be another day, she reminded herself, another opportunity to learn and grow.

"Sink or swim," she whispered, before closing her eyes and slipping deeper into the water, trying to drift away from the worries plaguing her thoughts.

# CHAPTER NINE

**Tuesday 3ʳᵈ May**

Nat checked the message on her phone.

"Twenty-three," she muttered, running her fingers up the buttons on the polished silver panel of the imposing building in one of Kensington's most affluent neighbourhoods. The number was right at the top—she assumed he must live in the penthouse apartment that crowned the exclusive development. The property developers would have never marketed these exclusive dwellings as a mere 'block of flats'. This was decidedly the epitome of extravagant living and Nat couldn't help feeling a tad underdressed and out-of-place amid such unapologetic luxury.

It shouldn't have come as a surprise—where else would the CEO of a successful social media company live? This was poles apart from the life of a failing interior designer. One who had no choice but to move out of a tiny flat and in with her brother. She looked up and felt even smaller at the overwhelming sight of the enormous building towering above her. The speaker crackled and Michael's voice boomed out.

"Come up."

The speaker clicked off and the sound of a buzzer made her jump. Nat was already on edge, her nerves like coiled springs and ready to snap at any moment. She pushed the heavy glass door open, took a deep breath, and stepped inside.

The foyer was airy, with pristine marble floors and contemporary art decorating the walls. Lush plants were dotted around, providing splashes of vibrant green against the neutral tones. Two comfortable leather sofas welcomed residents and guests to take a seat and admire the city views through the tall windows. This wasn't just an entrance space, this set the stage for the luxury and comfort that you could expect throughout the entire building. The place even smelt expensive.

Nat made her way to the lifts and pressed the button. She fiddled with her nails as she waited for it to arrive, watching the illuminated numbers count down slowly above the doors. They ticked down towards zero—a cruel timer set especially for the unfortunate fate waiting for her upstairs. When the doors finally whooshed open, she stepped inside, her heart pulsing in her chest. The speed of the lift caused her already sensitive stomach to lurch, and she placed her hand on the railing to steady herself.

The doors opened on the top floor. Nat stepped out and took a few paces forward to stand in front of a large black wooden door with polished silver numbers. Before she had a chance to knock, the door opened. Michael was on his phone and beckoned for her to come inside. She closed the door behind her and followed him through into an enormous open-plan kitchen, dining area and lounge.

Floor to ceiling windows took up two sides of the room, showcasing a sprawling city view of skyscrapers and tower blocks with the river carved right down the middle. Nat took in everything around her. Each piece of furniture was carefully placed to maximise the sense of space. Not that the apartment needed any help to feel any bigger. Her old apartment could have fitted into just the kitchen area.

The use of whites, greys, and blacks across the space complemented each other to highlight the light and dark, creating different zones. But something was missing. There was no colour, no sense of life, nothing that gave away Michael's personal identity. Nat guessed he had paid someone to furnish his apartment, but they hadn't taken the time to get to know him. Or he didn't want them to know him. She would have done a much better job, given the chance.

"Why don't you take a seat?" Michael had finished his call and signalled for Nat to take a chair up at the breakfast counter. "Can I get you a coffee?"

"Oh," Nat faltered. "Yes, please." She was hoping to get this over and done with as quickly as possible, assuming he would want to do the same. Maybe he was just being kind and doing his best to break the news gently?

"So, I thought it was best we did this face to face." Michael placed a capsule into the coffee machine and flicked the switch. Despite stating the importance of having the conversation in person, Nat noticed he was making every effort to avoid eye contact. "I can't afford for you to make these types of mistakes. The investor I took out for dinner last night could take the company to the next level. This is a crucial time, and securing finance at the moment is extremely challenging. They have to be sure we are taking any potential deal seriously." He placed a coffee cup in front of her.

Nat nodded solemnly as she listened to him scold her like a disappointed parent. She was all too familiar with that feeling.

"I'm really sorry." She pulled the drink towards her, trying not to spill the contents on the spotless counter.

"Milk?" He placed a delicate white porcelain jug down.

"Thank you." Nat reached forward, and as Michael moved his hand away, it brushed against hers. She flinched at the tiny electric shock that passed between them. Their eyes met. Did he feel it too? After a moment, he broke eye contact and turned away.

"I know it's only been a week—" he said.

"Please, it *has* only been a week," Nat interrupted him. "But it was an honest mistake. There was so much going on and I remember I couldn't get through on the phone, so I left them a message. They can't have picked it up." She took a sip of her drink, the cup wobbling slightly in her hand as she tried to steady her nerves.

"It's not acceptable." Michael looked at her, dissatisfaction sitting deeply in the lines carved across his forehead. "I've had enough problems with staff not doing their jobs properly. I took a chance with you and I'm starting to regret that decision."

His harsh words cut into Nat, and she took a steady breath to ward off the tears threatening to spill over.

"I really need this job." She pushed down the shame that came with her pleading tone. "Would you consider giving me some more time to prove myself? I promise I have learned from this, and I won't let you down again."

Michael continued to stare at her, a coldness to the intense blue of his eyes. He took a deep breath. "OK, I'll give you some more time."

"Thank you so much!" Nat let out a deep sigh of relief.

"But there are some conditions attached to this." He placed his hands firmly on the counter. "Your home environment is far too chaotic, and I need to make sure you're on track with what needs doing. If you can't find anywhere quieter to work, you need to get yourself to the office. When I'm in the office, you need to be there with me."

"Of course." Nat nodded.

"And there will be times when I'm working from home that you'll need to base yourself here. I know that is a little unconventional, but I think it's important until we can build more trust."

"Absolutely, whatever you need me to do." The tension in Nat's stomach finally began to ease.

"There can't be any more mistakes." Michael's expression softened a fraction. "I'll give you a month."

Nat nodded.

A month might be all she needs.

# CHAPTER TEN

**Wednesday 4ᵗʰ May**

T he following morning, Nat returned to Michael's apartment and set up her laptop on the dining table. The smooth glass top was a stark contrast to the rustic wood at her brother's house. Every time she put something down, the sound reverberated around the room. Michael sat at the end of the table, positioned to enjoy the incredible view and keep an eye on Nat at the same time.

Nat had a view of light grey walls and the uncomfortable sensation of being exposed from all sides. A plain black sideboard lined the wall, with a simple silver light stand and a large, empty silver bowl. There were no photographs anywhere to give her any clues about his life. The only sound filling the room, now she had finally settled herself down, was the rhythmic hum from the refrigerator and the gentle clicking of a mouse as Michael studied his screen.

She coughed, and Michael looked up at her.

"It's very quiet, isn't it?" Nat opened her notebook. The pages were still warped from their soaking earlier in the week.

"Just how I like it." Michael looked back down at his screen, putting an end to the conversation.

Nat sighed, reaching over to her bag and pulling out a pair of bright yellow headphones, eager to fill the silence. She made sure to unravel them slowly so as not to make too much noise. Michael watched her but said nothing as she stretched the thin wire between her hands and plugged the end into the laptop. She paused just before putting them on her head, feeling his eyes still on her. Selecting an upbeat playlist to lighten her mood, the music filled her head as she opened up a document and began typing.

A few minutes later, movement from the corner of her eye drew her attention. Michael's eyes were wide and his face had a look of exasperation. "Do you realise you are humming along?" There was a clear undertone of irritation in his voice.

"I can't help it." Nat shrugged her shoulders innocently. "It's just so quiet here and I needed something else besides the fridge and the sound of your constant disappointment."

A faint grin played at the edges of his mouth. Nat saw it just before he was able to hide his reaction and her stomach gave a little flip. Maybe she was going to win him over.

After an hour, Nat was pleased with the progress she was making on her work and decided it was time for a short break.

"I'll make us a coffee. How do you like yours?" She pushed back her chair. The legs scraped against the floor, making them both wince.

"Just black, please." Michael stretched, locking his fingers together behind his head.

She was momentarily distracted by how the pale blue shirt became taut against his skin. The fabric between the buttons gaped under the pressure, teasing her with a glimpse of what lay underneath.

"The coffee pods are just in that drawer."

"Oh right, yes." Nat's skin flushed bright red, and she turned her back on him.

"How are you getting on with your work?"

"Great." She knew this was a test. But this time, she was ready. "I've finished writing up the actions from the meetings last week and most of them have already been completed. You just need to sign off the latest HR policies so they can be issued. The notes for the finance team have been sent and I've checked—they should have completed their assessment of Ethica by the end of next week. The next meeting with Spinigma has been scheduled for Thursday morning and I have triple-confirmed a table for lunch at the new Thai restaurant. Apparently, their CEO has been desperate to eat there for weeks and not been able to get a booking."

Nat paused to place the coffee cup down in front of Michael, unable to take the satisfied smile off her face.

"Good." Michael lifted the cup and took a sip. She couldn't tell if he was pleased or not. "Let's hope you keep this up."

Despite his neutral tone, Nat took his comment as a positive and allowed it to lift her confidence. She sat down at the table with her own coffee, placed her headphones back on her head and nodded her head along quietly to the music for the rest of the morning.

The vibration of Michael's phone against the table caught Nat's attention. She pulled her headphones aside slightly and watched as he checked the message.

"I need to pop down and collect a delivery." He closed his laptop and stood up. "I'll grab some lunch while I'm out. Is there anything in particular you would like?"

"Oh, thank you." Nat's stomach growled at the thought of food. "I'm not fussy, you choose."

Michael grabbed a black leather jacket from a coat stand and made his way to the door. Nat watched him leave. His confident stride and the way he effortlessly pulled on his jacket triggered something inside her. The sight was so far removed from what she was used to—remembering the awkward way Joe carried himself. Joe didn't slide into his clothes. He wriggled and writhed, just like the snake he turned out to be. Nat shook her head. Now was not the time to be getting interested in another man. Especially not when that man was your boss.

She needed to stretch her legs. Sitting still for a living was not doing her any good. Her joints felt like they belonged to someone in their sixties, not someone who hadn't even reached thirty yet. Nat decided it wouldn't harm to explore Michael's apartment while he was out. Surely he wouldn't have invited her to work from here if he had something to hide? Plus, it was a good excuse as there was plenty of space to get her steps up.

As she walked around, she noticed the minimalist design and the absence of personal touches continued throughout. A large, pristine white sofa sat against one wall, looking inviting yet untouched. A perfectly aligned book sat in the middle of a sleek glass coffee table. It was the autobiography of a famous businessman. Perhaps an inspiration for Michael and what he hoped for his future?

Nat's attention was drawn to a framed black and white piece of art photography that hung on one wall. It added a touch of creativity to the otherwise sterile space. The lack of family photos or any personal mementos emphasised to her that Michael was a private man, keeping his personal life hidden from view. Hidden even in his own home, if you could call it that.

The kitchen was immaculate, with stainless steel appliances and a spotless counter-top. Nat noticed the fridge was almost empty, with only essentials like milk, eggs, and some fruit. A few bottles of beer rolled about in the bottom drawer. It was clear that Michael didn't spend much time cooking or grocery shopping. He probably had food delivered or just ate at fancy restaurants.

The apartment was a perfect reflection of Michael himself—cool, composed, and guarded. The quiet and emptiness that had initially unnerved her now made sense. Michael's world was precise and controlled, just like his business dealings. She struggled to reconcile this with the man who kissed her hand in the coffee shop only a few weeks ago.

Curiosity got the better of her, and she ventured a peek into the bedrooms. The first was a serene oasis in soft shades of beige and cream. A neatly made king-sized bed with crisp white linens dominated the room, flanked by matching nightstands. She guessed this was his room—a precisely hung suit jacket was the only item that betrayed his presence. She didn't step inside. Just looking felt like an invasion of his privacy that was overstepping a boundary.

The second bedroom also contained a perfectly made king-size bed, but this was a more functional room. A sturdy workout bench and set of dumbbells were carefully placed against one wall, indicating that it doubled as a home gym. A yoga mat was rolled out on the floor. This was yet another room that gave no clues about the owner of the apartment. Although, it didn't take a genius to know he was into his fitness. You just had to look at Michael's toned physique, and Nat didn't need any excuses to do that. The thought of his body made her blush slightly, even though there was no one around to see.

She pulled the door back until it clicked shut and sat back down at the dining table. As she began working on her laptop, she was even more intrigued by the man behind the quiet façade, wondering where the colour in his life was hiding.

Michael swung the front door open, balancing a parcel on his hip and carrying a couple of bags of sushi from a local restaurant. Nat leapt up from her seat and took the parcel from him, closing the door behind them both.

"Thanks. Would you mind popping it over there?" He signalled over to the kitchen counter.

"I'll grab some plates. Where are they?"

"That top one there."

Nat reached up and grabbed two plates from the cupboard, putting them on the other end of the table they had been working from.

"Oh." Her voice faltered when she saw Michael watching her with a strange expression on his face. "I'm happy to take mine outside if you'd rather have some quiet time."

"Don't be silly." His face relaxed into a smile. "It would be nice to have some company while I eat for a change."

"OK, as long as I don't have to eat in complete silence."

"No, you don't!" Michael laughed, and the sound triggered a tiny flutter in her stomach. "But you're going to have to ask the questions. I've never been great at small talk."

"OK, tell me all about yourself. Where are you from? Have you got any siblings? What do you like to do outside of work?" Nat placed a piece of sushi in her mouth and looked at Michael, her eyes wide and expectant.

"Wow, going straight into the deep stuff!" He picked up his chopsticks, taking his time to align them into the perfect position before picking up a California roll.

"Well, you did say I could ask the questions. And you have an advantage over me as you interviewed me." She paused to focus on aligning her chopsticks again. "I, on the other hand, know very little about you. Apart from the fact you are very serious and live in an apartment that looks like a show home."

"I didn't realise I was going to get an inquisition!" Michael picked up a napkin, folded it, and gently wiped the corner of his mouth. "I also didn't know I was that serious."

"You are kidding me?" Nat snorted, lifting her hand to catch a piece of rice before it fell and made a mess on the pristine table.

Michael shrugged his shoulders. "OK, I suppose I can be a little serious at times."

"When we first met, I told you my name was Nat, but you still choose to call me Natalie." She narrowed her eyes a fraction. "And I suppose you hate it if people call you Mike, rather than Michael?"

"I just prefer proper names, that's all."

"Don't you think that's a bit formal, and maybe why you come across as serious?"

"It's just who I am."

"Fair enough." Nat was starting to think stubbornness should be added to his list of personality traits. "So, where are you from?"

"I grew up in the Cotswolds with my mum and dad. No siblings. I left to go to university in London, travelled around for a while, then came back and set up my company."

Nat waited for him to carry on talking, but he kept his attention on the food.

"That's it? That's all you're going to give me?"

Michael nodded. "There's not much of a story to tell."

"Everybody has a story." Nat held his gaze for a moment. "You just have to want to tell it." As the intensity grew between them, she looked away and focused on eating the last bits scattered on her plate.

With lunch finally finished, Michael cleared his throat and stood up. "I'll get these dishes put away and then we'd better get back to work."

As the rest of the afternoon passed by, Nat noticed more and more of Michael's little habits. The way he paced up and down when he was talking on the phone. How when he concentrated, he fiddled with his watch strap and ran his tongue along his top teeth. That was by far the most distracting habit of his. She wondered whether she had similar quirks and if he had noticed them. As her mind drifted, imagining him concentrating on her and what he could do with his tongue, she felt a sudden heat rising up her neck and scolded herself for thinking about her boss like that. She knew it would be inappropriate for them to start any kind of relationship. Not that he would be remotely interested in her anyway, and she certainly wasn't ready for anything since her messy break-up with Joe.

A loud buzz from the intercom interrupted her wandering thoughts. Michael checked the screen and pressed the button to let a visitor into the building. Nat looked expectantly at Michael, but just as he was about to speak, his phone rang. The call connected, and he was immediately deep in conversation. A few moments later, there was a loud knock on the door and he motioned for Nat to answer it.

"Hey!" Nat greeted the visitor as she pulled the door open.

"Oh, hi! I'm Enzo." The newcomer extended his hand with a friendly infectious smile, his deep brown eyes sparkling with a hint of mischief. "And you aren't who I was expecting to answer the door!"

"Yes, sorry!" Nat laughed and shook his hand. "I'm Nat, Michael's new PA."

"Of course, he did mention you." He raised an eyebrow. "You've made quite an impression."

"Hmmm, not in a good way, unfortunately."

"You'd be surprised." Enzo laughed when he saw the puzzled look on Nat's face. "Anyway, don't mind him. He's very serious and his standards are incredibly high, but deep down he's a real softie. We've been best friends since primary school, so I should know!" Enzo's laughter was contagious, and Nat smiled in return.

He walked into the apartment, Nat following behind him. He was tall and lean, with flawless olive skin and a face framed by curly blonde hair. His whole demeanour exuded charisma, making him instantly likable. Nat couldn't help but notice the contrast between the quiet calm of Michael and Enzo's exuberant charm. She wondered how these two seemingly different people had become such good friends.

Michael had just finished his call and slipped his phone into his back pocket.

"Hey buddy!" Enzo grabbed Michael's hand and pulled him in for a half hug, the way men do, trying to seem macho when giving a public display of affection.

"Nice to see you, mate!" Michael returned the hug, then checked his watch and walked over to the fridge to grab a couple of beers.

"Thanks." Enzo took a bottle. "Where are your manners?" He raised an eyebrow at Michael and gestured towards Nat.

"Oh, sorry." Michael turned, a sheepish grin on his face. "Would you like one?"

Nat checked her watch, then shook her head. "No thanks. I'd better be getting back home."

"Ah, that's a shame. We're off out to watch the game tonight." Enzo took a swig of his beer. "You should join us."

"I'm sorry. I need to get back home as I'm babysitting for my nephew tonight." Nat was sure she saw a flicker of disappointment on Michael's face. "Maybe next time?" she added. He gave a slight nod and a smile.

Nat pulled on her coat and grabbed her bag from the chair. "Have a fun evening. It was nice to meet you, Enzo."

"Great to meet you, too. You're definitely coming out with us next time." Enzo winked at her. "Then you might believe me that Michael *does* have a fun side after all." They both laughed, but Michael remained silent, narrowing his eyes at them which only caused them to laugh harder.

"See you at the office tomorrow," she called out as she pulled the door closed behind her.

Nat stepped outside of Michael's apartment block and into the fresh air with a tiny bounce in her step. A bounce that had been absent for far too long.

# CHAPTER ELEVEN

**Saturday 7ᵗʰ May**

N at rolled her eyes at the sound of the horn. Lexi knew just how to make her presence known in a way that infuriated Simon, especially at nine a.m. on a Saturday morning.

"Nat!" Simon's voice, filled with frustration, echoed up the stairs. Nat grabbed her phone and sent a quick text to let Lexi know she was on her way, just in case she beeped again and Simon lost it completely.

"Bye!" Nat called out, pulling on her shoes and stumbling out of the front door. She climbed into the front seat of Lexi's old silver Mini and clicked her seatbelt in place before they sped off. Lexi's driving was a bit like her approach to everything—faster than necessary, somewhat reckless, and ignoring the directions to where she was heading. She had always been destined to carve her own path in life.

"So, two weeks down…" Lexi pulled onto the roundabout, accelerating quickly to avoid being shunted by a white van. "How is the new job going? Has it improved?"

"It's certainly going a lot better than the beginning of the week. I've got three weeks left of my probation period. Hopefully, I can get through that with no more disasters."

Nat shuddered at the thought of the restaurant booking. The telling-off she had received was still fresh in her mind. But her confidence had grown over the past few days and Michael didn't seem quite so disappointed in her. He had been trusting her with more challenging pieces of work, and she was enjoying the feeling of being part of a team. The world of interior design was incredible, but it could feel lonely at times.

"Doesn't it help that your probation officer is gorgeous, though?" Lexi flashed a wicked grin at Nat.

"How do you know?" Nat glared at her.

"So you agree?"

"No!" Nat protested a little too loudly. "Obviously he's good-looking, but I'm not interested in him like that."

"Hmm." Lexi didn't sound convinced. "Well, I did what most normal people do when they want to find out about someone—I looked him up on the internet."

"And what did you find out?" Nat sat up straighter in her seat, eager to find out what Lexi knew. She was excited by the possibility of finally knowing more about Michael. Despite trying hard all week, she had got little more than small talk out of him. It wasn't that she was looking for anything romantic, despite her wandering thoughts. After Joe, that was going to be out of the question for quite some time. But the less he told her, the more she wanted to learn. He felt like a challenge, one she couldn't refuse.

"Oh, so you want to know more? I didn't think you were interested?"

"Just spill it." Nat sighed, barely able to contain her impatience.

"Actually, it's nothing very exciting, if I'm honest. His social media accounts are completely locked down. The only reason I saw a photo was because they had his biography on the website for a conference he spoke at a few months ago."

"Oh." A tiny flutter of disappointment settled in Nat's stomach. "He really is a closed book."

"I bet you want to slip inside his covers, though!"

"Time to change the subject before we end up even deeper in the gutter. With your terrible driving, that's where we spend most of our time, anyway!" Nat punched Lexi playfully on the arm. "Let me talk you through where I've got to with the shop design before we get to the fabric shop."

Half an hour later and with a voice hoarse from singing along to their favourite songs, Nat recognised where they were.

"Pull up there, just on the left." She pointed to a small row of shops up ahead.

Lexi flicked the indicator, swerved up onto the kerb and brought the car to a sudden halt.

The bell above the door tinkled as Nat and Lexi entered the small, unassuming shop. The exterior was weathered, its paint faded and timeworn, but the space inside danced with a kaleidoscope of colours. Bolts of fabric stood tall, like sentinels guarding the entrance to a magical realm. The scent of aged textiles lingered in the air, mingling with a light floral perfume. The shop's owner was standing behind the cluttered counter. Silver hair framed a gentle face that crinkled with delight as soon as she spotted Nat.

"My dear!" she said, walking around and holding her arms out. "It's been too long."

"Hello, Mrs Thompson." Nat smiled and returned the older woman's gentle hug. The familiarity of the cosy space filled her with a sense of calm. "We're on a mission for the perfect fabrics today."

"Well, you've come to the right place." Mrs Thompson chuckled, her eyes sparkling. "Let me show you the treasures we have tucked away."

It was hard to believe that this warm soul was the same Mrs Thompson who had once loomed larger than life at the front of Nat's university lecture theatre. Back then, her fire and passion for her craft had been intimidating. But over time, Nat had grown to understand the depth of love and kindness behind her stern demeanour.

Her lectures were a dizzying whirlwind of vibrant colours, intricate patterns and a deep-rooted history of textile design. Mrs Thompson's enthusiasm was contagious, igniting a fire in Nat's heart that cemented her dreams of becoming an interior designer.

As she wandered up and down the narrow aisles, Nat allowed her fingers to graze delicate silks and textured linens. The shop provided a rich tapestry of possibilities for her to bring Lexi's shop to life. She inspected the different fabrics, imagining the stage with a dramatic backdrop for the performers. Lexi pulled out various textures and hues, each met with a thoughtful shake of Nat's head. The anticipation built with every unfurled roll and piece of fabric discarded on the old wooden floor.

"Wait, my dears." Mrs Thompson disappeared into the labyrinth. She emerged triumphantly, cradling a roll of deep claret velvet. "Draped correctly, and this will command attention and add a touch of elegance. And look here!" She produced a delicate gold fabric edging that sparkled under the dim shop lights. "You could add this trim to really take it up a notch."

"Oh, they're absolutely beautiful!" Nat's eyes widened, and she could not stop her jaw falling open. "That's exactly what I was looking for. Now, we need some wallpaper."

Nat's excitement was contagious as the trio continued their search, the small space pulsating with creative energy. Nat did a double take and stopped in her tracks. She delved into a cluster of rolls, frantically moving them to the side to reach what she was looking for. She turned to face Lexi and Mrs Thompson.

"I can't believe it!" She was holding a thick roll of silver wallpaper adorned with black musical notes. The serendipitous discovery almost left her breathless as she showed Lexi. "This will be perfect for the back wall. It's like it was made just for you!" She looked at Mrs Thompson with pleading eyes. "Please tell me there is more of this?"

Mrs Thompson disappeared upstairs into the stock room. The next few minutes felt like hours as Nat waited to see whether there would be enough to cover the space.

Finally, her voice floated down into the shop. "You're in luck! I have four more rolls up here and I can always order more in if you need it."

Nat let out a huge sigh of relief. "Fantastic. I'll take all of those, please." She ran up the stairs. "Let me come up and help you bring them down."

Nat picked up two rolls of wallpaper and turned to walk back downstairs. A flash of colour caught her eye. A stunning piece of abstract art was leaning up against the wall. Splashes of cerulean, crimson, and gold were intermingled with darker tones of navy and forest green.

"Where did this come from?" Nat's eyes were fixed on the artwork.

"A local artist gave me this print of his original piece for the shop, but it never felt quite right here." Mrs Thompson sighed. "It was lost amongst the fabrics, so I tried it at home. But it definitely didn't suit an old-fashioned bungalow!"

"Would you consider selling it?" Nat's eyes brightened with inspiration. Her thoughts immediately sprung to Michael's apartment and how it was calling out for a bit of colour. "I know just the place where its beauty would shine." Hopefully he would appreciate the offer, rather than be offended. He knew she was an interior designer, and it was a gift, after all.

"Well, then. You can have it. No need for any money." Mrs Thompson shook her head firmly. "It deserves to go somewhere it will be enjoyed, rather than gathering dust up here."

"Are you sure?"

"Absolutely." Mrs Thompson smiled. "You are my favourite customer, after all! Take it downstairs and I'll roll it carefully so you can frame it when you get home."

Back downstairs, Mrs Thompson put the fabrics and wallpaper through the till and Nat handed over her credit card.

"Oh, I almost forgot!" Mrs Thomson reached under the counter and pulled out a small black box. "I've been saving these for you." She opened the lid and held the box out.

Nat took it from her and carefully lifted out swatches of fabric that unfolded like lavish tapestries. Satins, rich as midnight, dripped between her fingers. She held up lace to reveal intricately woven floral motifs, each thread showcasing meticulous craftsmanship. Metallic brocades glistened with an elegant sheen, nestled amongst plush velvets. Each swatch was a miniature masterpiece infused with the essence of indulgence, beckoning with the promise of haute couture dreams.

"Are these...?" Nat's voice faltered and her eyes grew wide.

Mrs Thompson nodded, a warm smile on her face.

"OK, will someone please explain what is going on?" Lexi threw her hands up in the air.

"These fabrics are from a specialist design house in Paris," Nat explained, unable to tear her gaze away from the materials in her hands. "It has been my dream to be able to use their designs as part of a project. They only make so much of each of these different fabrics. One day, I might even be lucky enough to visit their boutique. It's just down the street from the Eiffel Tower!"

"Those are the last few pieces I will get for quite a while now, as the next shipment isn't due for a few months. Put them to good use, please!"

"Oh I will." Nat grinned. "I am pulling together a special portfolio at the moment and these might give me just the edge I need to win the contract!"

With the car finally loaded, Nat hugged Mrs Thompson goodbye and promised to visit again soon. Spending time immersed in her passion was just the reminder she needed that she wasn't ready to let go of her dreams. She was pleased the job with Michael was going well, but it was just a temporary measure until she was back on her feet.

Holding on tight to the box of special fabrics, she closed her eyes and imagined how impressive they would look lining the walls of a luxury country hotel. She smiled to herself as Lexi turned the radio up as loud as it would go, allowing the sensation of hope for the future to build inside her.

# CHAPTER TWELVE

**Wednesday 11<sup>th</sup> May**

"Good morning!" Nat grinned at the security guard, Alfred, as he held the door open for her. "Thank you so much."

"You're welcome!" Alfred smiled, giving a little bow.

Nat felt her morning instantly brighten. Alfred had been with the company for years and knew everyone by name. She enjoyed chatting with him and he always had warm words of encouragement for her. His pride and joy were his two grand-

children. He would spend hours proudly displaying photos
to anyone who expressed even the slightest interest. His other
passion was gardening. Nat didn't have the heart to tell him
she didn't have a garden. So, she nodded along eagerly to every
tip and trick he shared on pruning roses and the right type of
fertiliser for the camellias.

"I hope one of those is a latte with hazelnut syrup!" Alfred
nodded towards the two cups Nat was holding.

Nat pressed her lips together and lifted them up. "Sorry, these
are for me and the boss. Definitely next time, though."

"I'll hold you to that." He bowed again and waved as Nat
walked towards the lifts.

She stepped inside and punched in the button for the tenth
floor. As she waited for it to creak into life, she glanced at her
reflection in the mirror. Her dark hair was pinned up into its
usual bun a little more haphazardly than she realised. A few
wisps had escaped around her face, and she did her best to tuck
them back into place. She had paired her usual black trousers
with a soft teal cashmere sweater in an attempt at looking smart.
But as she looked at the woman staring back, she realised she
still had some way to go before she would properly fit in with
the London office crowd. Nat couldn't keep borrowing Lucy's
clothes—despite her insistence—so Lucy had made her promise
a shopping trip after payday as a compromise.

The lift doors opened on the top floor of the office block and
Nat stepped out. A muted grey carpet led the way down the
corridor and soft light spilled from fittings on the wall. Large
windows offered glimpses of the city as the hushed tones of

conversations and occasional laughter echoed throughout the modern space.

As she reached Michael's office, Nat looked through the window and noticed that he wasn't alone. An unfamiliar woman dressed in a perfectly tailored suit sat across from his desk. Every detail of her appearance spoke of sophistication. From the fitted jacket that emphasised her impossibly narrow waist, the subtle pattern of her silk blouse peeking through, to her fiery red hair cut into a sharp bob.

Nat knocked gently on the door before opening it. As she approached, she noticed the woman's high heels crossed neatly under the chair—sleek, black, and undoubtedly designer with their red soles. She couldn't shake the feeling of insecurity, acutely aware of the contrast between her inadequate laid-back outfit and the woman's impeccable sense of style.

The woman turned and looked at Nat with icy blue eyes. She made no attempt to disguise the fact she was openly examining her from head to toe, scrutinising every inch.

"Good morning. I'm sorry, I didn't see you had a meeting in the diary," Nat said, holding up the coffee cups. "Otherwise I would have got more drinks."

"Don't worry, this wasn't a planned meeting. Clara likes to stop by unannounced so we have to drop everything for her." Michael seemed very at ease with this casual teasing of their co-worker. "You haven't met Clara yet—she's our chief financial officer and only just back in the country after meeting with the financial director of our potential investor in the US. By the sounds of it, she has certainly been negotiating a great deal."

"It's nice to meet you." Nat placed Michael's coffee down on the table, then held her hand out to shake Clara's. "Would you like me to get you something?"

Clara stood up and took Nat's hand in hers. Nat shivered at the coolness of her fingers. The phrase 'cold hand, warm heart' sprung to mind, but Nat didn't think there was anything warm about Clara based on first impressions. Even her perfectly manicured fingernails looked like they might be tipped with frost.

"No, but maybe later on you could run out and get something for me." Clara retrieved her hand, then sat down and continued talking to Michael as if they were alone. "It's great you've finally got some admin to do your errands. Let's hope this one is better than the last few..." She paused for a moment, visibly considering her next word, "candidates."

Nat's eyes widened and she looked at Michael for support. He said nothing—not even a second of eye contact for reassurance. Instead, he gave a little chuckle and scolded Clara with a tut.

"I could do with running through a few things with you for the day." Nat pulled her notebook from her bag and opened the pages. She tried to squash the sensation that she was intruding into something very private. Clara let out a short, sharp cough and raised an eyebrow at Michael.

"Sorry Natalie, we'll have to do it later. I need to finish up here before my next meeting." Michael picked up a folder from his desk and turned his attention to continue the conversation with Clara. Nat flinched at his easy dismissal. Their daily check-in before starting the day properly had become a comforting routine that was slowly building her confidence. This sudden change had put her on the back foot and she left the office with a sense of unease for the day ahead.

Nat sat down at a desk, plugged in her laptop, and flipped the screen up. She stared blankly as she waited for the login box to appear.

"Earth to Nat!" Jamie threw his rucksack down onto the desk next to Nat and waved his hand in front of her face.

The office was set up to encourage people to work wherever they wanted in order to build good relationships across teams. Although Jamie worked in the technical team that generally preferred to sit together, he often made the effort to mingle with others and Nat had enjoyed the few times they had sat near each other. He was great fun and never took anything too seriously, unless there was some kind of security breach. Jamie was able to shift to serious professional mode at the flick of a switch. Fortunately those events happened rarely, so the time passed quickly with their gentle back-and-forth banter.

"Morning!" Nat pushed his hand away, laughing. "Sorry, I was completely in my own world there."

"How are you doing?"

"I'm OK." Nat let out a sigh, her tone a stark contrast to her usual cheeriness. "Just getting set up for the day."

"Oh, dear." Jamie sat down and wheeled his chair right next to Nat's. "Come on, spill the tea." He placed his elbows on the desk and cupped his chin in his hands. Nat knew there was no way Jamie would let her rest until he knew what was going on.

"So who's this Clara person?" she said, wanting to test whether she might have an ally in Jamie before she opened up.

"Ahhh. So, you've met the ice queen."

They shared a look and Nat laughed, relieved to know she had a safe space to share her feelings.

"Oh, my goodness." Nat's eyes grew wide. "She looked me up and down as if I was something she might have picked up on the bottom of her shoe!"

"Yes, she's a genuine delight." Jamie laced his fingers together and stretched them out in front of him. "The IT support team draws straws every time she needs help with something."

"How long has she worked here for?"

"I think she's been here right from the start. She knew Michael extremely well from before the company existed, from what I heard." Jamie raised his eyebrow, a suggestive look on his face.

"Oh!" Nat told herself the jolt in her stomach was from surprise, rather than a pang of jealousy, which it most definitely was not.

"Yeah, I'm pretty sure that was a long time ago." Jamie shrugged. "Apparently she's engaged to some hot-shot and makes sure everyone knows it. I'm surprised she can lift her hand up with the size of the rock she's got on that ring!"

Jamie brought his lips together in a pout and held out his left hand to show an imaginary ring on his finger. Nat burst out laughing, covering her mouth when she realised the noise had drawn the attention of the rest of the office.

"Surely she can't have made you feel that bad?"

"Well, it wasn't just her. The worst bit was Michael just dismissed me as if I wasn't worth his time." Nat pressed her lips together. "I know he can be serious, but he's never been quite like that before."

"Pay no attention." Jamie rubbed her arm. "He's oblivious to anything when he's in business mode. You should know that well enough by now. He's not the most socially aware at the best of times. Don't take it personally."

Nat smiled and nodded. "Thanks. You always know how to make me feel better."

"That's why they employ me. Not only do I give great advice, I also have the ability to communicate entirely through the use of amusing memes."

"Is that all?"

"Well, that and the fact I'm the only one that really understands the technical code. So, if something breaks—which obviously it rarely does as I'm so good at my job—they need me to fix it!"

Nat placed her hand on her chest. "Your modesty overwhelms me sometimes!"

"You know it!" Jamie winked, then wheeled himself back to his desk.

Nat typed in her login details, got her notebook out and began putting stars next to the most important tasks. She hoped the confidence she had built over the last week would see her through the rest of the day with no major issues.

"I'm going to set up the room for our team meeting," Nat said to Jamie, standing up. "Make sure you're early. I have a feeling I'll need moral support for this. I'll save you a seat next to me."

Jamie nodded and bowed. "Anything you say, boss!"

Nat stepped into the conference room and shivered. The air conditioning had been left on so she adjusted the dial up a few degrees. The atmosphere was going to be frosty enough with Clara in the room. She had to do something to bring warmth to the surroundings. She checked the cables of the laptop to ensure they were connected to the projector and brought the presentation up on the screen.

People began filing in, gradually taking up the seats around the large table. As HealthLink was still a small company, everyone knew each other well and the room was soon buzzing with chatter. Nat spotted Michael through the glass, making his way down the corridor. She went out to catch him for a quick chat before the meeting started. Every time she had tried to speak to him that day, Clara would appear out of nowhere, making it clear Michael didn't have time for her. She finally got his attention and motioned for him to come towards her. He smiled, but before he could get to her, Clara stepped out in front of Nat, right on cue.

"I need to speak to you before the meeting," she said, ushering him into a small room adjacent to the conference room. Clara turned briefly to look at Nat, her icy stare laced with an undertone of challenge—a daring invitation that further flamed the spark of unspoken tension between them. Nat was left in the corridor alone, surrounded by an overwhelming smell of sickly sweet perfume.

Nat took her seat next to Jamie and distracted herself by chatting with her other colleagues around the table. A few minutes later, Michael and Clara joined them, sitting together at the head of the table.

"Good afternoon," Michael began. "Let's get this meeting started."

Instinctively, Nat opened her notebook and held her pencil, ready to start taking notes.

"First of all, I would like to give an update on the progress of the company growth. As you know, we are in the fortunate position where our user base has expanded significantly over the last few years. In order to make this growth sustainable and take us to the next level, we need to secure more investment. We have narrowed it down to two potential investors. First, we have Spinigma, a US based strategic economic entertainment organisation..." Michael stopped speaking for a moment at the sound of gentle muttering. "Would anyone like to share their thoughts with the room?"

Jamie sat up straighter. "By a *strategic economic entertainment organisation*, do you actually mean a gambling company?" The room fell completely silent. Michael turned to Clara. She placed her hands together before speaking, as if surrounded by school children.

"If we were still in the 1980s, then yes. But we're not. We're in the 21$^{st}$ century and their business practices have evolved. Strategic economic entertainment is the future and generates billions of dollars of profit every year." She paused for a moment. "It's the future for those with the sense and intelligence to get on board. They would significantly accelerate our growth." Clara narrowed her eyes at Jamie, willing him to challenge her further. He just nodded his head and raised his eyebrows, clearly unimpressed with the explanation.

"Our second option is Ethica," Michael continued. "They are a UK based healthcare and nutrition company with an emphasis on the local supply chain and community development. Although our growth might be slower if we go with Ethica, there are advantages to this, so we need to carefully assess the options before making a decision."

Michael turned to the presentation on screen and began talking through the proposals in more detail, stopping for people to ask questions and make suggestions. Nat could sense Clara watching her as she scribbled furiously in her notebook. She looked up and they locked eyes.

"I think everyone might need to speak a bit more slowly." Clara's words interrupted the discussion as she nodded towards Nat. "It looks like the new girl is struggling to keep up with her notes."

"I'm fine," Nat replied, her tone composed despite the flush creeping up her neck. She was desperate to hide the infuriation and embarrassment that simmered within her. "Please, carry on." The room fell silent.

Michael looked at his watch. "Maybe we should stop for a quick break?" He seemed entirely oblivious to the uncomfortable exchange between the two women.

"Good idea. I think I'll have my coffee now, Natalie." Clara looked at her briefly, a tiny smirk tugging at the corner of her mouth. "A double espresso with a dash of hot oat milk. No sugar."

"I'll be back as soon as I can," Nat said, with a hint of sweetness to her tone that disguised the bitter taste in her mouth. "Would anyone else like something while I'm out?" Everyone shook their head, smiling sympathetically. At least Clara's behaviour wasn't entirely unnoticed.

"I'll give you a hand." Jamie stood up and linked his arm through Nat's, guiding her from the meeting room and out into the corridor.

"What the actual fuck?!" Nat whispered, clenching her fists together into tight balls.

"Shhh, wait until we're outside." Jamie pressed the button to summon the lift. "Don't let her know the effect she is having on you."

As soon as the lift doors closed, Nat let out a frustrated groan.

"Why is she such a bitch?"

"Don't worry about it. Everyone knows what she's like. No one will think any differently of you. She's the one who looks bad."

"I just don't get it. Why does she seem to have Michael wrapped around her finger?"

"There's a long-standing loyalty there. They go back a long way. Michael had a very difficult break-up a few years ago and apparently Clara supported him through that." Jamie shrugged his shoulders.

"I'm sure she did. She's such a kind hearted woman and there's absolutely no trace of possible ulterior motive there." Sarcasm dripped off her voice.

"Miaow! Put those claws away." Jamie laughed and Nat reluctantly joined in, letting go of her anger just a fraction.

"Come on then, let's get her highness that coffee." Nat gave an exaggerated curtsey. "I'm surprised though..."

"Why is that?"

"I would have thought iced tea would be more her thing."

Jamie tutted, a warm smile on his face, then followed Nat out into the sunshine.

As they reached the end of the meeting, Nat congratulated herself on remaining calm, despite the occasional snide remark from Clara. She couldn't help feeling disappointed that Michael did nothing to put a stop to it. Surely he couldn't be so blind to her behaviour?

Back at her desk, she began packing away everything into her rucksack. Her hand brushed up against the cardboard tube that was protecting the print she had bought for Michael. Today was the first day she had remembered to pack it since the weekend. She was eager to give it to him and see his response, reminding herself it was just a nice gesture from one colleague to another. There was nothing else to it, nothing at all.

"I'm off now," Jamie said. "Are you coming?"

"Not just yet. I need to catch Michael before I go. I'll see you later in the week, though."

"Bye then!"

She took a deep breath, held the tube in one hand, and pulled her rucksack onto her shoulder. Nat hoped he would be on his own for a change as she walked towards his office. She slowed down as she reached the door.

"Typical," she muttered under her breath on seeing a glimpse of Clara through the glass. She turned on her heels to walk away just as the door opened.

"The restaurant is booked for 7pm." She heard Clara say to Michael as they walked out. "So that means we have time for some cocktails beforehand."

Nat picked up her pace and let the rucksack drop from her shoulder. She shoved the cardboard tube inside and pulled the zip across roughly, catching her finger in the process.

"Shit." Her hands shook as she sucked her finger to ease the pain. The numbers showed the lifts were still on the ground floor. The last thing Nat wanted was to share a confined space with that woman. She couldn't bear the thought of any further humiliation, not in front of Michael. She pushed the door to the stairwell and began making her way down, her mood dipping a little further with each step.

# CHAPTER THIRTEEN

**Thursday 12<sup>th</sup> May**

Nat pulled up her hood and zipped her coat higher as she stepped off the bus. The recent spell of spring sunshine had been short-lived, replaced by a morning of torrential showers. It was only a short walk to Michael's apartment, so she picked up the pace to avoid getting drenched further. As she turned the corner, the large doors to Michael's building swung open. A figure stepped out holding a large black umbrella. Nat's stomach lurched and she stopped in her tracks. In a panic, she jumped into a shop doorway and shielded her face—just enough to not be recognised, but still able to peek out. She watched as Clara walked down the other side of the street and away from where Michael lived.

Nat's pulse raced, thumping against her chest until it almost hurt. She took a deep breath in through her nose. The damp air, heavy with acidic car fumes, flooded her lungs. She couldn't understand why her reaction to seeing Clara leaving Michael's apartment had been so intense. It wasn't like there was anything going on between them. The tiniest spark of attraction at his apartment the week before hadn't grown into anything significant. In fact, Nat questioned whether it had been entirely in her imagination.

When she was sure Clara was far enough away, Nat stepped out of the doorway and back into the rain. She waited at the edge of the pavement for the traffic to clear.

"Well, who Michael sleeps with has got absolutely nothing to do with me," she muttered to herself.

Just as she was about to cross the road, a cyclist sped past and straight through a puddle, sending spray in all directions. Nat let out a startled yelp and tried to shield herself. The freezing water soaked her clothes and drenched her shoes, leaving her shivering and deeply annoyed. She glared at the cyclist, who had already disappeared into the distance, oblivious to the chaos they had left behind. Sighing, she shook off the water and crossed the road, wondering if the day could get any worse.

"Hey!" Michael was smiling as he opened the door. "Oh, I didn't realise it was raining that much. I'll grab you a towel."

"Thank you," Nat said, pulling off her coat. "The speeding cyclist didn't help the situation." She untied her laces and worked her feet out of the soggy boots, leaving them in the corner.

"You do look very sorry for yourself!" Michael laughed as he took Nat's coat.

Nat narrowed her eyes at him. "And you look rather pleased with yourself. Did you have a good night?" The words, laced with annoyance, tumbled out of her mouth before she could stop herself.

"Yes, thanks." Confusion flashed across Michael's face and his eyes lingered on her face for a moment. "I'll hang this up and get you a cup of hot chocolate. You look like you need warming up."

Nat inwardly kicked herself as he walked off. The words had slipped out without a second thought, and now she was left feeling like a jealous schoolgirl. Michael came back with a soft grey towel and handed it to Nat.

"Here you go," he said. The friendly smile had returned to his lips.

Nat dried her face and hands, trying to shake off the damp chill that clung to her. She sighed and made her way to the table, hoping that throwing herself into her work would stop her feeling so irritated.

As she powered on her laptop, she stole a glance at Michael bustling around the kitchen. He measured everything to perfection—of course—ensuring the exact ratio of milk to chocolate flakes. It was the complete opposite to Nat, who threw everything in and hoped for the best. He stirred the pan continuously, pausing only occasionally to check the thermometer to ensure it reached the precise temperature. A few minutes later, he carefully placed the mug of hot chocolate on the table. The sweet aroma swirled around Nat's face. She lifted it up to take a sip, looking at Michael the whole time as he waited for her reaction.

"Oh, my goodness!" A wide smile spread across Nat's face. "Now, that has to be the best hot chocolate I have ever tasted!"

"Glad you like it." Michael nodded his head in satisfaction, then sat down behind his computer. "Now we've got you warmed up, we'd better get on with work. There's a lot to sort out over the next few weeks before we make any decisions on investments."

"Yes, I need you to review the notes I made at yesterday's meeting. I'm just sending them across to you now." She clicked to send the email. "They might not be up to Clara's standards, though."

"Oh, don't mind her." Michael glanced up at her. "She can be a bit bossy sometimes, but she doesn't mean anything by it."

"You mean rude and condescending?" Nat had bitten her tongue on how she felt for so long. She wondered if she'd gone a step too far with this outburst.

"Wow!" Michael's eyes widened. "She's really got under your skin, hasn't she?"

His inability to see her flaws was beginning to infuriate Nat. She laced her fingers together, rested her chin on top and looked expectantly at Michael.

"So, what's the deal with you two, then?"

"There's no deal." Michael tilted his head a fraction. "We studied at the same university. She was dating my flatmate, so she spent a lot of time at our place. We became good friends and kept in touch. When I was setting up the company, I needed someone with a good head for finance as I couldn't manage everything myself. She's incredibly bright and came top of her class. The job she went into after university wasn't fulfilling her and she was looking to push herself, so I offered her a job. So far, she hasn't disappointed."

"Ah, so there was never anything else?" Nat suddenly felt awkward at asking such a personal question. As always, her mouth engaged itself before she could think about what she was saying.

"Oh, no!" Michael laughed. "Why on earth would you think that?"

"I just assumed, because..." Nat stopped, deciding whether to continue. "She made such a fuss of you going out for dinner together last night. Then I saw her leave here just as I was arriving this morning."

"Oh, I see. So you assumed that as you saw her leaving, she stayed here and therefore we must have had sex?" Michael's expression stayed neutral. "What must the neighbours think of me with you coming and going all the time as well?"

"I, well I..." Nat stuttered, before Michael started laughing gently.

"I'm just messing about. You're right, she stayed here. But only because it was getting late by the time we had finished dinner..." He paused for a moment. "Dinner with our old university friends. Plus, she'd had an argument with her fiancée and wanted to teach him a lesson by letting him stew at home on his own."

"Right." Nat fiddled with her fingers. "Well, this isn't awkward at all."

"It's fine. Don't worry about it." Michael gave her a reassuring smile. "And please don't worry about her. She's just very focused on doing a good job."

"Even if that's at the expense of common courtesy?"

"I didn't think she was that bad?"

"Clearly not." Nat watched Michael for a reaction. His expression remained serious and she realised he really was oblivious to Clara's behaviour. "Well, talking of doing a good job, let's get on with what we need to do, shall we?"

"Yes, boss." Michael lifted a hand to salute Nat, then turned to his laptop with a faint grin playing at the edges of his mouth.

The day passed by quickly and Nat's confidence grew as each task became easier. She enjoyed the fast pace and took particular delight in surprising Michael with having what he needed ready exactly when he asked for it. The job didn't give her the same satisfaction as her interior design work, but it was good enough for now. Especially as the feeling of being a failure was finally ebbing away.

They had settled into a nice rhythm of companionable silence interspersed with light conversation. Nat continued to share personal information to a degree she often regretted, whereas Michael gave her snippets that only served to intrigue her.

As Nat leaned back into her chair, stretching her arms up and behind her head, a text message pinged through on her phone.

"Oh great," she muttered.

"What's up?"

"It's my friend, Lexi. I've been designing her shop ready for the launch in a couple of weeks. We've got loads to do still and she can't make it tonight. This means we'll have to spend the whole weekend decorating. Otherwise there's no chance it will be finished by the end of the month."

Nat contemplated telling Michael about the design contract she was preparing for. But everything had been going so well for the last couple of weeks, she didn't want him to think she wasn't committed to the job. Especially as there was no guarantee the contract would be hers.

"To be honest," she continued, "we've been working so hard on it, so having a night off to rest would be nice. I don't think I've ached this much in all my life!"

"There's a great pool here with a sauna and a steam room. You're always welcome to use it if you fancy somewhere nice to relax and wind down. You'll have to bring your stuff though. I'm afraid I don't have anything you could borrow."

"I'm surprised. What with all these women you have visiting all the time." Nat winked at Michael and he laughed awkwardly—unable to hide a trace of embarrassment.

"You're right," he said, recovering quickly. "Maybe I should get in a range of bikinis, just in case?"

Despite knowing he was joking, a tiny jolt of jealousy shot through Nat.

"Well, don't do anything on my account." Yet again, she immediately regretted speaking before thinking. "I'm going to head off soon. Is there anything in particular you need me to sort out before I go?"

"I don't think so." Michael paused for a moment. "Did you want a quick drink if you haven't got to rush off to the shop now?" His demeanour shifted a little. Nat couldn't help but wonder if he had become a little shy. "Clara opened a bottle of red last night but didn't finish it. It's a good one, so it would be a shame to let it go to waste."

"I suppose I could settle for her leftovers." Nat threw her hand to cover her mouth. "I'm so sorry," she said, her voice muffled. "I don't know where that came from."

"I get the impression you really don't like Clara."

She could tell Michael was trying to suppress a laugh.

"She just reminds me of the popular girls at school." Nat shrugged. "I never fitted in with that crowd and it's clearly left me damaged and insecure." She pulled a dramatic face and laughed to show she wasn't being serious, not really. She had no doubt that Michael would have been the type of boy that those girls spent all of their time trying to impress. Nat was also beginning to think that he was the type of boy that wouldn't have even noticed.

He grabbed a couple of glasses from a cupboard and placed them on the kitchen counter. Nat sat on one of the stools and watched as he poured the wine, mesmerised by the deep claret swirling against the sides. He pushed the glasses across the counter and took a seat next to her.

"So, tell me about this shop of Lexi's." He took a sip of wine. Nat did the same before she replied, enjoying the sensation of the rich liquid as it slipped down her throat.

"Lexi's dream has always been to own either a music shop or a cafe. The place she is renting gives her enough space to have both. When it comes to Lexi, she likes to have it all, so that's what she's doing!" Nat laughed. Thinking about her best friend always put a smile on her face.

"How much have you got left to do?" Michael's face was relaxed and Nat got the impression he was glad to be asking the questions for a change.

"The basics of the structural build is pretty much there now, but there's a whole load of painting to do. We need to set up the furniture and, once the paint has dried, there are musical instruments that need to be fixed to the wall." She paused to take another drink. The reminder of how much there was to do had suddenly become a little overwhelming.

"I'm happy to help, if you need it?"

"That's really kind of you. Have you done much decorating before?" Nat guessed what his answer would be. She only needed to glance around his apartment.

"Er, no." Michael pulled a face which confirmed Nat's suspicions were correct. This was not an area he was particularly familiar with. "But I'm a quick learner."

"Hmm, maybe another time. When the pressure to get finished quickly isn't so great?" Nat grinned sheepishly, hoping she hadn't offended him. "I don't think I could manage teaching you alongside getting things done myself."

"I understand." Michael grinned. "Take it from me—teaching a total novice when you're trying to do your own job is no easy feat."

Nat's face lit up with surprise. She punched him playfully on the arm and he reacted with a mock wince. She was struck by what might have been a spark of desire in his eyes as he gave her a sly grin. The interaction only served to heighten the tension between them. Nat was keen to loosen it before it became uncomfortable. What she didn't need right now was an overwhelming desire to kiss him.

"The offer is there if you want to take me up on it," Michael said, his tone genuine. "What's the bit you're most excited about seeing come to life?"

"There's this incredible wallpaper that I know is going to look fantastic. We bought it from my favourite shop..." Nat gasped and leapt down from the stool. "I almost forgot!" She paused to steady herself—the wine had already gone to her head. She opened her rucksack, pulled out a slim cardboard tube and handed it to Michael. "I saw this at the shop and thought it would fit perfectly in your apartment." She watched as Michael pulled the picture from inside and unfurled it. His expression gave nothing away. "I hope you don't mind, but I thought your apartment needed a touch of colour."

"Yes, I suppose you're right." Michael looked around. "I've never really given that type of thing much thought." He looked back at the print, studying it closely.

"It shows." Nat gave him a lopsided grin. "I know a great framing shop. Sorry I didn't get it done before, but I didn't fancy lugging a framed print around on the bus."

"Thank you. You shouldn't have, but I do really like it."

"You're welcome." Relief washed over Nat. "That's the thing about my passion—I'm always on the lookout for ways to improve my surroundings. I hope you're not offended."

"Not at all! How could I be offended at receiving a thoughtful gift from a beautiful woman?" Michael picked up his glass and drained the last bit of wine. He was clearly none the wiser as to the effect his unexpected words had on her. Nat shook her head. It must be the alcohol. He probably didn't even realise what he was saying and there couldn't be anything to it. It was just a throwaway compliment, nothing more.

Nat looked at her watch. "I should be heading back," she said, fastening up her rucksack. If she wasn't going to be working at Lexi's shop, it would give her some time to work on her portfolio for the country hotel contract. The deadline for that was creeping up on her quicker than she would like.

"Are you sure?" Michael held up the wine bottle. "There's a tiny bit left to finish if you want a top up?"

"I'm sure you can manage that."

"OK, well next time then," he said, more of a statement than a question.

"Next time." Nat nodded, knowing it was an offer she would find very difficult to refuse. "See you at the office tomorrow."

Michael tipped the last of the wine into his glass and tilted his head back, allowing the liquid to trickle down his throat. She watched the smooth lines of his neck, the muscles contracting and relaxing as he swallowed. A shiver ran down her spine.

"See you tomorrow." He wiped a finger and thumb against each corner of his mouth, removing any lingering trace of wine.

As Nat gathered her things and pulled on her coat and shoes, she looked up now and again. Michael was still sitting at the kitchen counter, watching her with a slight smile on his face. It was absolutely just the wine, she told herself. As she pulled the front door closed, she held up a hand to wave. He gave a single nod in return, his expression sending a fizz of something deep inside Nat. "Next time," she said to herself. "Definitely next time."

# CHAPTER FOURTEEN

**Friday 13th May**

Nat closed the cover of her portfolio, leant back in her chair, and ran her fingers through her hair. With just over two weeks left to go before she attended the interview, things weren't going as well as she had hoped. She had settled on the themes for the majority of the bedrooms, but something didn't feel right about the entrance. This was the most important part of the design—the bit that would wow the guests on arrival and take their breath away. At this rate, there was no way she would get through the interview. She decided it was time to do something more productive.

Nat found Lucy in the kitchen, busy preparing dinner and trying to entertain Louis at the same time.

"Hi, can I give you any help?"

"Oh yes, that would be great." Lucy thrust a bowl of potatoes into Nat's hands, along with a peeler. "If you wouldn't mind sorting those and bunging them into that saucepan." She nodded towards the side.

"Of course." Nat filled the saucepan with water and sat down at the table next to Louis. She let him dip his hands into the cold water. He squealed in delight and began splashing his fingers around.

"How was work today? Are things getting better?"

"Oh, much better than before. Apart from this woman, Clara." Nat pulled a grimace at Louis and pinched his nose gently. "She's a meanie." Louis giggled in agreement.

"Ah, the office terror." Lucy laughed. "There's always one."

"Honestly, she's vile. And she's got this weird hold over Michael that means he is blind to her behaviour."

"Do I hear a hint of jealousy in your voice there?"

"Not at all!" Nat threw a piece of potato peeling in Lucy's direction.

"Are you sure about that? You do go a bit starry-eyed when you talk about Michael." Lucy launched the peeling back at Nat. "Although, I wouldn't blame you at all. There aren't many hot, rich men working in the NHS, I can tell you."

"Well, it wouldn't be appropriate anyway, would it? Being as I work for him."

"Aha! So you have thought about it!"

Nat's cheeks flushed and she concentrated hard on peeling the potato in her hand.

"Every now and again. It does feel like there's this strange connection between us. I don't know, I'm probably just imagining everything. I don't think I'm the best judge of romantic situations after what happened with Joe." She dropped the slices of potato into the pan. Even though Nat was young and inexperienced when they started dating, she didn't know if she would ever be able to trust her instincts again.

"That was more about Joe being a dickhead and nothing to do with you." Lucy gently placed her hand on Nat's shoulder. "Well, this is all the more reason for you to win that design contract. Then you can quit your job and you and Michael can live happily ever after."

"There's another thing that's not going so well." Nat put her head in her hands and groaned. "I've got some of my portfolio exactly how I want it, but the most important bit just isn't coming together. There's no way I'm going to beat the competition. This is such a prestigious opportunity and I don't stand a chance."

"OK, you need to give yourself a break," Lucy scolded Nat. "You are very talented and have just hit a minor bump in the road. You'll figure it out."

"I know," Nat said, not really believing it. "It's just sometimes it feels like everything is conspiring against me."

"And that kind of attitude isn't going to help." Lucy paused to take the casserole out of the oven. "You know, you should show your work to Simon. I know he would love to see it. Who knows, a fresh pair of eyes might be all you need to give you some inspiration?"

"Maybe." Nat wasn't convinced her brother would be capable of providing any kind of useful contribution. He might mean well, but that didn't always translate into something that might be encouraging. "Right, are there any more kitchen jobs, or shall I get this little one bathed and ready for bed so we can relax and watch some trash TV after dinner?"

"Oh, you superstar. That would be great!".

Nat whisked Louis out of his highchair and tickled his tummy. "Come on, stinky. Let's get you smelling beautiful."

Nat began filling the bathtub, pouring in some lavender bubble bath and swirling the warm water around with her fingers. She lifted Louis and placed him gently down. He swung his little fists around and bubbles sprayed up into the air, landing on both of them. His clear green eyes twinkled at Nat, and the perfect dimples in his cheeks framed a cheeky smile.

Before she knew it, Nat was imagining what a child of hers and Michael's might look like. Would they inherit eyes with Michael's rich blue tone, or would they be more green, like Nat's? The hair would undoubtedly be brown, but dark chocolate like Michael's, or with Nat's chestnut hues woven in?

"Louis, I think I need my brain examining." Nat scooped up a handful of bubbles and rested them on his head. "I blame your mummy, putting these thoughts in my mind." He squealed in delight and patted his bubble-covered hands over his mouth. A few of the suds slipped inside and caused him to hiccup and cough. Nat rubbed his back gently. "Let's get you washed and then ready for bed."

She lifted him out of the bath and wrapped him up in an enormous fluffy white towel. As she carried him out of the bathroom and towards his bedroom, she passed Simon's office. The door was slightly ajar and she could hear his phone conversation. It sounded like he was having a heated discussion and his voice carried into Louis' bedroom as she dried and changed him.

"Sounds like Daddy has a few problems at work," Nat whispered to Louis. "You won't have to worry about that kind of thing for a long time." As she pulled Louis' sleep suit over his head, a familiar-sounding name caught Nat's attention. She placed Louis in his cot and set the nightlight going, then stepped back a few paces so she could hear Simon's conversation more clearly.

"We've got enough of an evidence trail now to finally put a stop to Spinigma. We need to start pushing the Gambling Commission to make a decision on when they will take action." Simon paused to listen to whoever was on the other end of the call. "But this isn't just about issuing a fine. That won't stop them. If anything, it will just spur them on, knowing they won't be held to account properly."

Nat heard Simon thump his fist onto the desk.

"No, I've got a strong case. Listen to me. I have evidence to show they are exploiting their users and not safeguarding them properly. A number of coroner reports for recent suicides have shown the links between gambling, and in particular with this company. This isn't just about people being made miserable—people are losing their lives, and these types of companies play a fundamental role in tipping them over the edge. They deliberately target the vulnerable and destroy them for profit."

Simon paused again and Nat held her breath, not daring to move in case he heard her outside his office.

"But that's exactly why we need to persuade them to take it one step further. Companies like Spinigma will stop at nothing to exploit people. Buying out social media companies to get access to their user base and aggressively marketing their products breaks so many—"

A cry came from Louis' cot, drowning out what Nat could hear. She went to him and settled him back down, before returning to the doorway and tuning back into Simon's conversation.

"We have to put effective sanctions in place to prevent any future investments, at least while I gather the final few pieces of evidence to put a stop to them for good. They have another deal lined up that they are trying to wrap up by the end of this month. If that deal goes ahead and the Gambling Commission don't take action until later, that could signal the end of the company they are investing in. They will quickly break any contract as soon as they have got access to what they are really after. No company will survive the scandal of giving away their user information to a gambling company."

Nat's head was reeling from the conversation. Surely the deal Simon was talking about couldn't be the one with HealthLink? But who else could it be with? There must be something she could do about it. She couldn't let Simon know she had heard his conversation. He would be furious with her for eavesdropping, even if it was accidental. If his law firm found out, he could be in serious trouble and Nat would never forgive herself.

It was clear that Clara was set on the investment with Spinigma. She was definitely more interested in profit than company values. Strong values don't buy Louboutin shoes. Nat would just have to work harder to ensure the deal with Ethica was given equal consideration, despite it not appearing to be a fair competition. She couldn't let Michael's years of hard work be taken away from him, not if she had any means to intervene. Friday the thirteenth had taken a darker turn than she had expected.

# CHAPTER FIFTEEN

**Saturday 14<sup>th</sup> May**

"Turn this one up. It's my favourite!" Lexi shouted across to Nat from the stepladder. Nat followed her instructions and Lexi began working the paint roller in time with the dance beat, balancing a little more precariously than Nat would have liked. The last thing they needed at this stage of getting the shop ready was any kind of injury to delay progress.

"Well, with this music motivating you, we might stand a chance of being finished just in time for opening." Nat wiped a bead of sweat from her forehead, leaving a trail of silvery paint in its place.

She stepped back and looked around the shop. It was coming together just as she had imagined it would. The red velvet drapes hung beautifully behind the retractable stage, as Mrs Thomson had promised. The perfect backdrop to make the performers feel special and add a touch of magic to their shows. That's what true interior design was all about—bringing together carefully selected items and visuals that created an entire experience, not just a random collection of stuff that faded into the background, unnoticed.

"How soon until we can break for lunch? I'm starving!"

"Oh my goodness!" Nat checked her watch. "It's midday now, and we've only been at this since eleven a.m. because of someone sleeping in this morning."

"I know, my bad." Lexi grinned sheepishly. "What can I say? I like my sleep!"

"We'll keep going for a little while longer. How about I pop out and bring us back some sandwiches at one?"

"Eurgh, another hour!" Lexi stamped her foot on the metal step, the sound making them both flinch as it echoed around the shop. "You're such a taskmaster!"

"If you want to launch this shop, you better stop moaning and get working!"

Lexi lifted the roller in reluctant agreement and got back to painting the walls.

"So, tell me the latest gossip," Lexi said. "That will help the time pass by more quickly. How's that gorgeous boss of yours? Have you found out if he's single yet?"

"He's fine, thank you. No, I don't know if he is single, and I wouldn't be bothered even if he was."

"You are such a liar!" Lexi threw a knowing look at Nat. "I can tell by the colour of your cheeks."

Nat brought her hands up to her face. "I'm just warm from all this decorating."

"OK, you just keep telling yourself that!" Lexi smirked and turned back to the wall, singing along to the radio at the top of her voice.

The mention of Michael turned Nat's thoughts to the conversation she had overheard last night. A tightness grew across her chest as she thought about the consequences if they chose the wrong investment partner. Michael's company was his passion, and he would be devastated if he lost it all. His employees weren't just members of staff, they all played their part in the success of the company. He did everything he could to make it a great place to work to reward them for their commitment. Nat knew she had to figure out a way to stop the deal from going through. She would have to talk to Jamie when she was next in the office. She was sure she could trust him, and there must be something he could do to help her.

Nat's stomach rumbled, a timely reminder of her promise to pop out and get lunch. "OK, the hour's up. I'll get us some food now."

"Finally! I was about to pass out!" Lexi lifted the back of her hand to her forehead with a dramatic flourish.

Nat slung her bag over her shoulder, laughing at Lexi as she pulled open the shop door. She turned to walk through, but found herself staring at the impressive chest of a tall man with broad shoulders blocking the exit. Broad shoulders encased in a perfectly fitted, spotless white t-shirt. Her eyes travelled upwards until they met a familiar blue pair looking down at her. Nat was sure she saw a trace of awkwardness on Michael's face, but his expression quickly shifted as he held up a brown paper bag and smiled warmly.

"Hi! What are you doing here?" Nat asked, pleasantly surprised.

"I've brought lunch." Michael shook the bag and then stepped aside. "I also brought reinforcement."

"Hi ladies, I hear there is a shop that needs finishing, and two fine, strapping young men are just what you need to make that happen!" Enzo appeared from behind Michael with a huge grin on his face and his hands on his hips.

"You really didn't need to," Nat said, stepping back inside the shop. What they might lack in skill, they certainly made up for with enthusiasm. "But at this stage, I will take any help I can get!" She held her hand out to invite Michael and Enzo inside. "Lexi, this is Michael and Enzo."

"It's great to meet you." Lexi shook both their hands, making no attempt to hide the fact she was checking them over. "Now hand over that food. This evil woman hasn't allowed me a single break all morning and I'm ready to chew my own arm off."

Michael laughed and handed the bag over to Lexi. Enzo followed her to the table and began helping her set out the food.

"You really didn't need to do this." Nat turned to Michael. "I'm also not sure you're suitably dressed for the occasion, either." She smiled and nodded towards his pristine t-shirt.

"I know, but I was at a bit of a loose end and I remembered you telling me how behind you were with the shop." He stopped to look down. "And don't worry about this old thing. Plenty more of those in the wardrobe."

"Well, it's really kind of you. Both of you."

"When I mentioned to Enzo what you were doing, he suggested we come and help. If I'm honest, I think he's hoping it'll swing him favour with the owner. He's something of a musician himself, so he'll no doubt negotiate mates rates before long. Plus, he's a sucker for a damsel in distress!"

"Well, judging by how well they are already getting along…" Nat nodded over at Lexi and Enzo chatting away like old friends. "I think those mates rates are a done deal!"

"He's such a charmer." Michael looked over at his friend and laughed. "It's always been the same, ever since school."

"I'm sure you charmed your fair share of girls as well." Nat kicked herself for making a flirty statement. Especially one she didn't want Michael to confirm as being true.

"I was never really that confident, to be honest." Michael shrugged his shoulders. "I was a bit of a nerd, so any girlfriends I had were usually the friends of Enzo's latest beau, not a result of my smooth talking."

"Latest beau!" Nat burst into laughter. "Did you grow up in the 19th century?"

"OK, now you're just being mean! His latest *girlfriend*, then" Michael made an extravagant show of being hurt. "I can quickly retract our offer of help." He raised his hands to show a friendly challenge.

"With both of you here, it would be a pity not to make use of those muscles."

Very fine muscles indeed, she added to herself. "Come on, let's eat and then we'll go through what needs to be done."

They worked hard all afternoon, keen to take new instructions from their leader as soon as they had finished each task. Nat enjoyed the feeling of having a team of staff that did exactly as they were told, even if some things took a little explaining. She occasionally slipped into daydreaming about what her future might look like if she won the hotel contract. With that under her belt, it wouldn't be long before she would need to take on some real employees.

"Earth to Nat!"

She felt a gentle pressure on her arm and swung round. Michael was looking expectantly at her.

"Oh, sorry! I was in a world of my own."

"What's next, boss?"

"Perfect timing. I need to hang this wallpaper and it must be carefully placed to match the pattern. An extra set of hands is just what I need."

"Well, my hands are all yours. Just put them where you need them."

The sound of Lexi sniggering nearby was a useful distraction for both of them to look away. Nat narrowed her eyes at Lexi, throwing her an unimpressed glare.

"If you could hold the paper there for a moment, I can judge the positioning better to get the pattern lined up."

Michael did as he was told and stood perfectly still in position against the wall. Nat took a few paces back, then slipped under his outstretched arms to adjust the wallpaper a fraction, becoming acutely aware of their proximity. She felt the gentle heat radiating from his body, which only made her shiver a little harder when the warmth of his breath flowed down the back of her neck. She swallowed hard, trying to maintain her focus on the pattern. He had on the same aftershave he was wearing the day he interviewed her at the cafe. The warm spicy scent took her straight back to the moment when he kissed her hand. The memory was starting to take on new meaning. Maybe there was more to it than just a kind gesture to get her out of an uncomfortable situation?

"I think that's just where it needs to be," she said, stepping aside and doing her best to avoid any form of eye contact. She picked up the smoothing brush and worked it gently over the paper. "There are just a few more strips to go."

As they continued working side by side, the intensity of feeling triggered by being so close began to fade and Nat allowed herself to relax. They soon fell into a comfortable rhythm as they hung each piece of wallpaper, conversation flowing naturally as they discussed books, films, and which restaurants they would recommend. With the final piece smoothed down, they both stood back to admire the finished wall.

"It looks great!" Michael's eyes sparkled as he looked up and down at their handiwork. "I can see why you love doing this."

"Feels good, doesn't it?" A wide smile settled on Nat's lips as she noticed the sense of pride and accomplishment on Michael's face. Seeing him experience such an intense response to her passion meant more to her than he would ever know.

The moment was interrupted as Nat laughed at the sound of Michael's stomach rumbling.

"I guess it's dinner time!" Michael grinned. "Enzo and I can pick up some takeout. Any requests?"

"Ooh, how about Indian?" Nat began scooping up the wallpaper trimmings from the floor. "I'm craving something spicy."

"Indian sounds perfect. That OK with you both?"

Lexi nodded and offered a paint-splattered thumbs-up. "We'd better start clearing away then."

"I'll grab my coat." Enzo offered his hand to Lexi to help her down the ladder. "Anything in particular you like?"

"A bit of everything?" Lexi threw her hands in the air and shrugged. "I'm terrible at deciding."

"We'll be back as soon as we can." Michael smiled at Nat as he held the door open for Enzo.

"So..." Lexi waited for only a second after the door had clicked shut. "You and Michael seem to be getting on well."

"Stop it! We're just work colleagues, that's all." Nat felt her cheeks flush, instantly betraying the fact that she had been thinking the same thing all afternoon.

"Mm-hmm, sure." Lexi pursed her lips together and folded her arms across her chest. "Because work colleagues always give up their weekends to help decorate a shop with absolutely no ulterior motive whatsoever."

"He's just a kind person who was at a loose end." Nat busied herself with tidying away the paint trays, doing her best to avoid Lexi's stare. "Anyway, talking about ulterior motives and getting on well. What about Enzo?"

"He is…" Lexi looked towards the ceiling, lost for a moment in her thoughts. "He is very lovely. But, as always, you are trying to shift the attention away from you." She shook her head and narrowed her eyes. "How has it been at work?"

"Since the incident a couple of weeks ago, it's actually been OK. Michael seems happy with my work, and it's definitely getting easier. I don't think it will ever be my dream job, but at least it keeps Simon off my back for a while."

Nat was surprised to discover how much she enjoyed updating Lexi about her new life in the corporate world, discussing office politics, and sharing the latest rumours of a potential romance in the accounts department.

"Oh, and then there's this woman Clara." Nat rolled her eyes. "I met her for the first time this week." Before she could go into any more detail, Michael and Enzo returned with arms full of food and a couple of bottles of wine.

"We're back!" Michael began spreading out the containers onto the counter. "I hope you're hungry."

"We've got enough food here to last a month." Enzo piled their plates high with aromatic curry and rice and brought them over to the table.

"It smells amazing!" Lexi reached for some glasses from the cupboard and handed them to Nat, ready to be filled by the bottle she had just opened.

"Cheers!" The sound of four glasses clinking together echoed around the shop, signalling the shift from hard work to play-time.

Nat leaned back against her chair and took a long sip of red wine, enjoying the feeling of warmth as it flowed down and settled in her full stomach. Across from her, Michael was smiling, his blue eyes crinkling at the corners. She had never seen him look so carefree before. As the evening progressed, laughter and conversation flowed easily. While Enzo entertained them with funny tales from his classroom, the wine bottles steadily emptied.

Lexi poured the last of her wine down her throat and jumped up from her seat. "We shouldn't just be sitting here. This is a music cafe." She made her way to the keyboard that was set up near the stage area. "It's time for some music!"

The melody of a lively jazz tune filled the air as Lexi's fingers flowed across the keys, accompanied by her beautiful voice. Enzo grabbed two wooden brushes and started drumming along on the counter, keeping a perfect rhythm. Nat watched as the pair grinned at each other, communicating the rise and fall of the song through unwavering eye contact.

Her attention shifted as she noticed Michael stand up, sway-ing a little tipsily to the music. He held out a hand to her, and she allowed him to pull her to her feet, giggling as they twirled around the cafe. Nat couldn't remember the last time she had laughed so much. As the wine kept pouring, her inhibitions melted away. She let Michael, his warm hand a perfect fit on the small of her back, lead her around the space that would soon be filled with tables, chairs, and happy customers. At that moment, the rest of the world faded away. It was just the two of them, lost in the music.

Michael gazed down at her, reflections from the light dancing in his blue eyes. Nat's heart fluttered in her chest. She tried to tell herself they must keep things professional between them. But it was so tempting to get lost in this feeling...this connection. The song slowed to a stop and they paused, holding each other close. Nat held her breath, wondering what was going to happen next. His face was just inches from hers.

Lexi's voice rang out in the brief silence. "Uh-oh, looks like we're out of wine!"

Nat and Michael stepped away from each other, the spell broken. Nat's cheeks flushed as she smoothed down her shirt, her attention suddenly drawn to a spot of stray paint on the floor. She used the point of her toe to release the fleck, taking much longer than necessary.

"Luckily, there's a shop just down the road. Enzo and I can go grab some more."

"Oh, you don't have to do that." Nat started to protest, but Lexi waved her hand dismissively.

"It's no trouble at all. We won't be long." She grabbed Enzo's arm. "Come on, we can carry on jamming when we get back. You're quite the talented drummer!"

"And that's just with paintbrushes. Wait until you have a proper drum kit, then you'll see what I'm capable of!"

The pair continued chatting as they disappeared out of the cafe, the door slamming shut behind them.

Nat and Michael stood awkwardly, unsure what to say now that they were alone again. At the start of the evening, the wine had softened Nat's senses, making her feel warm and fuzzy. But now sobriety was threatening to creep in. She snuck a glance at Michael, who was studying the floor with a sudden intensity. His shoulders were tense, hands shoved in his pockets.

He cleared his throat, running a hand through his dark hair. "Some more music might be nice?"

Nat was relieved he had finally broken the silence. She nodded and flicked the switch on the radio. As she turned up the volume, a slow, sweet melody filled the space between them.

Michael held out his hand once more. "May I have this dance?"

Nat smiled and took his hand. He pulled her in close and they swayed to the music. She breathed in his scent—clean linen and a hint of his cologne.

"You're a good dancer." He looked down at her, his voice low.

"You're not so bad yourself." Nat looked away, unable to hold his gaze.

With their bodies pressed close, she was hyper-aware of every point of contact. His leg against hers, his breath on her ear, the heat of his body. Her skin tingled everywhere they touched. She wondered if he could feel the rapid thump of her heartbeat where her body aligned to his. As she looked up, he tilted his head and their eyes met again. Being this close, she could see the different shades of blue in his eyes. This evening they were mainly azure, like the colour of a clear summer sky. But with flecks of cobalt, that brought a vivid intensity. She could study them for hours.

Nat's breath caught in anticipation as he leaned in. She closed her eyes as Michael's lips met hers in a gentle, tentative kiss. At

first it was soft and exploratory, both of them a little unsure.
Testing to see how the other was responding. But as the kiss
deepened, passion ignited between them. Michael's arms encir-
cled her waist, pulling her against him, and the kiss became more
urgent.

They jumped apart as the door burst open. Lexi and Enzo
tumbled through, joking around and completely unaware of
what they had just interrupted. Nat moved behind the counter
and busied herself tidying up the remnants of their impromptu
dinner party. Her lips still tingled from the kiss, her mind reeling
as she tried to grasp the magnitude of what had just taken place.
She had never expected him to kiss her like that, and now her
emotions were a tangled mess. Part of her wanted to grab him
and pick up where they left off. But the logical part of her knew
getting involved with her boss was a terrible idea.

Glancing over at Michael, she could tell he was also flustered.
He joined Enzo at the table and soon fell into easy conversation,
while Lexi uncorked a fresh bottle of wine. Nat paused to take a
deep breath, willing her heart rate to return to normal. It was a
mistake, she told herself firmly. A drunken moment of madness.
They were both under the influence and had let their guard
down. They would never speak of it, and it certainly wouldn't
happen again.

# CHAPTER SIXTEEN

**Monday 16<sup>th</sup> May, daytime**

The steady hum of the office greeted Nat as she pushed through the glass doors. Dark strands of hair fell around her face, shielding her from the outside world. She was back from lunch, the salty flavour of a sushi box still lingering on her palate, but her mind was elsewhere, caught up in the memory of the kiss that had triggered something unexpected. Despite her attempts to brush it off as a drunken mistake, she was struggling to ignore the thought that there may be something more. The potential for something to develop between her and Michael.

"Hey, Nat!" The booming voice of Mark from accounting cut through her daydream.

"Hi!" Nat's eyes widened with forced brightness as she offered a nod to him and a couple of other colleagues who greeted her in passing. She followed the corridors through the building. The soft flow of her loose trousers and simple t-shirt were a stark contrast to the sleek, efficient lines of the corporate environment.

Michael's absence all morning left a sense of unease that buzzed irritatingly at the back of her mind. She couldn't shake the feeling that their last encounter had shifted some invisible axis within her. She wanted to know if the same might be true for him.

She rounded the corner to his office and noticed the door was ajar. A knot twisted in her stomach as she glanced inside and saw the scene playing out. The woman with impossible-to-miss vibrant red hair was perched beside Michael, leaning in close enough for her perfume to mingle with the air he was breathing.

"See, if you adjust the parameters here..." Clara's tinny, assertive voice filled the room and floated out into the corridor. Nat could see freshly manicured nails—this time a bright red to match her hair—gliding along the screen to trace invisible lines.

Michael, ever the serious figure, was nodding along, his eyes fixated on the data before him and unaware of Nat's presence. But as she lingered unnoticed in the doorway, Clara's eyes flicked up, a spark of unpleasantness igniting within them. With calculated informality, her hands found their way to Michael's broad shoulders, fingers pressing into the fabric of his tailored jacket. Nat's heart hammered against her ribs, her eye drawn to every nuance of the deliberate display. Clara smirked at Nat as she leaned in closer to Michael. He remained blissfully ignorant, his attention never wavering from the task at hand. A hot anger flared, painting her cheeks with an unwanted flush of crimson. Without a word, without acknowledgment, she rushed away, desperate to avoid giving Clara the satisfaction of getting under her skin.

The click of her shoes against the tiled floor rang in her ears as she fled the scene, the image of Clara's hands on Michael branding itself into her thoughts. Nat had always struggled with confidence, her mother's perfectionism casting a long shadow over her aspirations. And now, with jealousy clawing at her throat, she felt the familiar tug of self-doubt. Despite Michael's reassurances that there was nothing between them, how could she, in her mix-and-match outfits and unrealistic dreams, compete with someone like Clara? It was another reminder of her failed relationship with Joe and coming second place to another woman.

Nat slumped into her chair, the cushioned back accepting her weight with a soft sigh. She flicked on her monitor, its glow casting a pale light across the clutter of paperwork that sprawled untamed across her desk. Her inbox chimed with the relentless tide of unread emails demanding attention. With each click, she reluctantly worked her way through the digital clutter, the tension coiled tightly within her as her mind replayed the scene in Michael's office.

"Rough day?" Jamie's voice sliced through the hum of keyboard tapping and distant phone calls.

She glanced over at him, his own screen reflecting on his glasses.

"You could say that."

"Let me guess, Clara was flaunting herself around Michael again?" He leaned back in his chair, an eyebrow arching in playful curiosity.

"What makes you say that, and why do you think that would bother me, anyway?" Nat instantly regretted her defensive tone.

"Well, ever since you arrived this morning, you've been on edge. I've lost count of the number of times you've walked past Michael's office to see if he was there." He paused for a moment. "Then I saw Clara and Michael go into his office while you were out at lunch, and I'm assuming you've just come from there?"

"I needed to talk to him about something important." Nat offered her defence, but Jamie was having none of it.

"Why not just drop him an email? And what's the important thing you need to talk about?"

Nat stalled, desperately trying to think up an excuse, but getting nowhere.

"Is it that obvious?" She exhaled slowly, dragging her fingers through her hair and pulling it into a loose ponytail with the band on her wrist.

"Pretty impressing for someone who's only just getting to know you, huh? Who says men don't have any emotional intelligence?" A smirk formed on Jamie's face. "Admit it, Nat, you've started catching feelings for him."

"It's not like that." A reluctant smile fought against the annoyance etched on her face. Nat knew he was right, but admitting feelings for Michael felt like stepping onto shaky ground. Ground that she wasn't ready for. "We should both get back to work."

"Yes, boss!" Jamie lifted his hand in a salute and turned towards his screen.

Nat's cursor hovered over an unopened email from Michael.

Subject line: URGENT–Investment Reports.

Natalie,
Spinigma are due at 2 p.m. Please get copies of the attached document printed and bring them to my office as soon as you can.
Regards,
Michael

Nat clicked the reply button and started to type.

Subject line: Re: URGENT–Investment Reports.

Michael,
Of course, I am doing it now.
Nat

She hesitated for a moment, contemplating whether to end her signature with a brief 'x'—a test to see how Michael might respond. How could a simple letter be loaded with such significance? Nat sent the message as it was, deciding she wasn't ready to find out just yet and certainly not in a way that might leave a digital footprint of any rejection. She put the thought out of her mind and turned to Jamie.

"Looks like we're close to sealing the deal with Spinigma."

"It's getting real." Jamie clicked the end of his pen repeatedly. "As long as we're willing to sell our souls to the devil, it could be a game-changer for the company."

"It could be." The sentiment in Nat's tone didn't match the excitement she knew others in the company were beginning to share about the deal. Especially knowing what it could mean if the court case was successful. She wanted to confide in Jamie, but there would be serious implications if Simon's firm knew he was the source of what Nat had discovered. She would have to tread carefully.

The machine produced a final hum and beep to signal the printing had finished. Nat gathered the warm pages, tapping them into a neat stack. She walked with purpose down the corridor, trying to shake off the tension from her earlier encounter with Clara that clung to her like a second skin. Pushing open the door to Michael's office, she found him engrossed in his computer screen, lines of concentration etched across his forehead. As she stepped inside, she inhaled deeply and braced for awkwardness, looking for any sign that Saturday's kiss had lingered in his thoughts as well as hers.

"Here are the documents you needed." Nat held her voice steady, despite the relentless fluttering in her chest.

"Ah, thank you, Natalie." Michael didn't look up. The use of her full name was a reminder of the formality and distance he liked to keep. He had fully returned to his business demeanour and Nat could sense no trace of the man who had looked at her so differently just days ago.

"The representatives will be here soon." He finally glanced up. "We need to have everything prepared in the room." Nat's breath caught in her throat as she tried to read behind his piercing blue eyes.

"Of course." A rush of mixed feelings washed over her. In some ways, Nat was relieved he was behaving as if nothing had happened between them. Working together could have been very awkward. But she couldn't help but feel a tiny pang of hurt. Even though she knew getting into a relationship was a terrible idea, a part of her was intrigued to see where things might progress. Deep down, she had hoped to see even just a hint that he might feel the same.

Clara sauntered back into the office, her hair a fiery halo around her pointed features. She leaned in close to Michael, her fingertips grazing his shoulder.

"I've just seen the car pull up outside. Perhaps Natalie should get the coffee ready." Her voice dripped with condescension. Nat hated the way she echoed Michael's use of her full name. With him, it felt like a special connection—something just between them. But when Clara used her name, the word felt tainted—thick with layers of belittlement and disrespect.

"Actually, I—" Nat began, but a sharp look from Clara cut her off. "Sure, I'll see to it." Each word tasted sour on her tongue as she left the office.

Back at her desk, the frenetic click-clack of Jamie's keyboard greeted Nat. She hesitated for only a moment before leaning towards him.

"Can we talk? Somewhere private."

Jamie raised an eyebrow but nodded, following her to a vacant conference room. Once inside, Nat closed the door and turned to him, her expression grave.

"I've stumbled onto something worrying about Spinigma."

"Trouble?" Jamie's features mirrored her concern.

"They're about to be taken to court for illegal practices. If they lose, our company could take a hit. A big one. I don't think we would survive."

"Damn. So much for *strategic economic entertainment organisation.*" Jamie flexed his fingers together and cracked his knuckles. "That's not good. Does Michael know? And how did you find this out?"

"No, he doesn't. It's not public knowledge. And I can't go into detail about my source. Not yet, anyway."

"Come on, you can tell me!"

"I can't. Please trust me on that."

"OK, we need a plan. There must be something we can do about it."

"I need your help. We have to figure out how to prevent this deal from going through. Clara is pushing it really hard, and I think we should find out why."

"OK, let me see what I can dig up." Jamie's eyes lit up with determination. "We'll sort this out."

"Thank you." The weight on Nat's shoulders eased a fraction. They would do everything possible to keep the company, and everything Michael had worked towards, safe from the impending storm.

Side by side, Jamie and Nat settled back into the rhythm of their work, their chairs occasionally bumping lightly against one another whenever they reached for a file or twisted around to grab a printout.

"Check this out." Jamie's voice was a low whisper as he tilted his screen towards Nat.

She peered at Clara's latest social media post: a selfie, with the Eiffel Tower just a blurry suggestion in the background, her red hair a stark contrast against the blue Parisian sky. Nat couldn't help but smirk at Clara's pout.

"World traveller and wannabe part-time model." Jamie scrolled through an endless feed of Clara's escapades. Each photograph had been carefully curated and filtered, accompanied by an endless stream of inane hashtags.

"Seems like full-time narcissist should be added to her bio." Nat was relieved that the uncomfortable annoyance from earlier was finally transforming into something far more entertaining.

The afternoon flew by as they tossed friendly barbs back and forth, laughter punctuating their more serious conversations about suspicious activity and tiny clues. With the clock signalling the end of the day, Nat began to pack up her things, sliding her laptop into its bag with practised ease.

"Got any exciting plans for the evening?" Jamie leaned back in his chair.

"Not really." Nat shook her head. "Probably just veg out on the couch with a takeout and bad TV."

"Living the dream." Jamie laughed. "Well, I'm heading to a mate's place for pizza and video games."

"I forgot you have the lifestyle of a teenage boy. Enjoy, see you tomorrow."

Nat pulled on her casual blazer and straightened it, a token effort at looking somewhat put-together before she approached Michael's office.

"Natalie!" Michael called out just as she was about to knock on his door. He was striding toward her. Clara was in tow, talking animatedly with the investors from Spinigma.

"Hey." Nat tried to calm the sense of trepidation bubbling up inside her.

"We're just heading out to dinner. If you don't have any plans, why don't you join us?" The invitation from Michael came easily and without hesitation. "It'd be good to have you there."

"The table is only booked for six people." Clara threw an unpleasant glance in Nat's direction. Her lips curled into a sneer and her eyes glinted, daring a challenge.

"I'm sure we can make room for one more." Michael countered smoothly, his gaze holding Nat's.

"Thanks, I'd love to." A warmth bloomed in Nat's chest despite Clara's attempt to unsettle her. She fell into step with the group as they headed out into the evening, the city lights beginning to twinkle awake.

# CHAPTER SEVENTEEN

**Monday 16<sup>th</sup> May, evening**

The lacquered door of the Golden Phoenix swung open and a wave of savoury aromas greeted them as they stepped into the impressive space. Nat's eyes traced the intricate patterns of jade dragons coiling around golden pillars, each scale carved with painstaking detail. The plush crimson carpets muffled their footsteps, and the soft tinkle of traditional music floated out of hidden speakers.

"I've arranged the best table for us." Clara's voice sliced through the ambiance with a tone that grated against Nat's ears. "Not an easy feat, but when you are friends with the owner..." She let the sentence hang, smirking at the investors who murmured their impressed acknowledgments.

Nat swallowed the tightness in her throat, feeling out of place amid the restaurant's grandeur. Her high street blazer and loose trousers were a stark contrast to Clara's fitted designer dress and perfectly matched high heels. To Nat's annoyance, Michael nodded appreciatively at Clara's efforts.

A hostess, adorned in a silk cheongsam that shimmered like molten gold, led them through the maze of tables. Nat's gaze lingered on the delicate porcelain dishes and crystal glasses that caught the light, casting rainbow prisms onto the linen tablecloths. No matter where she went, she was always on the lookout for design ideas, and this restaurant was a treasure trove of inspiration.

"Your private booth." The hostess gestured towards an intimate alcove shielded by a lattice screen interwoven with lush greenery.

"Perfect." Clara steered the group toward the secluded spot and slid into the curved seating, patting the cushion beside her. "Michael, here."

Michael complied without hesitation, taking the space next to Clara. She angled herself towards him, cutting off the flow of conversation to the rest of the table. Nat paused for a moment, then settled into a seat across from Michael, the distance between them amplified by Clara's strategic intervention.

As she tucked her hair behind her ear, trying to settle the fluttering in her stomach, Nat finally caught Michael's attention. His eyes offered a brief respite, a silent acknowledgment before Clara's laughter drew him back into her orbit. Nat directed her focus onto the grain of the wood on her chair, tracing the lines with her fingertips to settle the irritation.

She shifted in her seat, feeling the plush cushion shift beneath her as she tried to ease into the evening. Nat did her best to make conversation with the rest of the group—Steve with his salt-and-pepper hair, Karen's sharp eyes behind rimless glasses, Malik's booming laugh, and Poppy, her enthusiasm barely contained—were animatedly discussing the virtues of various cocktails.

"Nothing beats a classic Old Fashioned." Steve poured water from a jug over the ice in his empty glass.

"Perhaps." Poppy tilted her head. "But have you tried a Lychee Martini? Made just right, they are so refreshing and not too sweet."

As the debate continued, Michael joined in with talk of single malts, his voice confident and smooth. Nat snuck a glance across the table, catching his gaze for an instant before it was pulled away by Clara's insistent chatter about her fondness for expensive champagne cocktails.

"Excuse me." The hostess arrived at their table. "Are we ready to order drinks?"

"Could you recommend something?" Nat welcomed the distraction.

"Of course." A smile lit up the hostess' face. "Don't be put off by the name, but our Dragon's Breath is quite popular. It has a hint of spice balanced by the sweetness of passion fruit."

"Sounds delicious," Nat said, closing the menu. "I'll have one of those." The hostess smiled again and turned to the others to take their orders.

The conversation naturally flowed into the territory of business as the clink of glasses signalled the arrival of their drinks. Nat sipped her cocktail, the sweet burn invigorating her senses. As soon as the moment arose, she seized the opportunity to delve deeper into the workings of the gambling organisation.

"Malik, how does the risk assessment work for your high-stakes players?" Nat was genuinely curious, but also keen to uncover whatever she could that might help build her understanding of the extent of their malpractice. "Is there any protection in place to ensure they don't end up in serious financial difficulties?"

"Ah, Natalie, how sweet that you want to understand the technical stuff," Clara cut in, her tone laced with disdain. "This is a bit more complex than typing up minutes for meetings, though." She tipped back her head and laughed, then looked directly at Nat.

A flush of embarrassment crept up Nat's neck, but she avoided Clara's gaze, unwilling to show weakness.

"I'm sure Malik could explain it in simple terms for someone like me." She looked expectantly at Malik, before casting a quick glance at Michael, who merely adjusted his cufflinks, a silent spectator to the exchange. Yet again, his lack of defence stung more than Clara's taunts.

Nat nodded along as the table erupted into a lively discussion about probability algorithms and client vetting processes. But she could not ignore the weight of Michael's indifference pressing down on her as she watched the discussion play out.

The group was soon distracted by the scent of garlic and ginger filling the air as dishes emerged from the kitchen's swinging doors, carried by a steady parade of waiters. Steamed baskets of pork dumplings arrived, their pleated skins glistening under the soft light, accompanied by crisp Peking duck that was carved table side, its skin audibly cracking. A large steaming clay pot revealed tender beef stewed with daikon, while plump shrimp lay in a vibrant bed of stir-fried snow peas.

"Can we get some forks and spoons over here?" Clara waved down a passing waiter with an insincere smile. "I'm not sure everyone is adept with chopsticks." Her eyes flickered to Nat, whose hands were hovering nervously over the bamboo utensils.

Suppressing a frown, Nat picked up the chopsticks with more confidence than she felt and skilfully plucked a dumpling from the basket, imagining where she would *really* like to jab the utensils. She held Clara's attention as she popped the dumpling into her mouth, unable to suppress a satisfied smile as she felt the burst of savoury juices on her tongue.

"Michael." Nat shifted her gaze, hoping to draw him into conversation. "Have you tried the Kung Po chicken? It's supposed to be exceptional." She actually had no idea if it was any good, but it seemed like a good opportunity to play Clara at her own game.

"Oh no, I—" Michael began, but Clara leaned across him, her arm brushing his chest.

"Michael, you simply must try the duck. It's divine." Clara used her own chopsticks to hold a slice up to his mouth before he could protest. "Here, let me."

"Thank you." Michael's eyes met Nat's, his expression unreadable. His blindness to Clara's behaviour, yet again, was exasperating.

"So, Steve." Nat turned to the older man. "How did you first get into the gambling business? It seems like an interesting career path."

Steve chuckled, wiping his hands with a napkin. "Well, it certainly keeps me on my toes! I actually started out training to be an accountant, but found it dreadfully dull. My roommate in university had an uncle who ran a small betting shop. He got me a job there while I was studying."

Nat listened and nodded along politely as Steve shared his life story. It was a relief to have something to distract her from Clara and her relentless attempts to monopolise Michael's attention.

As the night progressed, the remnants of their dinner were spread out haphazardly on the table, creating a patchwork of half-finished plates and crumpled napkins. Nat toyed with her chopsticks, the lacquered wood cool and smooth between her fingers. The chatter around them had taken on a relaxed quality, punctuated by the clink of glasses and soft laughter.

Michael caught the waiter's eye and subtly gestured for the bill. As the waiter nodded and retreated, conversation veered toward continuing the night at a nearby club known for its exclusivity. Clara, yet again, was keen to show off her connections across the city.

"I think I'll call it a night." Nat stifled a yawn, picking up her phone to summon a cab with a few taps. She couldn't face spending any more time watching Clara drape herself over Michael and needed a quick escape.

"Already?" Clara's eyebrows arched in mock surprise, her red lips curving. "The night is young."

"Early start tomorrow." Nat took her time sorting the contents of her handbag, avoiding Clara's gaze. "Enjoy the rest of your evening, everyone."

Moments later, Nat was outside with the chill of the drizzle settling on the back of her neck. The neon sign of the restaurant flickered overhead, casting an eerie glow on the slick pavement. She wrapped her arms around herself, seeking warmth as she waited.

"Natalie." Michael's voice cut through the misty air as he stepped out, leaving Clara and the others behind to gather their coats.

"Hey." Nat acknowledged his presence without looking at him, her eyes fixed on the distant headlights that crept closer.

"Are you sure you don't want to come with us?" There was a note of something in his voice, perhaps concern, but it was hard to pin down.

"I'm very sure." She winced at the sharpness of her tone.

He hesitated, then shifted uncomfortably. "Is everything OK?"

Nat turned to him, her eyes reflecting the streetlights. "You might not see it, but Clara... she's always trying to make me feel small. Trying to undermine me. And you just, well, let her." Raindrops gathered on her lashes as she blinked away the moisture.

"Clara?" Michael sounded genuinely perplexed. "She's just being... Clara."

"Exactly. And you don't see it. Or you don't want to." Nat's words were cutting, exact.

"Nat, I—"

"Never mind." She cut him off, a hollow laugh escaping her. "I shouldn't have expected any different."

"Expected what? I don't understand." His brows knitted together in confusion.

"Nothing. It doesn't matter." The headlights she'd been watching pulled up to the curb and the taxi came to a gentle stop.

"Please, tell me."

Nat's breath caught in her throat, the words finally spilling out with a mix of hurt and frustration.

"I thought... after the kiss, I believed there could be something between us. But if you can't even stand up for me, then maybe it was nothing to you. Maybe it was just a mistake."

Michael's face fell, the realisation finally dawning on him. The rain grew heavier, each drop splattering on the pavement like tiny echoes of her disappointment.

"I—"

"It's fine. Really." She attempted a smile, but it faltered, betrayed by the tear that escaped down her cheek. "I clearly misread the situation." She stepped forward and pulled the taxi door open.

"Wait…" Michael reached out, his hand hovering in the space between them to stop her.

"Goodnight." She moved past him, her heart heavy, and slipped into the back seat.

As the vehicle pulled away, Nat pressed her forehead against the cool glass, the world outside blurring into streaks of light and shadow. She leaned back against the seat, her gaze fixed on the receding figure of Michael through the rain-spattered window. The world outside morphed into a slideshow of distorted shapes and colours.

A few moments later, her phone buzzed in her pocket. She pulled it out, the screen lighting her damp face to show a message from Michael. His words pierced through the noise in her head.

> I'm sorry about Clara. I will have a word with her. And the kiss wasn't a mistake, not for me. This is terrible timing, but I have to go away for a few days. When I'm back, please, can we talk?

The phone almost slipped from her grasp as a mixture of emotions surged within her. She read and reread the message, each word sinking in, carving out a space amidst the chaos of her thoughts. Despite everything, a faint smile tugged at the corners of her lips. As the city lights passed by, their reflections danced across her eyes, offering a glimmer of something like hope.

# CHAPTER EIGHTEEN

**Friday 20ᵗʰ May**

Nat sat at the antique oak desk in the corner of her bedroom, everything lit by the soft glow of the evening light as it filtered through the sheer curtains. Her fingers made precise adjustments to the sheets spread out before her. With Michael away for the last week, work had been quieter and she had arrived home on time most days. The space between them had created an opportunity for Nat to focus on finishing the portfolio, and she welcomed the distraction.

Each page bore the mark of her relentless dedication—the only part of her life where she was a true perfectionist. Meticulous sketches and swatches of fabric told the story of the transformation of a decrepit country hotel into a luxury traveller destination. With the tip of her pencil, she shaded in a corner of a drawing, giving depth to the design of an imaginary room she hoped would soon become reality.

She buzzed with a mixture of pride and apprehension. The contract was a big one—potentially career-defining—and while she wanted to believe the designs staring back at her were impressive, doubt crept into the corners of her mind. Was her work truly good enough? Could she stand out against the competition?

There was a soft knock on the door and Lucy peeked her head around the frame, her freshly curled blonde hair hung softly around her face.

"Off for your night out?" Nat got up from the chair to meet her sister-in-law.

"Yep." Lucy stepped inside the room. Her eyes scanned over the open portfolio. "How's everything going?"

Nat hesitated, aware that any mention of her self-doubt might cast a shadow over Lucy's rare escape of a night out. She opted instead for a half-truth that wouldn't draw Lucy into a conversation that would keep her away from her friends.

"Just putting the final touches on this." She looked back towards the desk. "It's shaping up well, and won't be too long until it's finished."

"It looks amazing. You're really talented and so lucky to have the opportunity to do what you love."

Nat detected a tinge of sadness in Lucy's voice.

"Thanks." Her cheeks warmed with the compliment. She turned her attention to the necklace Lucy was fidgeting with—a delicate silver chain that refused to clasp. "Here, let me help you with that."

Nat secured the jewellery around Lucy's neck, fastening the tiny mechanism and adjusting it so it rested neatly in the centre.

"There." Her hands fell away. "You look beautiful."

"Thanks." Lucy smiled warmly. "Louis is ready for bed. He's just playing at the moment, so if you wouldn't mind settling him down?"

"Of course, you go and have fun!"

Without needing any further encouragement, Lucy turned and left, leaving Nat alone once more with her thoughts and the soft hum of the heating as it came to life. She glanced down at her portfolio. With a deep breath, she closed the cover, tucking her hopes and dreams neatly within its confines, ready to be revealed when the time came.

Stepping outside of her room, Nat called out into the hallway.

"Simon, I'm putting Louis to bed. Can you order some takeaway? I'm starving."

"Sure!" The muffled reply came from the living room. "Pizza OK?"

Nat paused at the top of the stairs, a frown on her face. "I'm not in the mood for pizza. How about Thai?"

"Thai *again*?" Simon's voice carried an amused chuckle. "We just had that last week."

"Because it's delicious." Nat enjoyed nothing more than arguing back with her brother, especially when it was about food. "And if I'm going to comfort eat, it might as well be Pad Thai. With extra peanuts."

"Fine, fine," Simon conceded with mock exasperation, but she could hear the smile in his voice. "Your wish is my command."

With that settled, Nat turned to the nursery. Louis was sitting up in his crib, playing happily among a sea of toys. The glow from his nightlight cast shadows that danced across the room.

"Hey, little man." She reached down to stroke his cheek with the back of her finger. Louis looked up with his wide green eyes—a mirror of her own. The possibility of having her own child seemed so far in the future, it was almost unimaginable. Although the relationship with Joe had lasted almost five years, marriage and children never came up in conversation. Which, in the end, was a blessing in disguise.

"Time for bed now." Nat lifted him up into her arms and he clung to her with chubby hands. His small body radiated warmth, mingled with the smell of lavender baby shampoo. She hummed a lullaby passed down from her grandmother, the melody settling Louis until his tiny chest began to rise and fall with a gentle rhythm.

"Sweet dreams." She laid him down, tucking the edges of a soft blanket around him. His tiny hand gripped the corner of the fabric as his eyes grew heavy and began to close.

Nat crept downstairs, trying not to disturb Louis at the critical point when he was just nodding off. Simon was in the lounge, stretched out on a brown leather sofa with his feet rest-ing on the coffee table, a glass of wine in hand, another poured and waiting for her.

"I thought you might need this." He offered her the glass.

"Thanks." She accepted the gesture with a nod and settled into the curve of the sofa next to her brother. She closed her eyes and took a sip of the chilled white wine, feeling the light and refreshing liquid glide down her throat. Hints of green apple, lemon, and spring blossoms danced across her tongue.

As she enjoyed the wine, Simon scrolled through his phone to select some music. He settled on a playlist of modern piano music, and the room filled with the sound of relaxing melodies.

"Why don't you show me what you've been working on?"

Nat gave Simon an uncertain look.

"Lucy told me you've been pulling together a portfolio for a potential design contract."

"Oh, I see." Nat was briefly irritated that Lucy had told Simon when she had explicitly asked her not to. But she couldn't be angry for long, as she knew Lucy only ever had good intentions.

"I really would like to see it." His tone held genuine interest and, despite her hesitance, a flutter of excitement passed through her at the thought of impressing her brother.

"Sure." Nat placed her glass on the coaster and crept back upstairs.

She retrieved her work and returned to the couch, unfolding the binder and placing it in front of Simon.

"This is one of the luxury suites." Nat pointed to one of the drawings. "It's one of their most expensive rooms, and so everything in it has to make the guest feel like it's worth every penny."

Simon leaned in, his eyebrows furrowed as he studied her work. Nat guided him through each page, explaining how each choice was a piece of a larger puzzle and how they all come together to create a narrative throughout the hotel.

"These are... incredible." He looked up at Nat, a wide smile on his face. "You should be so proud of yourself."

"Do you really think so?" Nat couldn't quite believe his reaction. This was a rare and unexpected complement from her high-achieving brother.

"Honestly, it's great. I really had no idea you were this good."

"Thank you." Nat tried to tame her broad grin by taking a sip of wine.

"Maybe I should get you to make some suggestions for this house." Simon continued flicking through the pages. "It's about time we freshened this place up."

"I'd love to!" Nat leaned back into the sofa, enjoying the unfamiliar sensation of pride as it swelled within her.

With Simon in a good mood and relaxed after a glass of wine, Nat decided now might be the only chance she would get to talk to him about what she had discovered by accident.

"Er, actually there's something I need to talk to you about." The gravity of her tone pulled Simon's attention away from the designs. "I overheard your conversation the other night. When you were talking about Spinigma and taking them to court."

His posture stiffened. "How much did you hear?"

"Enough to know it's serious." She paused, fiddling with the stem of her wine glass. "I'm worried about what the impact might be on Michael's company."

"What do you mean?"

"HealthLink is at a crossroads with two potential investors." Nat lowered her voice to barely a whisper, as if the walls might be eavesdropping.

"Go on."

"They need to decide on which one will help the company grow and Clara, the chief financial officer, is advocating for the gambling company as the financial projections are better." The mention of Clara's name sat bitterly on her tongue. "She's pushing Michael towards a deal that I'm certain isn't right. It goes against his vision of being an ethical social media platform."

"What that company is doing couldn't be further away from being ethical." His jaw clenched visibly. "Their trademark move is to invest in companies where they can gain access to personal information without consent. They will then aggressively target those people and sign them up to accounts with credit to get them started on gambling. Before they know it, the customer is hooked and hundreds, if not thousands of pounds in debt to them. Lives have been destroyed and that company doesn't even bat an eyelid."

"If the deal goes through, Michael's company will be destroyed." There was a tremble in Nat's voice. "Not just financially, but his reputation will be ruined as well."

"You can't say anything about this." He shifted, discomfort apparent in the tight lines etched along his forehead. "It could jeopardise the entire case. And I could lose my job."

"Then help me stop it."

"Nat…" He sighed, dragging a hand down his face. "It's not that simple. Our investigation has to follow due process and at the moment it must remain confidential. If you say anything and they find out, we may never have another chance to stop them. The case would be compromised and they would take swift action to ensure what they are doing is buried."

"Please. Isn't there something we can do? Something you can do? You have to push this forward before the deal is signed."

There was a lengthy pause while Simon considered his options.

"I will do my best, but I can't promise anything. In the meantime, you have to do everything you can to persuade them to go with the other investors."

"Of course." Nat's stomach dropped at the thought of challenging Clara.

The chime of the doorbell cut through the air and Simon stood up quickly. Nat could see he didn't want to discuss the matter any more, and she felt uneasy that she had put him in an uncomfortable position.

Simon returned with bags of fragrant Thai food cradled in his arms.

"It smells amazing." Nat's voice was deliberately light as she arranged the dishes. "So Lucy mentioned something about her manager calling and asking if she is coming back to work."

"Yes." Simon paused, a prawn hovering halfway to his mouth. "I just think it will be difficult, with Louis so young. The shift patterns are really tiring and she doesn't need to work."

"Maybe." Nat shrugged her shoulders. "But she loves what she does. Isn't that important too?" She met his gaze squarely.

"I suppose." He shifted his focus to twirling noodles with his fork. "I just thought she enjoyed staying at home."

"She loves being at home and she's an incredible mum, but she's also an incredible nurse. She can do both. This is the—"

"I know, I know. The 21st century." Simon glared at Nat, but his face softened as she punched him lightly on the arm and laughed.

"You might be right." There it was—the slightest shift, a crack in the façade of his old-fashioned views. It wasn't a concession, not yet, but at least it was possible he was coming round to the idea.

Nat pushed back from the coffee table, her knees popping slightly as she stood up. An unwelcome reminder that she hadn't been to the gym in a long time and was very out of shape. She navigated around Simon's outstretched legs and padded towards the kitchen with their empty plates, her socked feet silent on the hardwood floor.

"Pick something to watch, will you?" Nat called over her shoulder. "But please, no action or horror tonight."

She loaded the plates into the dishwasher, then rifled through the wine rack, her fingers trailing along the bottles until she found a Merlot they hadn't tried yet. With two glasses in hand, she returned to the lounge.

"I thought this might be good." He motioned to the television with the remote at the frozen title of a recent comedy. Nat nodded, taking a seat beside him as she handed him a glass of red wine.

"Looks good to me."

As the film's opening scenes flickered onto the screen, Nat couldn't shake an uneasy feeling that had settled in her stomach. Despite Simon's encouragement earlier, she still felt unsure about her portfolio. That, coupled with the potential destruction of Michael's company, she knew it was going to be a difficult couple of weeks. And there was still the matter of the kiss.

# CHAPTER NINETEEN

**Saturday 21ˢᵗ May**

Nat perched on the edge of Lexi's cluttered dressing table with a glass of prosecco in one hand, while the other brushed against a sequined top that didn't make the cut. Lexi appeared from the en-suite bathroom wearing the tightest black leather trousers Nat had ever seen. She had paired them with a cropped red top that skimmed her ribs and exposed her perfectly flat stomach.

"Seriously, you're not going out in jeans." Lexi shook her head in despair, then began rifling through her wardrobe. "It's a club, not a coffee shop."

"I just wasn't really feeling in the mood to dress up," Nat said, letting out a deep sigh. "And nothing seems to fit me properly."

"Well, I've got the perfect thing for you." Lexi spun around, a short black dress in one hand and a pair of strappy heels in the other. "This is going to fit you like a glove."

Nat reluctantly accepted the outfit and let Lexi shepherd her into it. She had to admit, the fabric hugged her in all the right places. The heels gave her just enough height for her posture to shift into something that could almost pass as graceful. As she looked at herself in the mirror, she tried to suppress the feeling that she was dressing up as someone else — someone confident, someone who didn't second-guess herself at every turn.

"Time to add the finishing touches." Lexi gestured for Nat to take a seat while she plugged in the curling tongs. "Welcome to Lexi's salon. Why don't you tell me about your week, madam?" She waved the tongs with a flourish and Nat burst out laughing.

"Well, it's been a terrible week. Thanks for asking." Nat raised her glass and then took a large gulp. "I keep messing things up at work, and there's this awful woman called Clara. She's like a shark that's just caught a whiff of blood. Every time I think I'm doing OK, she's there, reminding me I'm just... not."

"Well, she sounds like a grade A bitch." Lexi released a curl and let it settle on Nat's shoulder. "And you know, you are good enough. More than good enough."

"Am I?" Nat searched her friend's face in the mirror. "Michael probably thinks I'm an utter disaster. The way we left things at the restaurant..." Her voice trailed off, the memory of their disagreement still stung even though the text message he sent had given her a fraction of hope.

"Michael won't think that at all." Lexi lifted another section of hair and wrapped it around the tong. "Don't stress about it."

"Maybe, but he should be back from his break now, and there's been radio silence."

"Listen to me." Lexi moved to face Nat, placing her hands on her shoulders. "You are talented, and you are such a kind, caring person. Michael would be an idiot not to see that. And if he can't, then it's his loss."

"I don't know." Nat shrugged.

"Look." Lexi paused for a moment, visibly considering what she was about to say. "I didn't tell you this before as I didn't want to break his confidence, but..."

"But what?" Nat's heart began beating a little faster.

"Remember when Enzo and I went to get wine last weekend when we were at the shop?" Lexi swirled the liquid in her glass, a twinkle in her eyes. "Well, Enzo may have let slip something about Michael."

"Let slip what?"

"It seems Michael might have liked you from the start. Before you even walked into that interview, he already knew he liked you."

"What do you mean, knew he liked me?"

"Yep." Lexi nodded for emphasis, a little too enthusiastically. "Enzo said that Michael had done his homework on you. He started doing it after his HR department kept employing people that weren't right for the company."

"OK, that sounds very creepy. I'm not sure I like the sound of him stalking me before we even met."

"It's very common these days in recruitment. Most companies do it. That's why Enzo is always nagging his students about being careful with what they put online." Lexi shrugged. "Apparently, as he went through your social media profiles to check out you and your work—making sure you weren't a complete weirdo—it seems he was a little intrigued by what he saw."

"Intrigued?" Nat repeated. "But why would he…"

"Because he saw you. Because he saw the beautiful, talented, funny, carefree you." Lexi set her wine down and reached out, taking Nat's hands in hers. "He saw *you*."

The revelation sent a shiver down Nat's spine. She thought of all the photos and memories he would have seen and made a mental note to look at the security settings before her next job interview. The stupid poses, the ridiculous memes, the rambling status updates that didn't quite make sense. She found it hard to believe that Michael, with his impeccable suits and perfectly organised life, had taken an interest in her. That her chaotic and messy existence had somehow caught his attention.

"It doesn't change what happened at the restaurant, though." Nat's shoulders slumped.

"Maybe not." Lexi gave Nat's hands a reassuring squeeze. "But it should change how you see yourself. Not that you need a man to change that, but you should know that you're a truly remarkable person. Anyone who's met you can see how special you are."

"Well, Joe didn't seem to think so." Nat's shoulders sagged a little further.

"You need to stop taking responsibility for other people's actions. Joe was an absolute dickhead, and everything he did was because he was selfish. And as far as Michael goes, from what Enzo was saying, he doesn't exactly have a huge amount of experience in the relationship department."

"What do you mean?" Nat looked up.

"Michael has always been so involved in his work and making a success of the company, he never really made time for relationships. The one girl where he did think it might be serious... she ended up cheating on him with one of his friends. Since then, he's not been interested in anyone else. Not until he met you, it would seem."

"Ah." Nat exhaled as a piece of the puzzle clicked into place. She lifted the gold chain from her neck and began running her fingers up and down the metal. It made sense now. The kiss on her hand in the coffee shop. The memory of his lips pressing against her skin. He had know exactly how she felt through his own bitter experience.

"Come on." Lexi clinked her glass against Nat's, drawing her back to reality. "Tonight is about us having fun. No work talk. No moping. Just dancing, OK?"

"Deal." Nat gave Lexi a broad smile, then spun back around to face the mirror. "You'd better finish my hair, otherwise we'll never make it to the club!"

"Done!" Lexi teased the curls around Nat's face, each one emphasising the range of tones in her chestnut hair.

With a final nod of approval at their reflections, they grabbed their bags and headed for the door.

"Here we are." Lexi reached forward to hand the driver some cash as they pulled up to the club. They stepped out into the fresh air and could feel the bass reverberating through the pavement beneath their feet. The club's exterior was an unusual combination of industrial steel fused with ornate Victorian elegance. Inside, the space continued with the theme of old meets new. Plush velvet fabrics and antique wood tables contrasted with sleek iron chairs and smooth marble topped bars. Nat, always on the lookout for inspiration for her designs, found this blend of styles jarred her senses.

"Let's get something to drink." Lexi pointed to a far corner and led the way.

They stood at the bar waiting to catch the attention of the bartender. With the lightest dusting of hair on his top lip, he looked like he had come straight from a day at secondary school. Nat fidgeted with the hem of her dress. Although she was a little tipsy from the drinks at Lexi's flat, she still felt a little self-conscious at how much of her legs were on display.

"Stop pulling at your dress." Lexi grabbed Nat's hands and placed them on the sticky surface of the bar. "You look stunning."

"If you say so." Nat rolled her eyes.

"Two gin and tonics, please," Lexi shouted to the bartender as he approached.

"Make those doubles," Nat added. Lexi nodded her approval, and he returned moments later with two large glasses. She tapped her credit card on the machine, then lifted her drink and clinked it against Nat's before taking a long sip.

Nat's eyes swept over the sea of bodies. The club was buzzing with energy as they navigated through the crowd in search of a vacant table.

"Over there!" Lexi pointed to a spot on the other side of the dance floor, but as they made their way, Nat collided with a familiar figure stepping back from the bar—Michael. His eyes, bright blue even through the darkness of the club, widened in surprise.

"Nat, Lexi! What are you doing here?" A wide smile grew on Michael's face. "Hey Enzo, look who's here!" Enzo appeared from behind Michael, holding a glass of beer.

"Hey, what a coincidence." Enzo looked directly at Lexi with a mischievous grin.

"Yes, isn't this such a coincidence?" Nat raised an eyebrow, glancing at Lexi whose cheeks had suddenly developed a deep shade of pink beneath the strobe lights.

"Oh, I love this song!" Lexi grabbed Enzo's hand. "Come on." She pulled him towards the dance floor before he could protest, leaving Nat and Michael standing side by side and watching them disappear into the crowd.

Michael turned to Nat. "You look really beautiful."

"Thank you." Nat blushed. She had always struggled to accept compliments, especially when it came to her appearance. "This is all thanks to Lexi. If I had my way, I'd be in jeans and a jumper!"

"Well, I'm glad you took Lexi's advice tonight. Shall we?" He gestured towards a corner table that had just been vacated.

"Sure." Nat took a seat opposite him and placed down her drink. She pushed down the annoyance hovering under the surface from his lack of contact all week. "Your holiday... how was it?" She leaned forward so he could hear her over the music, suddenly conscious of how much cleavage might be on show. She attempted to adjust the neckline without him noticing.

"Exhausting. Enzo and I were on a stag do for an old school friend. Lots of... festivities."

"Sounds hectic." Nat tried to picture Michael downing shots among a rowdy group of drunken men, leering at girls and making crude jokes. She just couldn't quite see it. He didn't seem like that kind of person.

"It was." He ran a hand through his hair, a habit Nat noticed when she knew he was feeling uncomfortable. "I'm sorry I haven't been in touch. I just thought it would be better to wait until I could see you in person."

Nat fidgeted a little in her seat and twisted the base of her glass. They lived in a world where everyone was used to communicating via text messages and social media. It made a nice change that Michael saved the difficult conversations for when they could talk face to face, where nothing could be misunderstood. Despite this, they sat saying nothing for a while until it was almost unbearable.

"About the kiss..." Michael finally broke the tension, his voice nearly lost amidst the noise.

Nat's stomach lurched. "Yes. I've been thinking about it." She felt a flush creep over her cheeks.

"Me too." He paused for a moment. "I meant it when I said it wasn't a mistake."

"It wasn't." She shook her head slightly. "But I'm not sure what it means."

"Neither am I."

They held each other's gaze, trying to figure out what the other was thinking. The words hung between them, waiting for one of them to break the tension.

"I haven't been single for long, you know." Nat looked down at her hands, twisting them awkwardly. "Since my last relationship ended, I've been trying to regain my confidence."

"I know." He nodded his head slowly. "I remember what happened in the coffee shop when you saw your ex."

Nat groaned at the memory. "Please, don't remind me."

"And then there's the fact that I'm your boss. It complicates things."

Nat found herself tracing the rim of her glass with a fingertip, a helpful diversion from the weight of their eye contact.

"Complications." She tilted her head as if considering the word from every angle. "They have a way of finding us, don't they?"

"They do. Look, I think we both know that mixing work with... anything else is far from ideal."

Nat nodded. The acknowledgment cut through her. It was one thing to know it, another to hear him say it out loud. They were taking it in turns to present the evidence towards a decision she didn't really want to make.

"Truth be told, I've never been very good at relationships. Business plans, sales pitches, strategies—that I can do. But this?" Michael gestured faintly between them. "It's not my strong suit."

She admired the bravery of his admission. It was oddly comforting to hear that even someone as confident and collected as Michael could have his own insecurities.

"Friends, then?" Nat forced the words out, knowing there wasn't really another choice. Being the first one to say it was just her way of taking control of the situation. Deep down, she knew she would rather follow a different path.

"Friends." He hesitated briefly. "Though, if things were different, if you weren't my employee. It would be—"

"Less complicated." Nat finished his sentence, allowing a little smile to develop at the corners of her mouth. "As much as I love working for you, I'm still set on my design business."

"That's good to know." Michael shrugged his shoulders. "Who knows what the future might hold?"

"Who knows." she echoed, her mind already spinning with the possibilities.

"Come on, let's not just sit here all night." Michael smoothed down his trousers as he stood. "If I remember rightly, you're quite the dancer."

She nodded firmly and downed the last of her gin and tonic.

"Looks like they're having the time of their lives." She gestured towards Lexi and Enzo as they danced provocatively, oblivious to everyone around them.

"Looks like they need some privacy!" Michael raised his eyebrows. Nat laughed as he grinned at her.

This is for the best, she told herself as they made their way across the dance floor. But the thought did little to soothe the sting of disappointment. The design contract could mean more than just professional success now. It could pave the way for the freedom to explore a future with Michael. She watched him as he joked with Enzo. Maybe, if she secured this contract, they could revisit the possibility of more. But for now, they were friends, and that would have to be enough.

# CHAPTER TWENTY

## Monday 23<sup>rd</sup> May

"I don't think I've ever been given flowers before," Michael said, eyeing the bunch of rainbow tulips in Nat's hand as he opened his front door.

"Well, there's a first time for everything." Nat stepped inside and handed the flowers to him. "I thought your place could do with a little brightening up."

"What do you mean?" Michael followed her inside and looked around. "I thought my apartment was very bright. There's lots of natural light."

"It might have *light*…" Nat paused and walked into the dining area. She turned to face Michael and stretched her arms out. "But where is the colour? Grey, black and white. That's not the most imaginative of decor. It's very… bland."

Michael looked a little despondent and Nat felt a brief pang of guilt. She had bought the flowers as a gesture to signify a fresh start for their friendship, but had ended up accidentally insulting his decorating choices.

"There is a slight problem." He placed the flowers on the kitchen worktop. "I don't actually have anything to put these in."

"Good thing I came prepared then." Nat pulled a simple glass vase from her bag with a flourish.

She moved to the sink and began trimming the stems, her movements precise and deliberate. Once satisfied, she arranged them in the vase, and soon the bouquet had been brought to life.

"Here." She placed the vase on the sideboard. It stood out like a beacon, radiating warmth into the cool, monochrome palette of the living space.

"They look… nice." There was a note of surprise in his voice. "A perfect complement to that." He gestured towards the opposite side of the room.

Nat's eyes fell on the print she'd given him, now hanging on the far wall.

"It looks great!" She sensed a gentle flutter in her stomach, wondering if he thought about her whenever he looked at the print. "See, your apartment doesn't have to be so sterile and grey, does it?"

Michael studied the print for a moment before nodding. "You might be onto something."

Nat smiled to herself as she took a seat at the dining table. It felt nice, knowing that there was a little part of her in his home. Her fingers tapped away at the keyboard as she made an effort to stay focused on her work. Michael was across from her in his usual seat, poring over a document with a furrowed brow.

She found watching him work mesmerising, noticing his little quirks and mannerisms. The way he chewed on his lip when he was trying to decide what to type next. The way he rubbed his jaw line when he was talking on the phone. He was usually so engrossed in what he was doing, he never noticed Nat watching him. She snapped out of her daydream and looked at her watch. The morning was nearly halfway over and she had a lot to be getting on with.

"Need a caffeine fix?" Michael pushed back from the table and stood up.

"Definitely." She threw him a grateful smile, watching as he strode towards his modern kitchen.

"How's Lexi's shop coming along?" Michael returned to the table with two cups. "It can't be long until the launch?"

"It's Friday evening." She accepted the coffee with a nod of thanks. "We're nearly there, just a few finishing touches left. It's nerve-wracking, but exciting." Her voice betrayed the unease she felt, the fear of everything not being perfect lurking in the shadows of her enthusiasm.

"You've put a lot of work into it. I'd like to see the finished place. I know Enzo would, too. Count us in for the grand opening, if that's OK with you?"

"Really?" Nat's heart lifted, and she forced a laugh to cover the surge of warmth his support sparked within her. "Of course we'd love to have you there, if you haven't got other plans?"

"No other plans. And if I did, I would cancel them." Michael held his gaze steady on hers. "Besides, Enzo never misses a chance for live music. He's quite the musician, remember?"

"Hard to forget!" Nat laughed. "Lexi will be over the moon if you could both make it." And so would she.

Nat sank into the armchair in the corner of Michael's living room, her legs tucked beneath her as she flicked through a design magazine. The remnants of their casual lunch lingered on the coffee table. A few traces left from their bowls of chicken salad and two empty glasses stained with bright green smoothie.

Since she had been working from his apartment, he regularly made lunch for them. Nat was used to sandwiches, crisps, and a fizzy drink when she was in the office. She was starting to enjoy the healthy options he would effortlessly rustle up. It wouldn't be long before he tried to persuade her to go to the gym with him, although maybe that would be a step too far. The thought of trying to do exercise alongside Michael in his sportswear, showing off his tight muscular frame, would surely be a recipe for disaster. They may have agreed on just friends, but that didn't mean she had to put a stop to her imagination.

As Michael logged onto his laptop for the board meeting, Nat found herself an unobtrusive spectator, absorbed in her magazine yet keeping an ear on the conversation.

"Good afternoon, everyone." Michael's voice shifted to the crisp, formal tone he reserved for business. "Unless anyone has anything they'd like to raise first, let's get straight down to discussing the investment deals on the table."

Nat listened as the voices of the board members trickled through the speakers, arguing over numbers and forecasts with a passion that contradicted the boring topic.

A gentle ripple of worry ran through her as she studied Michael's composed profile. She knew him well enough by now, the way his jaw tensed, how his blue eyes turned a shade colder when discomfort lurked beneath his polished exterior. He believed in doing things right, not just profitably.

The board's enthusiasm for Spinigma was palpable, their arguments circling back to bottom lines and market shares. But where was the passion for integrity, for the impact of their choices beyond the boardroom? Clara's influence on the group was clear—and it looked like her efforts to persuade them to choose her preferred investor were going to pay off.

"Michael?" One of the board members drew his attention. "Your thoughts?"

"Both offers have merit," Michael conceded after a pause. "We'll need to weigh them carefully. There are certain... complexities we will need to consider with Spinigma."

"Come on, Michael." Another board member was quick to scold him. "You know the kind of capital we're talking about with such an enormous organisation. We can't let sentimentality cloud our judgement."

The meeting continued, but Nat's mind churned with disquiet. This wasn't him. Michael set up the company with a very specific vision that set them apart from others in the market. He was passionate about the environment, the community, the message they sent. Yet here he was, acquiescing to a path she knew he couldn't truly believe in.

As the call ended, Michael leaned back with a sigh. Nat set the magazine aside and took a seat next to him at the table.

"Can I ask you something?" Her voice cut through the quiet.

"Of course." His eyes met hers, a weariness to them that she couldn't bear seeing.

"The deal... with Spinigma." Nat hesitated, searching his face for any sign of the misgivings she suspected. "Are you really OK with it? It just seems so at odds with what you've always stood for."

"It's complicated." Michael's posture shifted. He was closing himself off and retreating behind his professional façade. "The board has a point—we have to consider the financial implications."

"But that's just it." Nat wasn't quite ready to let go. "It feels like you're being railroaded into something you don't want. Since when did you start compromising your values for profit?"

He stiffened at her words. A flicker of vulnerability crossed his features before he smoothed it away. "I have a responsibility to this company and its shareholders. It's not just about what I want."

"But still." Nat sensed she needed to tread carefully. "If you have concerns about the ethical side of things, shouldn't you voice them? You're not just any board member, Michael. You lead this company. You set the direction."

He looked at her for a moment. Then, with a reluctant exhale, he nodded, his admission quiet but laden with significance.

"I do have concerns." The armour of his professionalism had finally cracked. "But questioning the consensus isn't simple. There's a lot at stake."

"Isn't there always?" Nat offered a supportive smile. "Standing up for what's right is rarely easy."

She watched as Michael's fingers drummed against the surface of the table. He looked up at her as a deep sigh escaped his lips.

"I'm not blind to the implications. But you have to understand—the board is breathing down my neck for growth. They don't care about the how, just the end numbers."

"But you do." Nat leant forward. "You care. Or am I wrong? Has the Michael I have got to know, who puts integrity before profit, changed?"

"Of course I haven't changed." A flare of frustration broke through his composure. "But sometimes we don't have the luxury of choosing. The board is convinced that this is the best move for rapid expansion. And they're not wrong about the potential financial upside."

"Potential at the expense of principles?" Nat could feel herself getting agitated. "Come on. You don't seem like someone that follows the crowd. Lead them instead. Show them there's a better way."

"It's easy for you to say." Michael stood up, towering over her, the lines of stress etched into his face. "But you don't have to answer to a room full of sharks waiting to attack at the first sign of weakness."

"Maybe not." The challenge to unsettle her only hardened her resolve. "But if they smell blood in the water, wouldn't you rather it be because you fought for something you believe in, than because you let yourself be devoured without so much as a whimper?"

He responded with a heavy sigh and turned away from her, walking towards the window to look out at the cityscape. For a long moment, neither spoke.

"I appreciate what you're trying to do." He finally broke the silence, his voice low. "But pushing this means risking everything I've built if the board loses faith in me."

"Isn't the company already at risk if you compromise on the values that built it?"

"I don't want to talk about it any more." Michael's expression was closed off, resolute. He turned his back to her. "I need to handle this my way."

Nat felt his words like a physical blow. She had pushed too far.

"I... I'm sorry." She stumbled over her words, the colour rising in her cheeks as regret flooded her body. "I shouldn't have got involved... Just forget I said anything, OK? It's none of my business."

Michael didn't respond. He shifted his attention to the laptop and quickly became engrossed in what was on the screen. Nat let out a long breath and tapped the keyboard to log back into her own computer, trying to focus on her work. An uncomfortable tension hung between them for the rest of the afternoon.

By five p.m., Nat's shoulders were aching from sitting still for so long. She had barely moved for hours, not wanting to distract Michael from his work. He'd made it clear he wasn't in the mood for light-hearted conversation and the weight of the decision ahead was clearly playing on his mind. After such a positive start this morning, she knew she needed to do something to turn things around. She didn't want to leave with such an awkward atmosphere between them.

"Hey." She emphasised a brightness to her voice. "It's getting late. How about we call it a day? I bought my swimming costume as I fancied a swim. Why don't you join me to unwind? It's been a bit of a heavy day, hasn't it?" She offered a wide smile as a peace offering.

Michael looked up and studied Nat's face for a moment. "Sure." His posture relaxed slightly, some of the earlier tension dissipating. "A swim sounds good."

Nat smiled and nodded, grateful she had taken the chance to salvage the remains of the day.

Her fingers trembled as she hooked the clasp of her bikini top. She took slow breaths to calm her nerves a little. She was now regretting the offer of Michael joining her for a swim at the realisation he would soon be seeing her semi-naked. The changing room, with its pungent scent of chlorine and humid air, felt claustrophobic. She pulled the bikini bottoms up over her hips, wishing she felt as bold as the pattern of tropical flowers decorating the fabric. She wrapped a towel firmly around her waist, clutching at the material to hide her insecurities. Her eyes flicked to the mirror, taking in the apprehension etched across her features.

"You're a grown woman, Nat. It's just a swimming pool, not a bloody catwalk," she told her reflection.

Drawing in a deep, fortifying breath, she pushed open the door to the pool area. The expanse of blue water stretched out before her, glistening under the bright overhead lights. There, poised at the deep end like a sculpture chiselled from marble, stood Michael. His black swimming shorts clung to his frame, hinting at the strength coiled in his muscled thighs. They underlined a subtle ripple of abs usually concealed beneath impeccably tailored suits. Nat found herself entranced by the contrast of his tanned skin against the dark fabric. His floppy hair now lay plastered to his head, droplets of water catching the light as they rolled off his shoulders.

Michael looked up. A flash of blue as bright as the water below met her hesitant features. He offered a nod, acknowledging her presence, before cutting through the air in a smooth arc to dive into the water. Nat was captivated as he reappeared, powering forward with a fast, efficient front crawl, each stroke slicing through the calm surface. Her own worries were momentarily forgotten as she admired the play of muscles along his back, the ease with which he guided his body through the water.

But as she watched him, that old, gnawing doubt crept back, whispering reminders of her shortcomings. She thought of all the ways she didn't measure up—not as an interior designer, not in her personal life, and certainly not standing here on the edge of a pool, too self-conscious to shed her towel and join him in the water.

As Michael turned at the wall and continued his relentless pace, Nat imagined what Lexi would say to her right now. She would be furious, reminding her of all the ways she was good enough. Nat allowed something to shift inside her, deciding right there and then not to let her fears control her. She took a deep breath, dropped her towel on a chair, and walked over to the pool with a newfound sense of confidence.

Nat tentatively dipped a toe into the shimmering pool, her breath catching at the touch of water against her skin. It was cold—colder than she'd anticipated—but invigorating as well. She climbed down the steps, feeling a wave of excitement tingling on her skin until she was completely immersed in the clear water.

She let herself drift for a while, feeling the water lifting her up. It was the total opposite to the heavy doubts that usually held her back. With a shiver, she knew she needed to move to warm up and pushed away from the edge. Her movements were easy-going, almost awkward next to Michael's graceful precision. But there was something endearing about her clumsy breaststroke—as if each paddle was a tiny protest against the need for everything to be flawless all the time on solid ground.

Nat relished the rhythm of her arms breaking the surface, followed by the gentle kick of her legs, creating soft ripples that lapped against the pool's edge. She wasn't fast or remarkably skilled, but here, in these leisurely laps, she found a rare sense of freedom from expectation.

After a few laps, with the taste of chlorine lingering on her lips and her muscles warmed from the effort, it was time for a change of pace. Nat made her way to the jacuzzi, where the promise of heated relaxation beckoned. As she settled onto the submerged bench, her eyes traced Michael's form once more. He was a mesmerising sight, his body cutting through the water, lap after relentless lap.

As she watched him, a part of her acknowledged that sometimes, life called for the warmth of bubbling waters and the pleasure of rest, rather than the ceaseless pursuit of achievement. There in the jacuzzi, with the hum of the jets and the caress of hot water against her skin, Nat closed her eyes and embraced the balance between aspiration and contentment—a compromise that felt just right.

Moments later, she heard the sound of wet footsteps approaching the jacuzzi. Nat opened her eyes to see Michael climbing down and taking a seat. She feigned interest in the swirling patterns of foam around her as he sank into the bubbling space opposite, close enough that their knees almost touched beneath the surface.

"You're quite the swimmer, huh?" Nat said.

"University swim team. I made it to nationals a few times."

"I could have guessed." Nat laughed, rolling her eyes. "You're such an over-achiever!"

"I'm just multi-talented." Michael's smile was filled with a sense of deep satisfaction, but one that didn't come across as arrogant.

Their legs brushed accidentally, causing a surge of energy to rush through Nat's body. The sensation stirred something deep within her—an attraction that felt both thrilling and dangerous. She shifted a little, the movement sending ripples through the water. This was Michael—determined, serious Michael—and she was Nat, the one who saw beauty in imperfection and was always second-guessing herself. Being so close to him felt like a magnetic pull she wasn't sure she could resist, not without breaking their agreement of just friendship.

"Do you have the time?" She attempted to maintain a neutral tone to her voice, hoping it would calm her racing heartbeat.

"Yes." He looked towards the clock mounted on the wall. "Just after six-thirty."

"Damn it." Nat leapt up, breaking the spell of their closeness. She couldn't shake the urge to protect herself. The chemistry was undeniable, but so was her fear of rejection. "Sorry, I've got to dash—babysitting duty calls."

Nat wrapped the towel tightly around her waist, using it as a shield against the feelings being so close to Michael had stirred up. Without waiting for a reply or glancing back, she hurried away. Feeling both relieved to have an excuse to leave and a hint of regret, she welcomed the chance to break free from the rising heat that had nothing to do with the temperature of the water.

# CHAPTER TWENTY–ONE

**Tuesday 24ᵗʰ May**

"I'm just going to pop out and grab some bits so I can make our lunch." Michael reached for his keys from the kitchen counter.

Nat looked up from her laptop where she'd been engrossed in responding to a chat message from Jamie. He'd found out something that could be important, but he wanted to wait until he was certain before he told her any more. They would meet to discuss it properly in the office tomorrow.

"Just pick up something easy." As much as she enjoyed their lunches, she didn't want him to go to any trouble. But Michael was shaking his head before she even finished her sentence.

"I'd rather cook something nice for us." He pulled on his jacket and smiled.

"OK, fine." Nat masked the warmth spreading through her chest with a roll of her eyes. It felt nice to be looked after by someone. Over the last couple of weeks, she had discovered how much Michael enjoyed cooking. After the scrutiny of his almost empty fridge when she first came to his apartment, her initial scepticism had turned out to be unfounded.

With Michael gone, Nat moved to the lounge area, spreading her portfolio across the coffee table. She smoothed out the pages, her gaze tracing the lines of her latest design for what had to be the hundredth time. The entrance space for the hotel was the most critical part, meant to welcome guests and fill them with awe. It was almost complete, and pride swelled within her chest as she allowed herself a moment to admire the work.

Pushing a stray lock of hair behind her ear, she reached for her sketching pencils, the tips worn down to nubs from use. There were only a few bits left to refine, a few strokes of colour that would breathe life into the drawings. Next week's interview was at the forefront of her mind, but as she made the finishing touches, the anxiety that usually gnawed at her insides settled into a quiet corner of her mind.

"Looking good," she murmured to herself, allowing a rare smile of satisfaction. This project could be the one to change everything. Just maybe, her mother and Simon would finally see that she was more than capable of running a successful interior design business.

Nat was so lost in her work, she barely noticed as Michael returned with brown paper bags brimming with fresh groceries. She glanced up from her sketches at the sound of rustling in the kitchen.

"Back already?" Her voice carrying a note of surprise as she smoothed down the edges of her portfolio.

"It was quieter than expected." Michael placed the bags on the counter with a gentle thud. He looked over at the open pages spread across the coffee table. "What's that?"

"Oh, it's nothing." Nat lifted the cover to close the portfolio before he could see any more. "Just a little project I'm working on."

"Nothing? It looked impressive from what I could make out." He didn't press further, and she was relieved he had respected the boundary she had quickly drawn.

Michael rolled up his sleeves and started lifting items out of the bags. "Let's get started on making lunch. How do you feel about smoked salmon with a fresh tomato salsa on homemade bruschetta?"

"That sounds wonderful." Her stomach rumbled in agreement as she joined him in the kitchen. "Let me give you a hand."

"Could you chop these tomatoes and onions for the salsa?" Michael slid a knife and cutting board her way as he busied himself with the bread.

"Sure." Nat picked up the knife and grabbed a tomato. She turned it round several times before deciding on the best angle to slice it. She watched Michael's precise, swift movements, a stark contrast to her own hesitant chops.

"Here, let me show you." Michael guided her hands. "A rocking motion, like this." His fingers gently overlapped hers, and for a moment, Nat was acutely aware of the warmth of his skin. Her body tensed and she held her breath. With the first tomato done, he stepped back to place the bread under the grill, leaving Nat to carry on.

She finally allowed herself to relax again, making a start on the onions. With each slice, Nat's eyes became more irritated by the pungent smell stinging her eyes. Tears gathered at the corners and she tried to wipe them away with the back of her hand.

"Why don't you let me?" Michael lifted his thumb to Nat's face, wiping the moisture away gently. "You'll only make it worse." He let his hand rest on her cheek for a moment and a hint of something flashed across his face. He broke eye contact before Nat could figure out what it was.

"These look perfect." He turned to admire the neat pile of diced vegetables, adding a large squeeze of lime juice. "Now, for the spice—how brave are you feeling?"

"Um, moderately brave?" She allowed herself to relax a little as he moved away, the intensity of his touch dissipating.

"Moderately it is." Michael reached for the chilli flakes. He sprinkled a conservative amount into the bowl before adding freshly chopped coriander and mixing it together. "Taste?" He lifted a spoon of the salsa and held it out for her to take.

"That's really good." The flavours exploded in her mouth with the perfect blend of heat and zest.

"Teamwork." Michael grinned. "You grab some drinks from the fridge while I get this plated up."

Nat took the seat across from Michael, their plates filled with the lively colours of the meal set out in front of them. Ever the interior designer, she found herself appreciating how the reds and greens of the tomato salsa popped against the soft pink of the salmon—a burst of food magic.

"OK, this looks amazing." She reached for her phone to take a photograph. "And to think, my biggest achievement is not burning toast. Lexi won't believe this!"

"Give yourself some credit. You were chopping those tomatoes like a pro by the time you got to the last one." He took a bite, his expression one of content satisfaction. "But maybe we should get you some goggles for chopping onions?"

For once, Nat accepted the simple and sincere compliment. As they ate, the conversation turned to stories of travels and the foods that marked the memories.

"I think my favourite had to be the summer I spent in Italy with Enzo's family." A smile lit up Michael's face. "That's where I really learned to appreciate cooking. His Nonna wouldn't let me leave the kitchen until I could make pasta from scratch."

"Really?" Nat's eyes danced with curiosity and a touch of envy. Travelling seemed like such a luxury now. She couldn't imagine her finances allowing that for a long time. "I bet it was gorgeous there."

"Absolutely. The rolling hills, the vineyards, the food—it was like stepping into a different world. A slower pace of life, you know?"

"Sounds perfect." She took a brief pause to imagine such a place, so far removed from the hustle and bustle of Kensington and the demands of her family's expectations.

As the last bites of their lunch vanished, Nat got up from the table and began gathering the empty plates.

"I'll clean up," she insisted, despite Michael's protests. "You always do most of the cooking, so I'll clear. It's only fair."

With a reluctant nod, Michael agreed. The clink of dishes and the hum of running water filled the room as Nat lost herself in the methodical task of rinsing and stacking the dishwasher. She turned off the tap, wiped her damp hands on the back of her jeans, and glanced back at Michael, who had already opened his laptop and was absorbed in work once more. The seriousness with which he approached everything was both intimidating and admirable. She could just imagine him in the Italian countryside, learning to make pasta under the watchful eye of a loving Nonna, meticulously following every instruction until each piece was perfect.

"Back to work then?"

"Unfortunately." Michael grimaced. "Thank you for helping with lunch. It was nice." His gaze lingered on her for a second longer than necessary before dropping to the screen.

"You're welcome." Nat smiled to herself as she sat back down and opened her own laptop. They definitely made a good team.


It was getting late in the afternoon when a brisk knock punctured the silence. Michael set aside his work and made his way to the front door, opening it to reveal Clara standing in the doorway.

"Hi." She stepped inside without waiting for an invitation. In her hand was a sheaf of papers that looked as crisp and precise as her sharply tailored suit. "I'm here to go through the finances."

"Why don't you come in?" Michael laughed, closing the door behind her.

Nat watched as she breezed through the apartment towards the lounge. Clara's gaze swept over her, cool and detached, before landing on the portfolio sitting on the coffee table.

"What's this?" Clara waved her hand over the table, setting her over-sized designer handbag dangerously close to Nat's work. She began flicking through the pages.

"Natalie is an interior designer when she's not working for HealthLink." Michael took the paperwork from Clara.

"Interior design, how quaint." Clara's lips curved into a condescending smirk.

"It's a tough industry to get into. I'm quite proud of my work." Nat's words lacked the conviction she was trying so hard to portray.

"Of course you should be." Her voice dripped with insincerity as she smoothed down her vibrant red hair. "Everyone needs a hobby, right?"

Hobby. The word echoed in Nat's mind, trivialising every ounce of effort she'd poured into her career. There was a brief pause, bordering on a standoff. The warm, comfortable atmosphere from earlier in the day had turned icy in Clara's presence.

Michael cleared his throat and directed Clara's attention back to the task at hand.

"Let's get started on this." He guided her to the dining table. "We have a lot to go through before Friday."

"Of course." Clara flipped open her folder with an air of self-importance. She perched at the edge of the table as she leaned in towards Michael to examine the document, her shoulder brushing his with every deliberate movement.

Nat watched from across the table, her fingers curling into tight fists on her lap. Her eyes, usually warm and vibrant, narrowed as she observed the scene playing out before her. She wanted to believe that Michael was oblivious to Clara's advances, but the doubt seeded by her presence left her own confidence wavering. Even with the knowledge that Clara was engaged, Nat knew this was all a game to someone like her. She thrived on attention from men, and would stop at nothing to get it from whoever she could. It was all the more fun when there might be some competition.

"Looks like we've covered everything." Michael closed the folder with a sense of finality.

"Perfect timing." Clara stood up and stretched, reaching her long, perfectly manicured fingers above her head. "I could use a glass of wine after all that work. What do you say?"

Michael checked his watch. "Sure, why not?"

Clara walked towards the wine cabinet. The sound of her heels clicking against the tiles felt like tiny hammers inside Nat's head. She opened the door to reveal rows of bottles nestled inside. Her hand hovered over the selection before she plucked a bottle of red and held it aloft like a trophy.

"Ah, this one is just what I was looking for." Clara looked directly at Nat. Although her expression made it clear who she was really talking to. "Michael, I remember you getting this when we were away on that trip to France. Visiting that vineyard together was so much fun."

Nat bristled at her attempt to show off her familiarity with Michael and his tastes. She bit back the retort that bubbled at the edge of her lips—the urge to tell Clara that she wasn't the only one who knew how to appreciate a good vintage.

Instead, Nat remained seated and just smiled. She wondered if Michael noticed her discomfort or if he was too preoccupied with business. For a fleeting moment, she longed for the simplicity of chopping tomatoes and laughter, for the easy back and forth that had been so unexpectedly delightful. She watched as Clara reached for two glasses, placing them on the counter and checking the drawer for a bottle opener.

"You'll stay for a drink, won't you, Natalie?" Michael reached for a third glass and placed it next to the others.

"I'd love to." Nat stood and walked to the counter, making direct eye contact with Clara. A hint of challenge flashed across her face. As the cork gave way with a soft pop, Nat braced herself for what was to come, fighting against the rising feeling of not being good enough.

Nat sat back on the couch and took a large sip of wine. The alcohol filled her with courage almost immediately as she listened to Clara brag.

"If this deal with Spinigma goes through, we will be on target to make the FTSE100 within the next couple of years." Clara smoothed down her hair. "And I will be the youngest female Chief Financial Officer in a social media company."

Nat couldn't hold back any longer. "I'd love to hear more about the reasons why we're considering partnering with an organisation that likes to make their profit from people who are addicted to gambling." She directed the request to Clara, a sense of boldness growing within her as she studied her face for a reaction. "Exploiting vulnerable people seems like a strange fit for a company that prides itself on being socially and morally responsible."

"Well, it's a solid financial move, Natalie. The revenue potential is immense. We'd be fools not to go for it." Clara took a steady sip of wine and narrowed her eyes. "But I wouldn't really expect someone like you to understand it. You'd be much better off sticking to organising meetings, making coffee, and playing with your house designs."

Nat's anger flared, but she tamped it down, humiliated once again by Clara's dismissive attitude of her passion.

"Surely there are other options that don't involve..." Nat's voice trailed off, her argument losing steam as she saw Michael nod in agreement with Clara.

"Sometimes the best opportunities require tough decisions." He shrugged. "We have to think about the company's growth."

Nat frowned. She knew Michael's words echoed Clara's sentiment rather than his own.

Clara smirked, her eyes glinting with triumph as she reached out to refill her glass. As she set down the bottle, in one careless motion her hand knocked against the glass. The contents spilt out, flowing like a crimson waterfall over Nat's portfolio.

"Clara!" Michael reached forward to stop the glass, but it was too late.

"Shit!" Clara's exclamation did nothing to undo the damage. She lifted the cover, causing the wine that had pooled on the surface to soak into the pages inside.

Nat lunged forward, desperately trying to salvage her work. The paper absorbed the wine greedily, staining the fabric swatches and carefully drawn plans.

"It's ruined." Nat's voice was barely above a whisper, her words laced with a mix of disbelief and despair.

"Sorry, it's just a bit of wine." Clara's apology was hollow. "I didn't think it was that important, anyway."

Nat gathered the ruined pages, cradling them to her chest as if she could somehow protect them from further harm. Her eyes found Michael's, searching for some sign of understanding, of shared disappointment. He only offered a helpless shrug.

"Excuse me." Her face was hot with embarrassment and anger. "I'd better get going."

"Natalie, wait." Michael jumped up from the couch. "Is there anything I can do to help?"

"No, just leave it." Tears stung her eyes. "It's too late."

Nat gathered her bag and fled, clutching the portfolio that represented so much more than just a little project. As she rushed through the door, her heart pounded with a mixture of fury and a painful realisation that she was never going to achieve her dreams. Her trembling hand fumbled with the doorknob as she pulled it closed.

"Nat?" A concerned voice cut through the air. She nearly collided with Enzo as he stepped out of the lift, his easy smile fading at the sight of her distress.

"Enzo," she choked out, wiping away tears as she recounted the disaster that had unfolded.

"Clara was just vile, as always. And now she has ruined all of my hard work." Nat held up the portfolio. A few drops of wine fell to the floor. "To top it off, Michael let her walk all over me again!" Her words carried the sting of betrayal.

Enzo's face softened, his head tilted in understanding as he listened.

"I'm so sorry about your work. Is it salvageable?"

Nat shook her head. "It's completely ruined. And Michael doesn't even care."

"You know he's not the best with difficult situations, especially when it comes to dealing with women. I hope you can forgive him." He offered a wry grin that didn't quite reach his eyes, hinting at a shared understanding of his friend's shortcomings.

"Doesn't that just excuse him, though? For everything?" Nat's voice was lower now, her anger giving way to weariness.

"Maybe," Enzo conceded, shifting on his feet. "But it's obvious to anyone who sees you two together—there's more to it than just work or friendship. Michael cares about you, really. It's just...he has this habit of showing it in the most unfortunate of ways."

Nat's gaze dropped to the soggy edges of her portfolio, a stark reminder of the evening's undoing. The idea that Michael could genuinely care about her seemed unlikely. If he really did care, surely there wouldn't be the cold lack of defence she'd experienced moments ago? He wouldn't allow Nat to be treated so unkindly by someone else.

"Give it time," Enzo encouraged, his voice gentle. "You don't strike me as the type of person that gives up easily. Not when something really matters to them."

She managed a small, uncertain smile. Enzo gave her shoulder a reassuring squeeze and headed towards Michael's door. As she disappeared into the lift, Nat took a deep breath. She didn't know how many times she would be able to overlook Michael's behaviour. Perhaps it was finally time to give up on the possibility of a future with him. She looked down at the mess in her hands. With the portfolio ruined, maybe it was time to give up on her dreams too.

# CHAPTER TWENTY–TWO

**Wednesday 25th May**

N at clicked her laptop shut and slid it into her bag. Jamie
was at his desk nearby, eyes squinting at the screen.

"Anything new?" Nat said, her voice low. The hum of elec-
tronics and distant chatter filled the space between them. Jamie
shook his head, pushing up his glasses.

"Just the travel logs to Boston so far." He tapped the keyboard to bring up a spreadsheet filled with dates and destina-

tions. "It's where Spinigma has its headquarters. That's all I've managed to get from the finance system."

Nat leaned over to glance at the screen. Rows of Clara's trips, with corresponding dates and times, were neatly lined up.

"That's a lot of visits to the same place."

"She does have some family out there, so it could be a coincidence." Jamie fiddled with the end of his pen. "But I'm not buying it. I'll keep digging. I need to look at the calendars to see if there have been any unusual meetings."

"Thanks. But please be careful. I don't want you doing anything that might get you in trouble." Nat straightened up, slinging her bag over her shoulder. "We've only got two days. Let me know if you find anything else. The meeting to sign the deal is happening on Friday afternoon. In the meantime, I'll see if I can persuade the other investors to stay interested. My source tells me the court case is scheduled for Friday morning. If we can't stop the deal and persuade Michael and the board to go with the alternative investors, our only hope is that the judge rules to make the details of the investigation public. That will put a stop to everything."

"Hey, Nat..." Jamie's voice held a note of caution. "Michael won't be happy if he finds out what you're doing. Be careful, OK?"

"I will." Nat gave him a half-smile and turned, making her way quickly towards the lifts. She had managed to avoid seeing Michael all day, answering emails promptly and taking care to avoid any chance encounters. Now wasn't the time for a discussion about the events from the previous evening. He wasn't to know the extent of the damage to the portfolio and the significance of it being lost, and Nat wasn't ready to tell him. She had resigned herself to letting go of the design contract and doing what she could to save Michael's company, despite how he made her feel.

She slipped out into the warm spring air and made her way to the bus stop. The bus arrived with a hiss and a sigh, doors folding open to welcome her inside. A seat near the window was free, so she settled in. The fabric was scratchy against her palm. She pulled out her phone and opened up the email app, taking a deep breath and clicking to start a new message to the CEO of Ethica. They had met a few times while both deals were on the table—before Clara pulled their proposal apart and planted the seeds of doubt with the other board members. She hoped getting in touch wouldn't turn out to be a big mistake.

Subject line: HealthLink Proposal

Dear Julia,
I was hoping we could arrange to speak urgently tomorrow morning. There may be an opportunity for HealthLink to progress with your investment proposal. Please let me know the best time for you and I will call.
Kind regards,
Nat

Nat hit send and locked her phone screen quickly, unable to take back what she had just done. Despite her frustrations at Michael, she couldn't sit by and do nothing. He had built his company from scratch and didn't deserve to lose it all. With the design contract off the table, Nat was going to need this job for a little longer than she'd bargained for.

The bus came to a halt just outside Lexi's shop. Nat stepped off and pushed the door open, the cheerful bell announcing her arrival.

"Hey, where are you?" she called out.

"Over here." Lexi's head popped up from behind a table where she sat on the floor, surrounded by an array of colourful prints.

"I'm trying to figure out if the vintage jazz poster goes here, or maybe there..."

"Why don't you leave the art to me?" Nat picked up the hammer and a handful of nails. "You still need to get the counter set up."

"Yes, boss!" Lexi pulled herself up from the floor in a single fluid movement and began emptying out the contents of a large box. "So, are you ready for next week?"

"Hmmm?" Nat pretended not to hear. She picked up a poster and held up against the wall. "I think this is better here. What do you think?"

"I think you don't need to ask my opinion on where to put that." Lexi gave Nat a piercing look. "What's up? You're not having second thoughts, are you?"

"Nope, not second thoughts." Nat placed the hammer down gently and paused for a moment, unwilling to say the words out loud that made everything real. "There isn't a portfolio to show."

"What do you mean?"

"When I was at Michael's last night, Clara was there. She spilled her red wine all over it." She shrugged her shoulders, already resigned to defeat.

"No," Lexi gasped, her hands halting mid-polish. "Deliberately?"

"She claims it was an accident, but it doesn't really matter. It's too late now."

"There must be something you can do?"

"I can't." Nat shook her head. "The special fabrics I used are from Paris, and there's no time to get suitable replacements. The portfolio is due on Tuesday, so it's too late."

"Why don't you take the next couple of days off work to sort it out?"

"Honestly, please just leave it. I've cancelled my interview slot, anyway. It's done." Nat turned away, signalling the end of the conversation. She could feel Lexi watching her, wanting to say something that might change her mind. It didn't matter now. The damage had already been done and there was no coming back from this.

To keep the silence from growing too heavy, Nat turned back to her friend and changed the subject.

"So, how's Enzo?"

Lexi looked taken aback by the sudden shift in topic. She blinked slowly, as if processing the question. "Enzo?" she repeated, the tiniest hint of blush colouring her cheeks.

"You two seemed to be getting on so well the last few times we've been together. I was just wondering if you've been in touch."

"We're just friends." Lexi turned back to emptying the box, but her words lacked conviction and she wouldn't meet Nat's gaze. "Anyway, he seems to spend all of his spare time marking student work and running their extra-curricular clubs. Plus, this shop has been my life for the last few weeks." Lexi gestured to the space around them. "We haven't had time yet."

"Yet!" Nat clapped her hands together. "So you are planning on meeting up?"

"I... well..." Lexi stammered, biting her lip as she shrugged. "I'm not sure. We've got a lot in common and I like him."

Nat couldn't help the broad smile forming on her face. She couldn't remember the last time her friend had been shy about anything.

"Well, this has to be a first!" Nat opened her mouth to interrogate further, but Lexi held up her hand.

"Enough! There will be no more discussion on the matter. I have a world famous music cafe to launch and boys are an unnecessary distraction right now." Lexi eyed Nat carefully. "You, of all people, should know that."

"Fine, point taken."

"Come on, give me a hand getting the till up on here."

The till in question, a vintage brass beast of a thing, sat on the floor beside them. It was one of the special touches that made Nat's style so unique. They heaved it onto the counter, its polished surface gleaming under the shop's spotlights. Stepping back together, they crossed their arms in unison and surveyed their work. The shop's layout was near perfect—open and inviting with the corner stage for hosting live music nights and a scattering of comfortable chairs and tables under suspended lights with individual lampshades. Records lined the haphazard shelves, and an assortment of eclectic instruments and antiques graced the walls.

"Looks like we're almost done here." Nat reached into her handbag, feeling around until her fingers clasped the edges of the surprise she'd been holding on to. "I've got something for you."

"What is it?" Lexi's eyes glinted with curiosity.

"Why don't you open it?" Nat presented a small package, wrapped in earth-toned paper and tied with a simple twine bow.

Lexi undid the knot, peeling back the wrapping to reveal two antique gold door signs. One commanded 'Open', while its counterpart stated 'Closed', both words in ornate lettering. Tiny musical notes were etched delicately along the borders, catching the soft light of the shop.

"They're beautiful!" Lexi held them up against the rustic wood of the door. She hung them from a tiny hook in the frame and adjusted them until they fell perfectly.

"Come on, let's take a look from outside."

They stepped out onto the pavement and admired what stood before them. The former rundown laundry had been transformed into a place that was appealing and full of character. The navy blue paint of the wooden frames contrasted beautifully with the gold-tone signage hung over the door—a cleverly stylised mix of musical notes and coffee beans welcoming customers to 'Java & Jazz'. Large windows invited potential customers to get a glimpse of the warm and welcoming interior of the shop with its antique furniture and quirky ornaments. It was a perfect reflection of Lexi's vibrant personality.

"Well?" Nat broke their silent admiration. "What do you think?"

"I think…" Lexi paused, stepping back to take in the entire view. "I think it's absolutely perfect."

"It really is, isn't it?" Nat found Lexi's hand and gave it a squeeze.

"I couldn't have done this without you." Lexi wrapped her arms around her, holding on as tight as she could. "You're amazing, you know that?"

"I'm so happy you like it." Nat allowed a delicious sensation of pride to wash over her. It wasn't often she allowed it, worrying that it might come across to others as arrogance. But today, side by side with her best friend, she knew she deserved this feeling, and she wanted to savour it.

"OK, that's enough standing around. Let's run through Friday night." Lexi rattled off details of caterers, live bands and timings as they walked back into the shop, settling down in one of the plush armchairs in the window. "But the most important thing to discuss is what are we going to wear?"

Lexi whipped out her phone and tapped on the screen before showing Nat an array of stunning dresses.

"This is definitely in the top ten." She pointed at an off-the-shoulder fitted red dress that finished just above the knee. She scrolled to another, a black jumpsuit with a high neck and long sleeves.

Nat peered at the images, making approving noises. The red one was definitely Lexi—bold, sassy, confident. The black one was a touch more reserved, but still stunning in its simplicity.

"Look at this one!" She turned the screen towards Nat so she could see the sleek, black dress with a plunging back and swirling silver embellishments. "Isn't it just perfect?"

"They're all beautiful. But you would make any dress look incredible."

"What about you?" Lexi carried on scrolling through, frowning as she tried to make a final decision.

"Me?" Nat hesitated, her fingers twisting a lock of hair as she ran through a mental inventory of her wardrobe. It didn't take long. "How about some skinny jeans and a nice top?"

"Absolutely not!" Lexi's face twisted into a look of complete disapproval.

"But you know I hate dressing up!"

"It's a special night. Not just for me, but for both of us." Lexi's face softened a little. "You designed this place! You should look and feel as amazing as your work."

"OK, you win." Nat knew admitting defeat was the only way. "Is there anything there that would suit me?"

After a few minutes of searching, Lexi stopped and held her phone out triumphantly towards Nat. Standing out on the screen was a dress unlike anything Nat would have picked for herself. Made from navy blue silk, it had an elegance about it that was both timeless and contemporary. The fitted bodice had a subtle sweetheart neckline, while the sleeves puffed gently at the shoulders before tapering to narrow cuffs. From the cinched waist, the skirt flowed in soft folds, cascading down to the floor.

"Wow! It's beautiful." Nat looked closely at the image, then drew a sharp breath when she saw the price. "It's also way out of my price range."

"But it's not out of mine." Lexi tapped on the screen a few times before locking her phone and placing it on the table. "Consider it my gift to you for all the work you have put into my dreams."

"You can't do that!"

"I can, and I have." Lexi nodded her head firmly. "The dress will be delivered to yours on Friday morning. Cinderella, you shall go to the ball."

"Why thank you, fairy godmother!" Despite her initial resistance, Nat felt a flicker of excitement at the prospect of wearing such a beautiful dress. It wouldn't take much to persuade Lucy to help her with the hair and make-up. She glanced at the clock hanging on the wall.

"I really should be going."

"Did you want a quick bite to eat first?"

"I can't. I've got a few things I need to get sorted for work." Nat pulled her bag over her shoulder and made her way to the door. "See you on Friday."

She crossed over the road and navigated her way through the busy street towards the bus stop. The weather hadn't decided if it wanted to be sunny or overcast, leaving the sky a mottled canvas of greys and blues. An early evening chill was setting in, prompting Nat to draw her jacket in tighter. The bus wasn't due for a few minutes, so Nat scrolled to her emails. At the top of the list was an unread reply to her earlier email from the other investment company.

Subject line: Re: HealthLink Proposal

Dear Nat,

Thank you for getting in touch. I was somewhat surprised to receive your email as it seemed pretty clear from our last correspondence with Clara that HealthLink wasn't interested in progressing with our proposal.

However, we very much admire the mission of your company and would potentially still be willing to make an offer. I am concerned at the timings as this is very late in the day and there are other opportunities for us that we are close to signing. I would be willing to speak to you at 9 a.m. tomorrow morning to discuss options, but I can't promise anything.

Best wishes

Julia

As Nat typed her reply confirming the meeting the following morning, she allowed herself to feel a fraction hopeful. Yesterday had ended with her own dreams in soggy tatters, ruined beyond salvation. But today there had been a shift in her resolve. Instead of allowing things to happen to her and drifting from one disaster to another, she had taken control. She had chosen to withdraw from the interview, and despite the sadness she felt, she knew it was the right thing to do. Turning up with an incomplete portfolio that didn't look its absolute best would have damaged her reputation. She just hoped that there would be another opportunity in the future.

In the meantime, she was going to put her efforts into doing what she could to help Michael's company. It was time to stand up for what she believed in and what she wanted.

# CHAPTER TWENTY–THREE

**Thursday 26<sup>th</sup> May**

Nat's fingers drummed nervously on the kitchen table, her gaze fixed on the clock in the corner of the screen as it ticked towards nine a.m. Adjusting the hem of her soft grey jumper, she picked at a stray bobble and let it drop to the floor. She reached for the headset and placed it gently, trying not to disturb her hair. The mic hovered by her cheek. As the number flicked over, she clicked her mouse and started the video meeting. Moments later, two faces appeared on the screen. Nat inhaled deeply, forcing a confident smile.

"Good morning. It's nice to see you both," she said, her voice steady despite the fluttering in her stomach.

"Good morning, Nat." Julia had a kind face that immediately put her at ease. "I think you've met Stefan before?"

"It's good to see you again." Stefan gave a brief nod. His demeanour was more serious, but Nat was determined not to let that derail her.

"Thank you for taking the time to meet with me this morning." Nat hesitated for a moment before plunging into her prepared speech. "I wanted to talk about our previous discussions regarding investment. HealthLink is considering the options available to us, and we think your offer might be worth reconsidering."

"We were under the impression that your company is finalising an investment with another party tomorrow morning," Stefan said, cutting straight to the chase. "Clara made it perfectly clear to us the projected growth with our investment wasn't impressive enough."

Nat hesitated for a fraction of a second, aware that her next words could tip the scales in either direction.

"Yes, there's a meeting scheduled," she conceded, twisting the ring on her left hand between anxious fingers. "But nothing has been signed yet."

She heard Stefan exhale sharply.

"What does Michael have to say about all of this?" Julia's question gave Nat the opportunity she was looking for.

"He's in a difficult position. The board is pushing him to make a choice based mainly on the finances. I believe your offer might be more aligned with the long-term vision of the company, despite what Clara has told you. I'm asking you to reconsider. We need options, and your involvement could be exactly what we need to avoid a decision purely based on greed and ambitious financial projections."

"It's very late in the day for us to be having these discussions." Stefan seemed to enjoy playing the role of bad cop. "We are in talks with other companies that would welcome our money."

"I know, and I appreciate you meeting with me today. I wouldn't be asking if I didn't think it was important and worth your time."

The call went quiet and Nat held her breath, waiting for the verdict.

Julia broke the silence. "OK, we're willing to reconsider. We'll review the paperwork and get it across to you by the end of the day."

"But this is the last chance." Stefan's tone was firm, but not unkind. "If this deal doesn't go through, we won't consider any future investment deals with your company. This has taken a great amount of time and effort on our part."

"Of course." A wave of relief washed over Nat.

"Look out for an email from me later on today," Julia said.

"Thank you so much. Goodbye both."

Julia and Stefan disappeared from Nat's screen and she was left staring at her own image, a face lined with uncertainty. Nat closed the lid of her laptop and sat quietly for a moment, thinking about the risks she had just taken. If the deal with

Spinigma went through tomorrow and the investigation went public, there would be no coming back from this for Michael's company and she would have lost their last chance for redemption.

Her gaze wandered to the window where the morning light seemed too bright. She closed her eyes and took a deep breath to steady herself. Had she done the right thing? She had to believe that she was capable of making the right decision, that she wasn't as incompetent as she so often felt. The thought of going up against Clara filled her with dread, but she had little choice if she was going to change the outcome.

Nat opened her eyes and looked at the clock on the wall. It was nine thirty a.m. and Simon wouldn't be home until late. The day stretched out before her like an endless expanse of uncertainty. She needed to keep busy, to distract herself from the doubts that plagued her mind.

The sun had already set when Nat heard the front door open. Her shoulders tensed at the sound of Simon's footsteps in the hallway. Her back was aching from sitting at the kitchen table for the last couple of hours, scrutinising the investment proposal that finally landed at six p.m. It was nearly eight now, and she was eager to find out from Simon what was happening the next day. But as soon as his briefcase hit the floor, he disappeared upstairs to the bathroom and the sound of the shower running filled the house.

"Simon?" Her voice barely reached beyond the kitchen. With a sigh, she turned back to the proposal. The numbers danced in front of her on the screen.

Simon finally appeared, his hair damp and face freshly shaven. Dark circles sat under his eyes and his skin was pale. He looked exhausted.

"Long day?" She watched as he set the timer for the microwave and leaned back against the counter, his arms crossed.

"Never-ending." He adjusted his glasses up his nose. "How about you?"

"I managed to persuade the other investment company to resubmit their proposal for consideration."

"OK." Simon looked closely at Nat. "That sounds like a good thing, so why do you look so concerned?"

"If everything goes wrong tomorrow and I can't persuade them to go with Ethica, it will be a disaster. Michael could lose everything and there will be no coming back from it."

The microwave beeped and Simon retrieved his dinner. He joined Nat at the table and began to eat methodically, silently.

"Simon?" Nat tried to keep her voice steady. "What happens if my plan doesn't work? What's going to happen tomorrow?"

He paused mid-chew and lowered his hand. The fork clattered against the plate.

"We're due in court at nine a.m." His voice was laced with weary resignation, showing the stress he was under. "The first battle is to get the judge to make the initial decision on proceeding with prosecution."

"Prosecution?"

"Yes. We know there is already a case for enforcement action, which is only a warning and a large fine. But for a company like this, the fine is just loose change and doesn't act as a deterrent. Because their violations are so serious and persistent, we are taking the next step and seeking to prosecute them. The impact of a successful prosecution would be much more significant. If we can get the judge to agree there is merit to our investigation, we can start legal proceedings. Due to the nature of what we are doing, everything has to remain absolutely confidential until the judge confirms they will allow us to proceed. Gambling companies still have protections under law that prevent unnecessary speculation or harm to their reputation. Unfortunately, the judge will not care about the potential deal with Michael's company. They are interested in upholding the law and following due process. Only once they have made that initial decision would the company be formally notified of the charges, and everything from that point is in the public domain."

"So how long will it take for them to make that decision?"

"We have the morning to present our initial evidence. The judge will review it and hopefully make a decision by lunchtime. If they agree, we will be in a position to notify the company and make a public statement in the afternoon." Simon rubbed his hand across the back of his head. "By that point, we'll have secured what we needed and you'll be able to share the information."

"It's cutting it very fine." Nat slumped a little in her chair. "The board is meeting in the morning, and representatives from Spinigma are due early afternoon to sign the deal."

"I'll do what I can to let you know the outcome as soon as possible. Once the decision is made, I will send across the public statement that will follow later on in the day. That should be all you need to stop the board from signing the paperwork if you haven't been able to change their minds in the morning."

"Tomorrow is... it's big then, for both of us." She shifted in her seat. There was a pause as they contemplated the fear and uncertainty about what lay ahead.

"Come watch something on TV with me?" Simon's invitation broke the silence, a lifeline amidst the chaos. "It'll take our mind off things for a while."

Nat reluctantly agreed, shutting her laptop and packing it away into her bag. She couldn't do any more tonight and hoped what she had planned would be enough. There was no other option. It had to be enough.

# Chapter Twenty-Four

**Friday 27<sup>th</sup> May, daytime**

Nat arrived at the office early, dressed more smartly than usual in a black pencil skirt and crisp white blouse. Her dark hair was pulled back into a sleek ponytail that swung with every step as her heels clicked against the polished marble floor. She carried herself with an air of forced determination. Although the knot in her stomach was there to remind her that confidence did not come naturally.

"Well, you look like you mean business." Alfred's words were exactly what she needed to hear in that moment. "Whatever you've got planned today, I hope they know what's coming!"

"Thanks Alfred." Nat's smile grew as some of the nervousness began to fade. "Let's hope I can pull it off."

"Of course you can!" He gave her a reassuring wink and waved as she made her way to the lift.

The conference room was large, with high ceilings and tall windows that let in plenty of natural light and offered a panoramic view of the bustling city below. A long, polished wooden table dominated the space, surrounded by a dozen executive chairs. Nat placed copies of both proposals neatly on the table, making sure a set was within easy reach of each board member. Sitting down for a moment in her usual seat, she flicked through the paperwork she had annotated for herself. As she read the details, she muttered under her breath, trying to commit each important point to memory.

Once satisfied she was as prepared as possible, she filled the water jugs to the brim, ice cubes clinking gently against the glass. With the last glass placed on the table, she checked her watch. At just before ten a.m., the door opened and the board members began to file in—a steady procession of power suits and polished shoes. Michael led the pack, his bright blue eyes scanning the room. His tailored navy suit wrapped around his muscled frame in a way that was both elegant and commanding—every inch the successful CEO.

Behind him trailed Clara, not a hair out of place in her sleek bob. Her thin lips curled into what might have been a smile or a sneer—it was hard to tell. Beside her, Rita, the chief technology officer with a constant frown, took her seat and immediately placed her laptop on the table, getting lost in an email. Then there was Colin—the head of HR—whose jovial demeanour and round glasses gave the impression of an affable uncle rather than a corporate heavyweight.

One by one, they found their places at the table, the shuffling of papers and low murmur of voices filling the space as Nat stepped back to observe the scene. Her heart raced with the knowledge that today's meeting could change everything. She clasped her hands together, fighting the urge to smooth down her skirt, trying to appear every bit as collected as she needed them to believe.

"Good morning." Michael's voice carried the weight of authority as he took his place at the head of the table. Nat met his gaze, finding an unreadable expression that made her insides twist.

Michael's brow furrowed as he leafed through the two proposals.

"Natalie," he said, his voice quiet to draw her attention. "Why are there two proposals here? We'd agreed to move forward with just one. Representatives from Spinigma are due here this afternoon to sign the contract."

"Yes, about that—" Nat felt every pair of eyes turn towards her.

"Probably just another mix-up," Clara interrupted smoothly. "You know how she struggles to keep on top of things."

Nat resisted the urge to shrink under Clara's patronising gaze and cleared her throat. "Actually, I'd like a moment to talk to the board if that's OK?"

After a moment's hesitation, Michael nodded. "Fine. Make this quick."

"Thank you." Nat took a deep breath, feeling the weight of the opportunity pressing against her chest. Every insecurity she harboured about not being good enough seemed to converge, threatening to silence her before she even began. "I know you have already discussed it, but I think it's important we reconsider the proposal from Ethica as they have amended it since the original discussions."

A ripple of murmurs skittered around the table.

"Their investment might not bring a rate of growth as fast as Spinigma," she continued, her voice calmer than she felt. "But it will be steady and the changes they are offering opens up future growth that could match what Spinigma has proposed by year five."

She spoke of the potential for partnerships, the positive PR, and the benefits beyond the bottom line. With each point made, Nat felt a flicker of hope that maybe, just maybe, she could sway them.

"On top of that, their vision aligns more closely with our values and long-term goals. They are innovative, community-oriented, and have an ethical approach to investment that could redefine our industry."

The room was quiet when she finished, the board members exchanging glances. Nat looked slowly around the room, her heart sinking as she realised their faces were etched with polite indifference.

"Thank you, Natalie," Michael said finally, his voice measured. "Would anyone like to offer their views?"

"This new proposal is certainly more impressive than before." Rita flicked through the pages, underlining figures in a red pen. "However, it doesn't quite match what we need for the technology to meet our growing user base."

"Oh, Natalie. What were you thinking?" Clara shook her head. "We have been over this before. Those investors have been discounted. The numbers just don't add up. Why are you wasting our time?"

One by one, the rest of the board members muttered their agreement. Nat felt a wave of anger wash over her.

"Because they're the right company for us, Clara," she snapped back, her voice echoing around the room.

"Enough," Michael said. The room fell silent. "While we appreciate your input Natalie, I think it's best we proceed as originally planned." Michael cast Nat's work aside and reached for the agenda.

Nat managed a nod, her hands clasped tightly under the table to steady her shaking fingers. As the discussion moved on to logistics and financial forecasts, she retreated into herself, painfully aware of Michael's icy gaze from across the table. Clara, perched at the other end like a cat who got the cream, sent a smug glance in Nat's direction every so often, relishing the tension that simmered between Nat and Michael.

The meeting dragged on, each tick of the clock stretching longer than the last. Finally, they agreed to break for lunch before their afternoon session. The board members filed out, their chatter echoing hollowly in Nat's ears. Michael lingered behind, his posture rigid and hard lines carved around his mouth.

"Can we talk?" His voice was barely audible above the shuffle of papers and closing doors.

"Of course." Nat followed him out into the corridor, away from the curious eyes still inside the room.

"I'm really disappointed." Michael turned to face her, his eyes betraying a flicker of hurt. "You went behind my back, presenting a proposal we'd already decided against. It makes me look like I don't have control of the company. That I can't manage my staff. What were you thinking?"

"I was thinking about what was the right thing to do," Nat shot back, her frustration boiling over. "How can you stand there and act like this isn't a terrible mistake? This deal with Spinigma—it goes against everything you've said you wanted for the company."

Michael's jaw clenched, and he looked away for a moment. "It's not that simple. There are other factors at play—financial stability, shareholder expectations. We have been over this before."

"Since when do you prioritise money over integrity?" She crossed her arms.

"Since I became responsible for the livelihoods of everyone at this company," he said, his own arms mirroring hers. "It's not black and white."

Nat searched his face, looking for the man she knew cared deeply about his work and the impact it had. A face of hard stone stared back at her and she flinched at the anger in his eyes. This time, she wasn't going to back down.

"Well, I'm not going to seek your forgiveness for standing up for what I thought was right. I just hope this decision doesn't come back to haunt you." She turned and walked away before he had a chance to respond. She didn't want to hear any more of his excuses.

Her heart was still pounding from the confrontation with Michael as she made her way across the office.

"Jamie," she called softly when she spotted him by the vending machine, his tall frame slightly hunched as he fiddled with a stubborn button.

"Hey. How did it go?" Jamie straightened, offering a sympathetic smile when he saw the look on her face. "Oh, that bad?"

"Understatement of the year." Her words hung heavy with defeat.

"Come on, let's grab some lunch. You look like you could use some air."

They found a quiet corner in a nearby deli, away from the lunchtime chatter and the busy counter. Over sandwiches and iced tea, Nat recounted her ill-fated attempt to change the board's mind.

"I just thought if I could show them—make them see the other side. But it was like talking to a brick wall."

"You did what you could," Jamie reassured her. "You put up a good fight for what you believe in. That counts for something."

"Maybe." Nat nibbled on the edge of her sandwich. "But it wasn't enough. And Michael is furious with me."

"Hey, there's still a chance, right? The court case?"

"Right." She perked up at the mention of what her brother was dealing with. "If the judge agrees the prosecution can go ahead, the board will drop them like a hot potato."

"Exactly."

"But we're running out of time." Nat checked her watch. "If there's any kind of delay with the judge's decision, it will be too late."

"Don't give up hope." Jamie placed his hand on Nat's, offering her an encouraging grin. "It's not over until it's over."

Feeling slightly better, Nat returned to the office and left Jamie at his desk, buried once more in the world of code. The Spinigma representatives would be arriving soon, and she needed to be ready to greet them, no matter how much her mind was elsewhere. Pulling out her phone, she fired a quick text to Simon as she walked towards the bathroom.

> How's it going in court? Any news?

She opened a small, tatty make-up bag and pulled out a face compact and lip gloss. She applied the powder, dabbing gently against her cheeks, forehead, and nose to take away the shine. A thin layer of gloss was just enough to add a hint of colour, and she pressed her lips together. She wiped under her eyes where a few flecks of mascara had settled and made a mental note to throw it away and buy a new one. It had been lurking around in the depths of her bag for far longer than she could remember.

She took a deep breath and prepared herself for what was going to be a stressful afternoon.

The response came just as she reached the lobby. Simon's message was brief but positive.

> Evidence presented well. Waiting to be called back in. Will update ASAP.

A small flutter of hope stirred in Nat's chest. Maybe they had a fighting chance after all. She slipped the phone back into her pocket and pasted on a professional smile, ready to face what lay ahead.

Nat hovered by the door of the conference room as the representatives from Spinigma filed in. Steve, Karen, Malik, and Poppy were dressed in designer suits and their stiff nods exuded an air of arrogance and importance. She caught glimpses of silk ties and polished brogues, the air thick with expensive cologne and the scent of ambition. Their formality was a far cry from the casual dinner they shared less than two weeks ago.

Steve was the last to take his seat. The room settled into an expectant hush, the prelude to decisions that could alter the course of the company. Nat lingered at the edge of the room, waiting until everyone was there before she sat down.

Michael started the meeting, welcoming everyone to the company offices and running through the items they would be covering that afternoon. Nat focused on making detailed notes, the perfect excuse to avoid eye contact with both Michael and Clara. Time was passing too quickly and they were heading closer to the formal signing. Nat slid her phone from her pocket and tapped out a message to Simon.

> **The meeting is well under way. Any news?**

She placed the phone in her lap before returning to her notes. Moments later, her phone buzzed against her thigh.

> **Just been called in. Need another 10 mins. Stall them.**

Her mind raced, considering her options. It was Clara who unwittingly offered one up with a dismissive glance at her empty coffee cup.

"Let's move onto the next item." As always, Clara was keen to keep the momentum going.

"Actually, we've been here a while," Nat said. "I'm sure our guests would welcome a short comfort break while I arrange another round of refreshments. How does that sound?"

A few heads nodded in agreement.

"Fine," Clara said, letting out an impatient sigh. "But make it quick."

"Of course." Nat smiled politely and offered to show people where they could find the toilets.

Nat's fingers fumbled with the filter as she set up the coffee machine in the kitchen. The office sounds around her faded into a dull hum. Every ounce of her attention was fixed on her phone, willing it to vibrate with the news she was waiting for. Finally, it came. The message blinked back at her from the screen.

> Judge agreed. Check email for public announcement.

Swift and overwhelming relief flooded her body. She hurried to her laptop and logged into her email, fingers trembling as she hit the keys. There it was—the official statement that would be released that afternoon. She sent the document to the printer and then messaged Jamie. With the freshly brewed jug of coffee in one hand and a tray of assorted cold drinks in the other, she left the kitchen.

The conference room door opened with a gentle push from her shoulder and Nat stepped inside. She felt Clara's eyes on her, but Nat ignored her, focusing instead on steadying her shaking hands.

"Here we are." She set down the tray and began distributing the cups. Jamie appeared beside her and pressed a sheet of paper in her hand. He winked at her, then slipped out of the room. Nat placed the document on the table before taking her seat, feeling every gaze shift to what was lying innocuously among the glass coasters and leather-bound notebooks.

"What's this?" Michael's eyes flicked curiously towards the page.

"I thought this might be relevant to our discussions."

She settled back into her chair and watched as Michael began to read. He looked up at her, his eyes searching hers to see if it was really true. Nat nodded her head in confirmation.

Michael cleared his throat. "It seems there have been some unexpected developments." His voice was calm despite the shocking information he had just received.

"What kind of developments?" Clara's face twisted into an unpleasant snarl.

"Perhaps Natalie should explain to the rest of the room what's on that piece of paper." He looked over at her expectantly.

"Are you sure?"

"Go on." Michael nodded.

Nat took a deep breath. "We have just been informed about a court ruling regarding the company we're about to sign a significant investment deal with." Her voice steadily gained strength as she turned to look at the board members in turn. "Spinigma is being prosecuted for a number of serious charges. Associating with them would irreparably damage our reputation and potentially destroy the company."

Murmurs broke out around the table as the gravity of her words sank in. The representatives from Spinigma glanced at each other as they scrambled for their phones to verify the information.

"This has to be a joke," Clara said, snatching the piece of paper. Nat watched as she scanned the words, her face contorting from shock to anger as each one sank in. "I don't believe a word of it. For some reason, you've been desperate to stop this deal from going through. I don't know what that's all about, but this time you've gone too far. We'll be lucky if Spinigma even wants to do business with us after this outrage." She cast a look towards the company delegates as a show of apology.

"It's not me who's gone too far, Clara." Nat emphasised her name with a deliberate undercurrent of insinuation. They may not have got to the bottom of Clara's connections, but seeing the colour drain from her cheeks told her everything she needed to know.

"Are you absolutely certain?" Colin asked, his eyebrows knitted together in concern.

"Absolutely." Nat gestured toward the announcement. "It's being made public right now. We can't go through with this deal."

"Look, we're not sure what's going on." Steve was the first one from Spinigma to speak. He was visibly shaken and clawed the paperwork back into his folder. "We need to get back to the office to figure this out. We'll be in touch as soon as we can."

Without another word, Steve, Karen, Malik, and Poppy gathered their belongings and left, their abrupt departure leaving the rest of the room reeling in shock.

Nat turned to Michael. "Can we talk?" she whispered, watching as the tightness in his jaw began to relax. He nodded, and they stepped aside into a quiet corner of the room. Her heart hammered against her ribs, but she held his gaze.

"Do you understand now? I know you are angry at me for going behind your back, but I couldn't sit by and let this happen."

"You should have told me what was going on." Michael ran a hand through his hair, a mix of frustration and relief in his eyes.

"I couldn't. My brother could have lost the court case. He could have lost everything. I had no choice but to try to persuade you to make the right investment decision. When that didn't work out…" Nat's voice trailed off.

"That was too close for comfort. We were about to sign the deal." He hesitated, then sighed. "You were right. We would have lost everything. I would have lost everything."

"But you didn't. And there is still a way back from this." Nat reached into her bag and passed him the other proposal. "That wasn't the only deal on the table."

A shiver ran down Nat's spine as Michael placed his hand on her arm and squeezed gently.

"Thank you. For not giving up on the company. For not giving up on me."

"You can make it up to me with a drink tonight."

"Tonight?"

"Lexi's launch party for the music cafe?" Nat tried to hide the flash of disappointment that crossed her face.

"Of course! Drinks are on me all night." Michael's reassurance that he hadn't entirely forgotten eased Nat's mind. "I suppose I had better salvage what is left of this meeting."

She nodded, smiling to herself as he took his seat back at the table.

"Given recent developments," he began, "I think we should revisit the alternative proposal."

There was a collective shuffle of papers as the board members reached for the second set of documents placed before them earlier that day. Nat watched the rest of the afternoon play out before her. She relaxed into her seat, enjoying seeing the passion back in Michael as he talked through the details of the new investment deal and the potential for the company. Even Clara's continued attempts to patronise and belittle Nat did nothing to flatten the swell of pride she felt at what she had achieved. She thought about the evening ahead—tonight would be a double celebration. After what felt like months of chaos and uncertainty, she had a newfound sense of empowerment and control over her life. For once, she was excited for what would come next.

# CHAPTER TWENTY–FIVE

**Friday 27th May, evening**

Nat raised her glass of champagne and clinked it against Lexi's, the liquid fizzing against the rim. The music cafe buzzed around them—a hive of laughter and conversation lit by the warm glow of the lights suspended from the ceiling.

"This is incredible." Nat looked around. "You must be so proud of what you've achieved."

"Thank you." Lexi beamed at her, her eyes sparkling. "I can't believe my dreams have finally come true."

The party was well underway, with smartly dressed guests mingling and chatting as they listened to a young woman on the stage. She was strumming an acoustic guitar and singing a cover of a modern country song.

"Look who's finally here," Lexi said, nodding towards the door. Nat followed her gaze to see Michael and Enzo walking in. They were both incredibly handsome, but in very different ways. Michael always looked smart, even when he was trying to be casual. His dark trousers fitted so well they could have been designed just for him. The pale blue shirt, even with the top buttons loosened, was perfectly pressed. Not a wrinkle in sight. Enzo, by comparison, had a rugged, boyish charm with messy curls and olive skin courtesy of his Italian heritage. His faded jeans were clearly well-loved and complemented the t-shirt, which bore the name of an American rock and roll band from the 1980s.

"Sorry we're late," Michael said, the apology softened by his smile as he greeted Nat and Lexi with a kiss on the cheek. Nat could feel the warmth radiate from his lips, leaving a tingle behind that she did her best to ignore.

"Michael couldn't decide what to wear." Enzo's laughter was infectious as he winked at Lexi, who rolled her eyes playfully in response.

"Too busy making sure every hair was in place, huh?" Lexi grinned, watching Michael smoothly brush off the comment with a shrug.

"Can't let Enzo outshine me, can I?" Michael said, his eyes briefly meeting Nat's before darting away.

"So, what do you think?" Lexi handed over fresh glasses of champagne.

"You have done an amazing job." Michael sipped his drink. "The place looks incredible."

"It's all thanks to this clever girl." Lexi waved her glass towards Nat.

Nat flushed with pleasure at the compliment. "Thanks." She took a sip of champagne, hoping the cool liquid would wash away the heat that had settled in her cheeks.

The four of them carried on chatting for a while, the conversation flowing easily. Nat couldn't ignore the way Michael kept his eyes on her, his gaze intense and unwavering. They had agreed on 'just friends', but it seemed the dynamic was shifting and she was beginning to feel flustered and self-conscious.

The buzz of chatter mingled with the last strum of the guitar as the performer took her bow and applause erupted around the room.

"Time for me to get the next lot set up." Lexi placed her glass on the side. "Enzo, once this next band has finished their set, we're moving to more of an open mic style. You have to promise me you'll be up on that stage." Her tone left little room for negotiation.

"Only if you're up on stage too," Enzo said, his smile easy and charming.

"Deal," Lexi shot back with a grin, making her way to the door. "Now why don't you put those muscles to good use and give me a hand?"

Enzo downed the remaining dregs in his glass and dutifully followed Lexi to the van outside.

"Those two get on really well, don't they?" Nat said, hoping Michael might give a little insight into how Enzo felt about Lexi. Although Lexi had made it clear she didn't have time for anything romantic at the moment, Nat was already contemplating the future potential for double dates. She couldn't resist the thought of such a serendipitous cliché.

"They do." Michael nodded. "Although, from what I've seen of Lexi, she's very feisty. So is Enzo. If they did become a couple, there is a high likelihood of explosive arguments and drama. We wouldn't want to get caught up in the middle of that."

"Lexi is definitely feisty, but she is also a real softie deep down. She just doesn't like to show it. I hope Enzo likes being kept on his toes."

"I'm sure he'll give Lexi a run for her money on that front!"

The ambient hum of conversation filled the silence as Nat stood beside Michael, both looking out across the room.

"So..." Michael cleared his throat. "I can't thank you enough for today. After you left, I reached out to Ethica. They're eager to meet on Tuesday morning to finalise everything. It looks like we should be able to secure their investment, and that's down to all the work you did to secure their latest proposal."

"I'm glad it all worked out in the end." Nat glanced at Michael for a moment before looking away. "I'm just sorry I had to go behind your back."

"I understand why you did it." He placed his hand on Nat's arm. She became acutely aware of Michael's proximity, of the way his body seemed to be gravitating towards hers. Before she could respond, Lexi and Enzo returned with a fresh bottle of champagne.

"I hope you guys aren't talking work?" Lexi scolded, topping up each of their glasses.

"Guilty as charged," Michael admitted, holding up his drink with a grin. "Just thanking this incredible woman for saving my company. You know, just your average day at work." He winked at Nat, squeezing her arm gently. "So, what's on the horizon for this place?"

As Lexi launched into an enthusiastic rundown of upcoming events, Nat's attention was drawn to the cafe door. It swung open to reveal Clara, accompanied by a woman Nat didn't recognise. Her vibrant hair was unmistakable from across the room. A knot formed in Nat's stomach and her fingers tightened around her champagne flute as she watched Clara weave through the crowd.

"Michael, Nat," Clara called out as she approached, her friend trailing behind her. "Such a quaint little shop, isn't it?"

"Clara." Nat greeted them with a wide smile, a fraction too forced. "What are you doing here?" She caught Lexi's eye, whose eyebrows shot up immediately at the mention of Clara's name.

"Well, Michael mentioned to me earlier that he was coming to this little party." Clara waved her hand around dismissively. "Tia and I were at a loose end, and thought we might come and join the fun."

"I'm Lexi. It's lovely to meet you." Lexi stepped forward, holding out her hand for Clara to shake. "This is my quaint little shop."

If Clara had noticed Lexi's mocking tone, she didn't let on. "I hope we're not crashing your party." Her voice dripped with fake sweetness.

"Of course not! The more the merrier."

With perfect timing, the band interrupted the false pleas-
antries, kicking off their performance with a lively pop song
with infectious beats and catchy melodies.

"Let's get this party properly started!" Tia suggested, already
moving to the rhythm of the music.

"Come on, Michael. I know you'll dance with me." Clara
reached for his hand.

"Maybe later." He extracted himself politely. "I don't think
I've had quite enough champagne for dancing."

"Your loss." Clara shrugged and dragged Tia towards the
band, leaving Nat watching as they disappeared into the crowd.

Nat let out a breath and the tension that had coiled within her
began to ease, if only slightly. Michael's refusal to join Clara in
her flirtatious game was a small victory, but Nat couldn't shake
the annoyance that came with her presence.

As the night wore on, the alcohol flowed more freely and the
guests became increasingly relaxed. The music was getting live-
lier and more people were up dancing. Nat navigated through
groups of guests with Lexi by her side, chatting about the shop
and how Lexi's dreams had finally become real. Every now and
then, she looked over to where Michael and Enzo stood, deep in
discussion. Michael would return her eye contact occasionally,
nodding his silent support as she was dragged into yet another
conversation about her designs and the inspiration. Although
she loved the compliments, Nat would much rather be on the
sidelines than in the limelight. That was much more Lexi's
forte.

The band's lead singer tapped on the microphone to grab everyone's attention.

"Alright, beautiful people!" His voice cut through the buzz of conversations. "It's time to see every single one of you on your feet!"

The musicians behind him struck the first notes of an upbeat classic that never failed to fill a dance floor. Lexi grabbed Nat's hand with a mischievous glint in her eye. "Let's go. It's time to flaunt that dress properly." Excitement bubbled in her voice.

Nat couldn't help but laugh as Lexi pulled her onto the dance floor, twirling her around like a ballerina. She allowed herself to be swept up in the infectious energy of the crowd. The band worked in partnership with the audience, sensing when to introduce faster songs, and when to slow things down. She felt a rare sensation of elegance as her dress swirled around, the fabric soft against her skin as she danced. She could feel the warmth of bodies around her as they moved in sync with the music.

But as she glanced across the room, Nat's heart began to race and an awful queasiness settled in her stomach. Clara was with Michael on the dance floor, moving her body in a way that screamed for attention. Every twist of her hips was deliberate, as if trying to pull him closer. Nat felt a stab of annoyance, but tried to remind herself it was unwarranted. Despite their growing closeness, she and Michael had agreed they were just friends and nothing would change while they still worked together.

"Excuse me," Nat murmured to a group of guests, slipping away to seek refuge at the edge of the room. She poured herself a glass of iced water and took a large gulp, feeling the chill as it crept down her throat and fanned out across her chest. Condensation formed quickly on the outside of the glass, mirroring the sweat that had begun to bead on her forehead. She leaned against the side, allowing herself a moment to steady her heart rate and settle her stomach.

"Mind if I..." Michael's voice broke into her thoughts. She turned to see him standing beside her, gesturing towards her drink.

"Go ahead." She slid the glass across the counter.

He took a swig, his Adam's apple bobbing with the swallow.

"You look a bit... Is everything OK?"

"I'm fine." She didn't want him to see how upset she was. "I just needed some water."

Michael studied her face as he considered her explanation.

"OK, I was annoyed that Clara showed up." Nat finally admitted. "I don't know why she came. It's making me uncomfortable, especially as she seems to take so much pleasure from making me feel terrible."

"I'm sorry. To be honest, I didn't think she would just turn up. I only mentioned it in passing. If I'd known it would affect you so much, I wouldn't have mentioned the party at all."

"Well..." Nat paused, weighing up whether to say anything. "When it comes to me, she just seems to have a knack of knowing exactly what to say and do to get right under my skin."

"I'm sure she doesn't mean it."

Nat was instantly irritated by Michael being so quick to dismiss Clara's behaviour again. They stood in silence for a moment, both lost in their own thoughts. Before either of them could say anything else, the crowd shifted a little and Clara stumbled into Nat's space. The impact jostled her hand and ice-cold water poured down the front of her dress.

"Oh my gosh, I am so sorry!" Clara feigned concern as she gave Nat the insincere apology.

"Let me grab you some tissues." Michael disappeared towards the toilets.

"Really, Clara?" Nat's voice was a low hiss, barely audible above the music. Anger bubbled up, hot and unwelcome. She fought to keep it submerged.

"I'm just so clumsy! Remember the time I spilled wine all over your little design project?!" Clara let out an unpleasant laugh.

Nat's cheeks flushed with rage. She leaned forward slightly, a whisper away from confrontation.

"What exactly is your problem with me?"

"Problem? Why would I have a problem with dear little Natalie?" Clara looked over Nat's shoulder in dismissal. "Although I really don't know what Michael sees in you." She stared directly at Nat, a challenge in her eyes. "Incompetent doesn't even begin to cover it."

The accusation hung heavy in the air, and Nat felt every hair on her body stand on end.

"Excuse me?" Nat's voice was a dagger of ice.

"Come on, you've struggled from the start. Remember your first week? Michael told me all about it. You messing up the restaurant booking? He really wasn't happy at all. And now this deal—the company will be lucky to survive after you messed everything up. It's a wonder he keeps you around. I think he feels sorry for you."

Nat's heart pounded in her chest, but before the tears that were threatening could escape, Lexi was there at her side.

"That's enough, Clara." Lexi's firm tone left no room for debate.

"I think it's time for you to leave." Nat pointed toward the exit with unmistakable intent.

Clara opened her mouth, perhaps to argue or insult further, but then closed it. With a huff, she made her way towards Tia, grabbed her arm and weaved through the crowd. Nat watched them go, her gaze unwavering until the door swung shut behind them.

Lexi's face was stern, relaxing only when she turned to look at Nat. "Are you OK?"

"I'm fine," Nat lied, her voice not quite steady. "I just need some fresh air."

Without waiting for a response, she threaded her way through the throng of party-goers and stepped out into the night air.

She pressed her body against the cold brick wall, gulping in breaths that came fast and uneven. She couldn't shake the feeling of betrayal. Why would Michael say something like that about her to Clara, of all people? Clara, who had never been nice and always seemed to have it in for her. It made no sense.

"Natalie?" Michael's silhouette emerged from the doorway. "What's wrong?"

She didn't turn to face him, afraid that the sight of his usually serious face softened by concern would undo what little composure she had left.

"How could you? Clara..." Her voice wavered. "You told her about my mistakes at work."

Michael moved closer, his shadow merging with hers on the pavement.

"I—"

"Did it ever occur to you to support me? To stick up for me?" The question hung heavy between them. "Every time she belittled me, you said nothing."

"I was just frustrated when I told her about that stuff and I didn't really know you then. Not like I know you now. I didn't think she would tell you what I said."

"And what about when she was deliberately putting me down at work?"

"I thought you could handle it. If I'd known how much it affected you, I would have said something."

"It just feels like you don't..." Her voice trailed off.

"Like I don't what?"

"That you don't care."

"I do care," Michael insisted. "More than you know," he added, his voice low.

"I know we agreed on just friends." Nat finally turned to look at him, her eyes glistening with the onset of tears. "But if you really cared, you wouldn't have said those things."

"Nat, I..."

"Please, just..." She couldn't let him see the tears now streaming down her cheeks. "Tell Lexi I'm sorry I had to leave." Her words came out in a rush as she brushed past him, her heart sinking with every step away from the warmth of the party—and away from him.

"Please wait!" She heard his voice in the air, but it was too late. She was exhausted and wanted nothing more than to just disappear into the night.

# Chapter Twenty-Six

**Saturday 28<sup>th</sup> May, morning**

Nat's eyes blinked open to the harsh morning light, her head pounding like a drum. She groaned and pulled the covers tighter over her aching body. The events of the previous night replayed themselves in her mind. She squeezed her eyes shut, willing the memories to blur and dissipate. The argument with Michael had escalated quickly. Her response to finding out he had confided in Clara about her shortcomings at work—a trusted old friend—felt like an overreaction more suited to a teenager. Her tongue felt like sandpaper, and the room spun slightly as she shifted under the covers. Last night's mascara itched against her cheeks, a grimy reminder of the tears shed.

A knock interrupted her self-pitying thoughts.

"Nat? Are you awake?" Lucy's voice drifted into the room as she opened the bedroom door.

Nat grumbled something unintelligible in response.

"You have a visitor downstairs," Lucy said, her tone low and mysterious. Nat sat up, wincing at the pain in her head from the sudden movement.

"Who is it?"

"I think you need to find out for yourself." Lucy pulled a face.

"Can't they just leave a message?" Nat was not prepared for unexpected company. She hoped Lucy would have some sympathy and give her an easy escape.

"Trust me, you're going to want to see who it is." There was a pause and a shuffle of feet. "And, um... maybe wash your face first. You know, freshen up a bit. You look like a panda caught in a downpour."

Nat exhaled, a wry smile tugging at her lips despite herself. Leave it to Lucy to deliver a brutal truth with the softest blow. With considerable effort, she peeled herself off the bed, every joint protesting.

"Fine." She wriggled herself into a dressing gown. "But this had better be good."

"It will be," Lucy reassured her. Mischief danced in her eyes, suggesting she knew more than she was letting on. She closed the door and disappeared downstairs.

Nat made her way to the bathroom, grimacing as she caught a glimpse of her reflection in the mirror. She rinsed her face under the cold tap. The biting chill helped banish some of the fog in her head. With a squeeze of toothpaste, she began scrubbing her teeth vigorously, hoping the minty flavour would settle her queasy stomach. She swept a cotton pad dampened with make-up remover over the dark rings around her eyes, revealing puffy lids and bloodshot whites. After splashing some cold water on her face again, she felt a little more human, though her pulsing headache was a harsh reminder of last night's overindulgence.

Nat rummaged through the clothes in her drawers, finding comfort in the soft fabric of her jogging bottoms and an over-sized sweatshirt. Both items were reassuringly familiar after a night spent in clothes she wasn't used to wearing. The navy silk dress was beautiful, but it was definitely something just for special occasions. A pair of fluffy sock soothed her feet, still aching from dancing in high-heeled shoes.

She took a deep breath and made her way downstairs. The sound of muffled voices came from the kitchen and she paused at the doorway, bracing herself for whatever lay beyond. As she rounded the corner, the sight stopped her in her tracks. Michael was leaning against the counter-top, casual in a way that felt very unfamiliar to Nat. His usually perfectly styled hair hung loosely in waves, framing those intense blue eyes that could see right through her. As his eyes searched hers, Nat felt her cheeks heat up. She didn't know if she was ready to deal with this right now.

"Hi," she said finally, her voice coming out a little breathless.

"Hi." Michael gave Nat an awkward smile. "I'm sorry to bother you on your day off."

Simon stood next to him, taking the role of makeshift barista very seriously. His movements were methodical and precise, ensuring the perfect blend and temperature.

"Morning," he said, without looking up. He was mid-pour, the rich aroma of coffee filling the space between them. "Coffee?"

"Please," she croaked, her voice betraying the remnants of last night.

Simon slid a steaming mug across the island towards her, the black liquid sloshing perilously close to the rim.

"Thanks." Nat reached for the drink, wrapping her hands around the warmth. She hesitated before taking a sip, allowing the bitterness to snap her awake.

"Right, I'll leave you two to it." Simon adjusted his glasses with an air of finality.

The air shifted with his departure, charged with an unspoken tension that buzzed between Nat and Michael. The silence stretched out, filled only by the tick of the clock and the occasional shuffle of their feet.

"Nice sweatshirt," Michael said after a moment, a ghost of a smile playing on his lips.

"Um, thanks." A hint of self-consciousness crept up into Nat's cheeks. She pulled the fabric closer around her and felt an unexpected sensation in her throat. "What can I do for you?" She tried to swallow the lump down.

"I wanted to talk to you." Michael's jaw tightened and he took a deep breath. "About last night. I'm sorry for what Clara said. I'm sorry that I talked about you to her and made you feel like I don't care." He set down his coffee mug with a soft clink against the granite counter-top and ran a hand through his hair.

"It's OK." Nat forced a smile.

"But it's not OK. I need you to know how much I do care, especially now I know what happened with the design contract."

"What do you mean?" His admission took Nat by surprise.

"After you left last night, Lexi told me everything. About the portfolio and how, after Clara ruined it, you gave up on your dream." His eyes filled with sadness. "You gave up trying to fix it so you could help save the company."

His words unfurled a wave of anxiety inside Nat that she tried to settle with a sip of coffee.

"It doesn't matter," she mumbled, avoiding his gaze. "I probably wouldn't have been good enough, anyway."

"We both know that's rubbish." His voice was firm. "So, I want to make it up to you," he added, before Nat had a chance to disagree with him.

"How do you plan on doing that?" She tried to keep her voice steady. She wasn't sure there was anything he could do to make it right.

"I've got a surprise for you." Michael smiled, a hint of mischief in his eyes. "Get a bag packed. I'll wait here."

"Where are we going?" Nat frowned, confused by his request. She had expected him to give her more explanations, more excuses, or maybe even an enormous pay rise. The suggestion of a trip somewhere was a total surprise.

"You'll see. Just pack for this kind of weather, and maybe something nice to wear for dinner this evening."

Nat hesitated, torn between her desire to know what Michael had planned and her reluctance to put herself through another potentially disheartening experience. But something in his eyes told her he meant well, that he wanted to make things right.

"OK." A mix of trepidation and excitement played in the corner of her mind. "Give me twenty minutes."

"Twenty minutes." He nodded and a satisfied grin settled on his lips.

Nat's hands shook as she zipped the overnight bag shut, her mind racing all over the place. She'd stuffed everything in without much thought—a couple of shirts, jeans, a smarter pair of trousers, a hoodie, and her toiletries. She had taken the opportunity to change into something a bit more respectable than her joggers and sweatshirt. The lightest layer of make-up was just enough to conceal the dark circles under her eyes. Taking a deep breath to steady herself, Nat slung the bag across her shoulder and headed back downstairs.

Michael was waiting for her in the kitchen, a smile on his face. "Ready?"

Nat nodded, following him outside. To her surprise, Simon was there, waiting by his car.

"Are you driving us somewhere?" Nat said.

Simon grinned. "I'm giving you two a lift to the airport."

"The airport?" Nat's jaw dropped. "But won't I need my—"

"Passport?" Simon finished for her, extending the small navy booklet towards her. "It's a good job Lucy knows where you keep things. I would have been searching your room for hours!"

"Thanks." She took it with a shaky hand, still unable to fully comprehend the reality that she was leaving the country. With Michael. "Come on, you have to tell me. Where are we going?"

Nat's eyes darted to Michael, who simply shrugged, an unreadable expression on his face.

"You'll see." There was a hint of playfulness in his reply.

"Come on, we should get going. You don't want to be late." Simon gestured towards the car, ever the pragmatist.

"Have fun!" Lucy appeared at the front door, carefully balancing Louis on her hip as she gave Nat a hug. "I can't wait to hear all about it when you get back."

"Thanks!" Nat kissed Louis on the top of his head. "Be good little one. I'll see you soon. Whenever that may be!" She shared an excited grin with Lucy and climbed into the back seat of Simon's car, settling into the leather with a building sense of excitement.

The sliding doors of the airport admitted them into a bustling world of departures and arrivals, the morning light filtering through the expansive windows. Michael navigated through the terminal with an assertive stride that Nat found herself matching. There was something undeniably competent in the way he moved, effortlessly threading through the crowd and leading her to the check-in counter.

"We'd like to check-in for our flight please," he said to the attendant, his voice business-like.

Nat's heart skipped a beat as he handed over their passports. Reality set in as she watched the boarding passes being printed.

The soft whirring sound of the machine confirmed that this was all actually happening and she would soon be stepping on a plane for a mystery adventure.

"Let's head to the lounge. We've got some time before our flight." Michael offered her a small, cryptic smile as he pocketed their tickets.

As they made their way to the business lounge, Michael's hand occasionally brushed against hers in silent reassurance. The lounge was an oasis of calm, away from the frenetic pace of the terminal. They helped themselves to the breakfast spread, Nat selecting a croissant and some fruit while Michael opted for black coffee and a bagel.

Sitting opposite each other at a quiet table, Nat couldn't hold it in any longer.

"OK, you have to tell me now. Where are we going?"

"We're off to Paris," he said, finally putting her out of her misery.

"Paris..." Nat repeated.

"Yes, Paris." A hint of a smile played on his lips. "There's a special fabric boutique there that I think you'll love."

"You don't mean?" Nat's eyes widened.

Michael nodded. "I figured you might have just enough time, if you agree to my help, to get that portfolio finished."

"But I cancelled my interview!"

"I found out the details and managed to reinstate it for Tuesday morning." Michael smiled hesitantly.

Her silence was not giving away whether she was furious or ecstatic. She could only stare at him, her mind racing. Was this really happening?

"How did you…why would you do that?"

"Because I believe in you. I think you're talented, and I want to see you succeed. You saved my company and my dreams. Now it's my time to save yours."

"Thank you," she said, her voice quiet. "For all of this."

Michael's response was a simple nod.

The intercom crackled to life, calling for passengers to start boarding the flight to Paris.

"Ready?" He held his outstretched hand towards her.

Nat's stomach fluttered as she placed her hand in his, enjoying the gentle touch of his skin against hers.

"Ready." She nodded, a smile spreading as they moved together towards the gate.

For the first time in what felt like forever, she felt hopeful. Maybe this weekend would be the start of something new, something wonderful.

# CHAPTER TWENTY–SEVEN

## Saturday 28ᵗʰ May, evening

Nat stood in the bathroom of the hotel suite, leaning in closer to the mirror to apply a subtle smoky eye-shadow that had promised to play up the gold flecks in her eyes. It was much harder than expected and she had to repeatedly wipe off where she had added too much before starting all over again. She wasn't one for wearing much make-up, and this time Lucy wasn't around to give her a hand. She wore fitted black jeans that hugged her figure, while the floaty top with its floral pattern danced around her waist as she moved. Her dark hair fell in loose waves around her shoulders.

"OK, not too bad," she murmured to herself, scrutinising her reflection with a critical eye that saw imperfection where others would only see beauty.

Her phone buzzed on the counter, breaking her focus—it was Lexi video-calling, desperate to find out more about Nat's unexpected trip.

"Hey, how's it going with your knight in shining armour?" Lexi's cheerful face appeared on the screen.

A broad smile lit up Nat's features. "Today has been really nice. We went to this quaint little bistro for lunch. You would have loved it."

"And the hotel setup?"

"Two rooms. He had pure intentions for this trip." Nat felt a mixture of gratitude with a tiny fraction of disappointment at Michael's gentlemanly gesture.

"Pure intentions, huh?" Lexi brought her face closer to the camera so Nat could see her raised eyebrows.

"The purest." Nat considered adding "for now", but changed her mind so as not to get Lexi's, or her own, hopes up.

"Let's have a look at what you're wearing, then."

Nat pressed a button to switch the camera and held it up to the mirror.

"You look fantastic!"

"Really?" Nat never quite embraced her own beauty, forever comparing herself to glossy images or her mother's exacting standards.

"You just don't know how beautiful you are." Lexi shook her head. "Well, have fun tonight. See you when you get back. I can't wait to hear about it. About *all* of it."

"Thanks, I'll try." With that, she set her phone down, her conversation with Lexi leaving a warm glow that battled the cool uncertainty she felt about the evening ahead.

Nat stepped back into the bedroom and selected a pair of silver hoop earrings from her jewellery box. As she sat on the edge of the bed, the soft fabric from the boutique they visited earlier that day spilled out beside her. The place she had dreamed about for years had been a revelation—an Aladdin's cave of luxurious textiles and intricate designs that far exceeded her highest expectations. She couldn't wait to transform the fabrics into her own unique creations. Each piece was a critical part of the portfolio that could make or break her career. Her heart fluttered with nervous anticipation at the thought. She reached out, fingers tracing over a particularly exquisite piece of silk, letting the smooth material calm her nerves.

A sudden knock on the door snapped her out of her thoughts. She checked her watch. Michael had a knack for perfect timing, and he was right on schedule. She took a deep breath and walked over to the door, smoothing down her top and adjusting her jeans.

"You look beautiful." He stood there in a tailored navy blazer that accentuated the width of his shoulders. Underneath it, a crisp white shirt was unbuttoned just enough to be inviting. His dark jeans were a casual concession, but they did nothing to lessen the impact of his figure.

"Thank you." Nat felt a blush warm her cheeks. "You look nice too." Her compliment came out like an awkward after-thought, but he still acknowledged it with a charming smile.

"Shall we?" He gestured towards the corridor.

Nat nodded and walked out of the room, allowing the door to close behind her as she fell into step beside him.

The soft clinking of cutlery on plates echoed through the restaurant as Nat speared a bite of her starter. Across from her, Michael watched with an intensity that was doing nothing to settle her nerves. They had spent the day together, enjoying each other's company with the easy banter of a secure friendship. However, the intimacy of the restaurant had somehow elevated the increasingly familiar underlying feeling that there could be something more between them.

"So..." Michael dabbed the side of his mouth with a napkin. "Tell me more about your family."

"Not much to tell, really." She pushed the food around her plate, considering what to say. Then, with a deep breath, she opened up to Michael in a way she never had before. "I grew up in the shadow of my brother, Simon. Everything he did set the bar. He was always the successful one, the driven lawyer. My ambitions... they always felt a bit silly next to his. Mum and Dad—well, more Mum really—she always seemed so dis-appointed in me. I suppose I've never really been good enough."

Michael listened intently, his eyes never leaving her face.

"You are good enough," he said, his voice soft. "You might have had a wobbly start in your job, but you've been amazing.

I mean, let's face it, you pretty much saved the company." He laughed and tilted his head, giving Nat a lopsided grin.

"Well, yes, there is that small matter," Nat conceded with a smile, her cheeks flushed with pleasure and embarrassment all at once.

"And your designs are incredible. Do you think I would have flown you to Paris if I didn't think you stood a chance at winning that contract?" He raised his eyebrows in a gentle challenge.

"Thank you. So enough about me. What about you?" Nat was keen to divert the attention away from herself.

"I was an only child. My parents both ran their own businesses—success was the only option. Failure? It wasn't even in our vocabulary. Everything was black and white, no room for error."

"A bit like your apartment, then?" Nat laughed.

"Yes, very much! At least you came to save me from that. You have certainly brought colour into my life," he admitted, his face brightening with a smile that revealed the hidden meaning behind his words.

As they ate, they talked and laughed, sharing stories of their childhoods, families and dreams for the future. Nat couldn't help but notice how different they were to each other, but maybe that was a good thing? Over the last few weeks, she knew she had grown in confidence, facing challenges she didn't think she would ever be capable of. And sitting here watching Michael, more relaxed than she had seen before, maybe he was changing too?

As they left the warm glow of the restaurant, the cool night air blew away the fuzzy sensation from just a little too much food and wine. The city's lights twinkled around them, reflecting off the water as it lapped against the banks of the river. Nat wrapped her arms around herself, the thin fabric of her coat offering little resistance against the evening chill. Michael noticed and, without a word, draped his jacket over her shoulders.

"Thanks," she said, pulling it tighter around her. The scent of his aftershave hit her, instantly triggering the memory of when they first met. The feel of his lips against the skin on her hand. Despite the warmth radiating from his jacket, she shivered a little.

They walked side by side, their footsteps synchronising on the cobbled riverside walkway. The soft murmur of distant conversations and the occasional laughter from other late-night wanderers filled the spaces between them. It was getting late, and Nat could feel the weariness seeping into her bones. She did her best to stifle a yawn.

"Shall we find a taxi?" Michael suggested.

"Sounds good."

The ride back to the hotel was quiet. Nat relaxed into the seat, listening to the hum of the taxi's engine and watching the city as it flashed by. When they arrived, Michael paid the driver and walked Nat to her room.

"I've had a lovely evening, thank you," Nat said, suddenly aware of her heart beating a fraction faster. "For today as well, for everything."

"You're welcome." Michael smiled at her. "It has been my pleasure."

They stood in silence for a moment, before Michael looked at his watch.

"I should probably get going," he said, something reluctant in his tone. "Goodnight, Natalie." He leaned in, pressing a kiss against her cheek, then moved back in one effortless move. He brushed a stray stand of hair from her face, his fingers trailing softly down her cheek. Nat closed her eyes, and moments later felt his lips, soft and warm, on hers. She lifted her hands up to his neck and he responded by placing his arms around her waist, pulling her in as he deepened the kiss.

He finally pulled back, locking eyes with her.

"I couldn't help myself," he confessed, his voice almost a whisper. "I know we agreed just friends. I didn't come here expecting..."

Nat could only nod in reply, her heart now drumming wildly against her ribs.

"I had better go," Michael said.

"Goodnight." Nat's voice was thick with tangled emotions.

With one last look, he turned and walked down the corridor, leaving her standing in the doorway. She watched him until he disappeared around the corner and then she slipped into her room, her mind replaying the kiss as she leaned back against the closed door.

The quiet of the hotel room settled over Nat, her thoughts a whirlwind of "what if" and "maybe". She stood motionless for a moment, before coming to a sudden realisation.

"Fuck it," she said, conviction swelling inside her chest. Without allowing herself a moment of doubt, Nat opened the door and made her way down the hall, her steps resolute. The soft carpet muffled her steps, but each one rang like thunder in her ears.

She paused before his door, her breath catching. This was crossing a line they had carefully drawn together, but the confines of those boundaries now seemed suffocating. With trembling fingers, she clenched her fist and knocked.

After a moment that lasted longer than Nat felt necessary, the door swung open. The buttons of Michael's shirt were undone, the fabric hanging loosely to reveal his toned body and smooth skin. His eyes searched hers, asking an unspoken question. Nat didn't give him the chance to voice it.

"I don't think just friends is enough for either of us." She held her voice as steady as she could manage.

For a moment, he simply looked at her, those bright eyes reflecting a whirlwind of emotions. Then something shifted in his gaze, and he stepped forward, closing the distance between them. He captured her lips with an intensity that took her breath away. This kiss was nothing like the one they had shared earlier. It was intense, a mix of longing and newfound bravery. It revealed hidden desires and unspoken truths, and as Nat wrapped her arms around his body, she poured all of her emotions into the embrace.

They stumbled backwards into the room, their kiss never breaking, and the door clicked shut behind them. He led her into the bedroom, his hands exploring the contours of her back, sending ripples of anticipation coursing through her. Nat's skin burned beneath her clothes and the air between them crackled, charged with the electricity of long-denied attraction.

As Michael's hands removed the layers of clothing between them, Nat let go of her doubts and finally allowed herself to believe that she was good enough. Good enough to be desired, good enough to be successful, and good enough to be loved. And as they came together, everything else seemed unimportant, leaving only the undeniable truth that they could no longer be just friends.

Michael's chest rose and fell with a measured calmness, his breath a soft whisper against Nat's temple as she nestled closer into the smooth lines of his body. The crisp linen sheets, once neatly tucked and undisturbed, now lay in a tangled mess around them.

"Are you OK?" Michael's voice was a low rumble.

"More than OK," Nat murmured, her words muffled against his smooth skin. She could sense the rhythmic pulse of his heart against her cheek. It was a stark contrast to the energy that had possessed them moments ago. The urgency of their movements had given way to a peaceful calm that now enveloped them. With every breath, Nat felt the lingering traces of doubt evaporate, brushing away the shadows of insecurity that had clung like cobwebs. Michael's fingers traced idle patterns on her back.

"You're amazing, you know." His voice was soft, breaking the comfortable silence. "Before you, everything was just... shades of grey. Now, there's colour everywhere."

Nat lifted her head to meet his gaze and smiled.

"You're not so bad yourself," she whispered, a soft giggle escaping her lips as a smile formed on her face. "Thank you for believing in me."

As sleep began to tug at the edges of her consciousness, Nat allowed herself one last moment of awareness—to memorise the feeling of being held by someone who saw her for all that she was, flaws and dreams intertwined. In the protective circle of Michael's arms, Nat drifted off to sleep with a faint smile of happiness—the kind that comes from knowing you're exactly where you're meant to be.

# CHAPTER TWENTY-EIGHT

**Sunday 29<sup>th</sup> May**

Nat stirred awake, her eyes blinking open to the dimly lit room with a hint of morning light peeking through the curtains. She shifted slightly, the bed sheets rustling softly against her skin, only to find herself gazing into the calm blue eyes of Michael. He was already awake, propped up on one elbow, a content smile playing on his lips as he watched her emerge from her dreams.

"Morning," she murmured. Her eyes were still heavy with sleep.

"Good morning," he replied, his voice smooth and reassuring, the mere sound of it easing her worries that he might have somehow regretted the night before.

She noticed a softness to his gaze, a contrast to the usual seriousness that was his default at work. A knock on the door jolted them from their peaceful bubble. Michael glanced towards the interruption, then back at Nat.

"Breakfast is here." He peeled back the covers to get out of bed. As he padded across the room, Nat's attention followed the stride of his legs, toned muscles only half-covered by his boxer shorts. She surprised herself that such a simple act—a man walking across a hotel room—could stir such desire within her.

She brushed her hair away from her face, aware of a warmth creeping up her cheeks as she watched him talk briefly with the waiter. Michael took the tray and closed the door with a soft click.

"I hope you're hungry." He returned to the bed with a tray laden with the promise of a good start to the day.

"Starving." Nat sat up and rearranged the pillows behind her for support.

The crisp layers of the croissant crumbled softly as she tore into it, buttery flakes sticking to her fingers. She took a sip of freshly squeezed orange juice, its zest jolting her fully awake. Across from her on the white hotel sheets, Michael mirrored her movements, albeit with a precision that made even breakfast look business-like and efficient.

"Nothing beats fresh pastries in the morning." She eyed the golden-brown crust before taking another bite.

"Agreed." Michael paused to take a sip of his coffee, the steam rising up around his face. "Our flight is in a few hours." He cast a glance at the clock by the bed.

Nat nodded, a knot of anxiety forming in her stomach at the reminder of what awaited her back home.

"I guess when we land, it's straight to work for me. I've got this afternoon and tomorrow to get everything perfect."

"Hey." Michael reached out to place his hand over hers, halting her mid-tear as she continued to attack her croissant. "I'll be there to help you finish. If you want my help, that is?"

Her eyes met his questioning gaze, and she felt a surge of gratitude.

"Of course. At this stage, I need every bit of help I can get if I'm going to be ready on time."

Michael's smile turned playful, with a mischievous glint in his eye that made her heart skip a beat. "But, you know…" He leaned in closer, causing the bed to shift slightly with his weight. "I think we can spare a few moments for…other activities before we check out."

"Other activities?" Nat feigned ignorance, but the heat in her cheeks betrayed her.

His grin widened. "Yes, I believe we have just enough time for a proper send-off before we face the real world again."

The suggestion hung in the air, charged and tempting. For a moment, Nat hesitated, the old fears threatening to undermine her newfound confidence. But as she looked into Michael's eyes, filled with warmth and understanding, she knew it was time to let go of her insecurities.

"Then I suppose…" She leaned across the scattered breakfast remnants. "We shouldn't waste any time."

## Monday 30th May

The sun had long dipped below the horizon when Nat, fingers stained with ink and her mind a whirlwind of fabric swatches and colour palettes, finally leaned back from the desk. Weariness tugged at her shoulders, yet there was finally a sense of accomplishment that had been elusive for so long. Michael, who had been her faithful assistant since their return from Paris, glanced up from where he was organising a stack of sketches.

"It's looking really good." His voice was tinged with pride. "What's left to do?"

She rubbed her temples, trying to soothe away the tightness that had developed over the course of the afternoon.

"Just a few more sketches need tweaking. It won't take long." Her tone did nothing to hide the exhaustion she felt. "Most of them made it through the wine incident unscathed." The memory of red wine seeping into the delicate fibres still made her wince, but she pushed it aside. There was no room for dwelling on what had happened before, not with her future inching closer with each passing minute.

She stood up, stretching her limbs as she moved towards the portfolio fanned out on her bed. She ran her hand across the cover, grateful for its resilience despite the unfortunate soaking.

"Fabric samples all accounted for?" He got up too, standing beside her with an air of solidarity.

"Secured. Every single one."

"You're going to knock this out of the park." Michael's eyes scanned the pages, his expression one of admiration. "This is exceptional work."

"Thanks to your help," she said, her voice soft, acknowledging the support he'd offered without reservation.

"It's a pleasure, I know how much this means to you. What else can I do?"

"You've done more than enough." Nat slipped her arm around his waist and leaned in against him, lifting her head to kiss his stubbled cheek. "It's time for you to go home and get some rest. It's a big day for both of us tomorrow. Don't forget about your meeting with Ethica."

"They are going to be really disappointed you can't be there to finalise the deal with me." Michael leaned down and kissed Nat on the top of her head. "Julia couldn't stop raving about you and how lucky the company is to have you. How lucky I am to have you." He paused to look at her, his gaze telling her instantly what he really meant.

"I do really wish you could stay, though," Nat said, a tinge of sadness in her tone.

"There will be plenty of opportunities for sleepovers." Michael pulled her in closer. "Especially now we've established we're probably not cut out for just friends."

"No, I don't think we are." Nat laughed, stopping abruptly when Michael leaned in, his hand cupping her chin as he kissed her. Her body tensed for a second in surprise, before relaxing into his touch. She lifted her hand to run her fingers through his hair, feeling the urgency of his tongue quicken and his breath become more rapid. He moved his hand to find a gap between where her jeans and t-shirt met. She tensed again as his palm pressed against her back, the warmth tingling against her bare skin. She felt him lean closer into her, closing any gap that dared to exist between them, before pulling away.

"I had better go, otherwise you will have to drag me away," he said, clearing his throat.

"That's probably a good idea." Nat leant against her wardrobe and watched as Michael gathered his things. She followed him downstairs and waited inside the porch as he pulled on his shoes. The silence was comfortable, yet charged with a desire she knew they were both fighting to keep at bay. They looked at each other and, for a moment, Michael hesitated, as if debating with himself. Then, with a clear determination, he closed the gap and his lips found hers again.

"Call me after the interview?" he murmured against her mouth.

"I will." Her heart raced.

With a final glance, he turned and walked out of the front door. Nat stood in the stillness of the porch and a sense of calm washed over her. She smiled to herself as she made her way into the kitchen and reached for a glass. She filled it with water and drank slowly, the chill of the liquid doing little to quench the warmth that his kiss had ignited.

"Well, don't you look like the cat that got the cream?" Lucy's voice sliced through the silence, her figure appearing at the doorway with her arms crossed. Nat startled, her heart jumping into her throat.

"You scared me." She attempted a laugh, but it came out like a nervous hiccup.

"Sorry." Lucy's eyes narrowed with curiosity. "But seriously, what's going on? Was that Michael only just leaving?"

"Um…" Nat started, struggling to find the words while her mind raced. She didn't want to share too much, yet the truth was threatening to bubble up, almost impossible to contain. "Yeah, it's been a nice couple of days. He's been helping me out with my portfolio since yesterday afternoon."

"Wow." Lucy pushed off from the doorframe, her expression shifted to one of intrigue. "He's really smitten, isn't he? It seems you both are."

"Maybe." Nat's cheeks flushed. She slipped a band off her wrist and pulled her hair back, tying it into a loose ponytail. She was suddenly conscious of how dishevelled she must look.

"And he was just helping you with your portfolio? This late?" Lucy's tone took on a teasing edge, her eyebrow arching suggestively.

"Just helping with my portfolio," Nat confirmed, trying to sound nonchalant. "It turns out he's quite the gentleman."

"Really?"

Nat bit her lip, wondering how much to reveal. Finally, she let out a sigh, feeling the weight of the secret too heavy to keep from her sister-in-law.

"There might be… more to it."

"More to it?" Lucy repeated, tilting her head, her eyes wide with excitement.

"In Paris, we…" Nat allowed the silence and the look on her face to finish her sentence.

"Really?" Lucy's face lit up, a smile breaking through. "That's so exciting! I mean, as long as you're happy."

"I am. We have definitely become more than just friends." Nat smiled to herself at the thought. They had tried hard to keep it that way, but in the end, it was never going to stay like that. "But it's all so new, you know?" she added, her newfound confidence wavering a fraction. "And with everything that happened with Joe…" Her voice trailed off.

"Hey." Lucy stepped closer and placed a hand on Nat's shoulder. "Just take it one step at a time. You deserve happiness, and Michael might be just the person you need right now."

"Thanks." Nat managed a grateful smile.

"I'm off to sleep. Don't stay up too late."

Nat watched as Lucy made her way out of the kitchen, leaning against the kitchen counter and replaying the confession in her mind. She couldn't believe that she had admitted there might actually be a relationship on the cards. With Michael, of all people. They were opposites, but maybe that's what made it feel so right.

# Chapter Twenty–Nine

**Wednesday 1ˢᵗ June**

Simon weaved through the music cafe with an air of concentration that was typical of him as he balanced a tray heavy with glasses. He approached the table, setting down the drinks as carefully as possible, trying not to waste a drop. Nat watched him, unable to hide her amused smile. Her brother, always the high achiever, even with the simple task of fetching a round.

"Here we are," he announced, pushing his glasses up the bridge of his nose. "Drinks for everyone."

"I hope one of those is for me!" Lexi arrived at the table like a summer storm, all energy and apologies. "Sorry, I had to finish unpacking boxes in the storage room," she said, squeezing a chair in between Nat and Enzo and flashing her wide, infectious grin.

Nat reached out, her fingers brushing against the cool surface of her glass, drawing patterns in the condensation. As well as Simon, Lucy was there and excited at the prospect of a rare night out together. Only once they had found a babysitter that wasn't Nat for a change. Michael was by her side, his serious blue gaze scanning the room, with Enzo opposite, laughing at something Lexi had just whispered to him.

"I'm such a terrible friend. It's been so crazy here, I haven't even had time to ask you—how did your interview go yesterday?" Lexi looked expectantly at Nat.

"It went well, I think." She had hoped to sound casual, but wasn't convinced she had pulled it off. "But honestly, I won't hold my breath. The competition was really tough." Her eyes met Michael's for a fleeting second, searching for reassurance.

"Nat's being modest." Simon's voice was tinged with the pride of an older sibling. "She's got talent pouring out of her ears. They would be lucky to have her."

"Thanks." Nat offered a small smile, hoping to convey gratitude while her mind spun with doubts.

"Hey, you've got this." Lexi bumped her shoulder against Nat's. "You're going to win that contract, no question about it."

"Absolutely," Michael added. "I think we all know how good you are."

"Let's not jinx it." Nat laughed, trying to keep the mood light despite the tension coiling within her. "Why don't we talk about something else?" She was keen to change the subject and turned to Lucy. "So, have you decided about going back to work?"

Lucy's eyes brightened. "Yes, we've agreed I'm going to go back next month. Maternity leave has been wonderful, but I miss nursing."

Simon leaned back in his seat and put his arm around Lucy in a rare show of affection. "I'm so proud of you." He smiled at her. "And I've decided to cut back on my hours at the office so I can help more at home with Louis."

"Really?" Nat beamed, her expression a mix of surprise and pleasure. Maybe Simon really was capable of changing his old-fashioned ways after all.

"Absolutely." Simon planted a quick kiss on Lucy's cheek.

"Speaking of busy schedules," Enzo said, turning to Lexi. "How's everything been going with the cafe?"

"It's been crazy this weekend. I've managed to book music acts for every Friday and Saturday coming up the next few months." She glanced around the room, a flash of pride on her face as she looked at the busy tables around them. "But it looks like I'll need to hire more staff soon."

"Need a charming Italian barista?" Enzo joked with a theatrical waggle of his eyebrows. "I make a mean espresso."

"Your students would miss you too much," Lexi teased. Something about the look on her face told Nat that Lexi would love nothing more than to take him up on his offer.

"So, how's everything at the company since that mess with the gambling firm?" Simon asked Michael, the lawyer in him never quite off-duty.

"Actually, it's all going to work out OK," Michael said, turning to look at Nat. "All thanks to you and your sister. We've just signed a deal with Ethica. It's a solid partnership that aligns perfectly with our company values."

"Ethica," Simon repeated, nodding approvingly. "Sounds like you've made the right choice."

"Indeed." Michael took a sip of his drink. "And there's more." The weight of his tone suggested this was no trivial update. "It turns out Clara had—let's say—*inappropriate* associations with Spinigma. We mutually agreed it would be best for her to leave the company."

The revelation hit Nat like a wave, her heart hammering against her ribcage as she processed the news. "What do you mean?" She tried to find her voice, but it was barely above a whisper, lost in the noise of the cafe.

"Well, it seems she has been in a secret relationship with one of the partners in the organisation." Michael raised his eyebrows. "It had been going on for some time and explains why she was so keen for the deal to go through."

"But surely that's a conflict of interest?"

"Exactly. That's why she kept it a secret. That and the fact she was engaged to someone else."

"Yes, what about her fiancée?" Nat felt a surge of satisfaction at recognising from the start that she wasn't a woman to be trusted.

"I think it's safe to assume the wedding is off."

"Why didn't you tell me before?"

"With everything that happened, I thought you had probably had enough of hearing about her." Michael squeezed her hand. "And to be honest, I didn't know how to tell you. I was a little embarrassed."

"Embarrassed?"

"Yes, the way she treated you. It turns out you were right all along. She really wasn't the person I thought she was."

Nat opened her mouth to speak, but the ring of her phone sliced through the moment. She fumbled in her bag and her stomach flipped as she recognised the caller ID.

"Excuse me." She pushed back from the table. As she stepped outside, she held the phone to her ear and braced herself for whatever came next.

Nat leaned against the cool brick wall, watching as clouds raced across the evening sky. The conversation she had just finished raced through her head as she tried to process what had just happened, a cocktail of disbelief and elation bubbling in her chest.

"Is everything alright?" Michael's voice was full of worry as he joined her outside. "You've been gone a little while."

She turned towards him, eyes wide with astonishment.

"I... I got the job," she stammered. "That was them. They want to offer me the contract!"

In an instant, the distance closed between them as he pulled her towards him, his arms wrapping around her. Nat could feel the steady beat of his heart against her own as it raced wildly in her chest.

"That's incredible!" Michael leaned back just enough to see her face, his eyes full of admiration. "I knew you would."

For the first time, she allowed herself to bask in the feeling of accomplishment, casting sunshine onto the last shadows of doubt that remained. Rising on her tiptoes, she gently cupped his face and leaned in, feeling the warmth of his breath against her lips. With a sigh, she kissed him for what felt like forever. As they broke apart, Nat's smile was beaming, all uncertainty replaced with overwhelming happiness.

"I guess I should start drafting my resignation letter, huh?" A smirk danced on her lips.

"Really?" Michael raised an eyebrow. "I'd better get my money's worth before you finish, then."

"Ah, but that's the thing," she said, her voice light with the tease. "You technically already gave me one month's notice."

Nat saw the momentary surprise register on Michael's face before he let out a soft chuckle.

"Well, I suppose this means there won't be any more—"

"Complications." Nat smiled as she finished his sentence.

"This makes everything much simpler," Michael added, his gaze lingering on her, reflecting something more intimate than his words could convey.

"Simple is good." Her heart finally settled into a steady rhythm after the excitement of the last few minutes.

"Good." He reached out, taking her hands. "Because I think we've had enough complications to last us a lifetime."

The laughter that bubbled up from Nat's throat was genuine and free. They stood there, two opposites who had somehow found common ground. And as she looked up at Michael, with his dark hair ruffled by the wind and bright blue eyes shining with hope for their future, Nat realised that perhaps she had always been enough—enough for the job, enough for this moment, and enough for the man who stood before her, now open-hearted and unguarded.

"Thank you," she whispered, her gaze locked with his. "For believing in me, even when I couldn't."

"Always," he said, his voice certain and reassuring.

And as they stood outside wrapped in each other's arms, Nat knew this moment was more than just a happy ending—it was the beginning of everything she had dared to hope for.

## Acknowledgements

This book wouldn't be possible if it weren't for the wonderful people I am lucky enough to have in my life. My husband and two beautiful daughters are my absolute world. I hope you are as proud of me as I am of you. Mum, Dad, Matt and all of the Ball clan – you made me who I am today and I couldn't wish for a better family. And to the Sahota tribe, who welcomed me in and hold me tight – I am lucky to be part of such a wonderful extended family.

Midway through writing this book I was diagnosed with breast cancer. Focusing on my writing and getting the book finished has played a vital part in my positive approach to tackling such an immense challenge. I have had so much support throughout my treatment, there are no words to describe how grateful I am.

Thanks to Sam, who took a risk with me on my first children's book and helped me develop my confidence in writing. If it wasn't for you having faith in my ideas during our lockdown walks, I don't think I would have ever got to the point where this book was possible.

Thanks to all of my early draft readers, beta readers and proof readers, in particular Linda, Margot, Yvette, Madison, Etty, Hazel, Sarah, Emily and Mum. Your feedback and advice has been invaluable. And special thanks to Mikey Simpson for your help with the early cover concepts.

## About the author

Katie Lou is a versatile author who has explored various genres aimed at both children and adults.

In 2023, Katie was diagnosed with breast cancer, a challenge that only strengthened her resolve and motivated her to fully commit to her writing during treatment. Drawing from her personal experiences, she aims to create stories that not only entertain but also provoke thought and provide solace to readers facing their own battles.

When she's not crafting captivating tales, Katie finds joy in spending time with her family and friends, running and visiting garden centres.

With a talent for crafting engaging narratives across genres, Katie's ultimate goal is to transport readers into immersive worlds and leave them with memorable characters and themes that linger long after the final page.

You can sign up to Katie's newsletter and find out more on her website and social media channels:

https://katiesahota.com/
https://www.instagram.com/katie_lou_romance
https://www.facebook.com/katiesahotaauthor

## Also by the author

## Children's Fiction

(Writing under Katie Sahota)

Little Glow
The Cats Who Wanted More

Printed in Great Britain
by Amazon